The Last Pirate

A novel by Wilson Hawthorne

School's out for the summer in Florida. For young Harley Cooper, that means endless days of adventure on the bays and cays around Pine Island. With his sea-going black lab, Hammerhead, by his side, Harley fishes the pristine waters for blue crab to help his mom make ends meet.

When he hauls up an ancient treasure map one day, summer vacation explodes into a hunt for Spanish gold.

A mysterious hermit, known only as Salt, steers Harley toward hidden doubloons with swashbuckling tales of the infamous pirate Gasparilla. But, does the hermit have reasons of his own?

Or will nature have the final say when she sends a monster hurricane to hammer the coast?

Harley Cooper explains it all in an action-packed diddie he calls

The Last Pirate.

The Last Pirate, a novel by Wilson Hawthorne

Published by Eyeland Telemedia, Inc.

This is a work of fiction. Names, characters, places and incidents are either the product of the author's mind or are used fictitiously. Any resemblance to actual persons, living or dead, events, or locales is entirely coincidental.

ISBN 978-1-793-98916-1

Printed in the United States of America

Eyeland Telemedia, Inc.
Cape Coral, FL

www.EyelandTelemedia.com
www.TheLastPirate.net

12 11 10 9 8 7

For my children,
who have
inspired and demanded
stories such as this.

And for my wife, Gail,
the embodiment of
encouragement and love.

"We sail our ship across the seas,
For loot found on the blue.
Me pappy was a pirate,
And I be a pirate, too!"

- Captain Squid

The Last Pirate

A novel by Wilson Hawthorne

Calusa Gold

Diddies. That's what Salt called his pirate stories. I used to think he made them up. That all changed the week one of his diddies came true.

Unfortunately, something else came that week, too – a category four hurricane named Charley.

Now, I don't consider myself a narrow minded kid, but what I'm about to tell you seems too crazy to be true, even to me. If somebody started yakking to me about treasure maps and lost gold and the sea rising up to swallow an island whole, I'd probably tell them to go check their head for bats. The problem is it didn't happen to somebody else. It happened to me.

Salt always said we make our own history just by living life – best to live it well. I really don't know if I lived it well or not, but I figure what happened that week was big enough to at least put down on paper. So here's my diddie, from the top. And for that, I have to go way back.

About two hundred years ago, there were a bunch of pirates living on the west coast of Florida. They had been there for years looting merchant ships in the Gulf of Mexico.

Their captain, a big Spanish dude named Gasparilla, had deserted the Spanish navy to become a pirate. He had stolen one of their finest warships, sailed it to an island near my home-town, and built his hideout. Gasparilla, also known as

The Terror of the Southern Seas, stood over six feet tall, a giant in those days. He was meaner than a water moccasin and clever, bloodthirsty and bad enough to have an island named after him. Just google Gasparilla Island, Florida. You'll find it.

The pirates' only neighbors were an Indian tribe known as the Calusa, which means "fierce ones." They didn't mess around. These freaks were total warriors. I mean, they killed everybody. And there was only one thing they were scared of – nothing!

Well, just like the pirates, these Indians started swiping gold from merchant ships; only they couldn't just go out and attack big sailing ships because they only had little canoes. Instead, they'd wait until the Europeans wrecked during a storm or ran aground in shallow water, then they'd paddle out and kill them all. When they paddled back to shore, their dugouts held as much treasure as they could carry. The Calusa traded it for stuff in Spanish towns like Havana and Tampa.

Now, the pirates hated those Indians, hated them even more for taking what could have been pirate gold. But, they left the savages alone because the Indians fought like demons. The Calusa felt pretty much the same about Gasparilla and his men. They tolerated the Spaniards as long as they kept to themselves. That went on for years until 1804, the year the Calusa came down with the measles, a little gift from Spain.

One by one, the measles killed off the Calusa, and there was nothing the warriors could do to stop it. When the pirates found out how sick the Indians had become, the buccaneers attacked.

According to Salt, one battle took place in the summer of 1804 on Joseffa Island. Gasparilla's warship, the Florida Blanca, sailed up the channel that runs from the Gulf of Mexico to the backwaters of Pine Island Sound. He anchored in front of Joseffa and aimed his guns at the Calusa's village, high atop the island's tallest hill. After pounding the village with cannon fire all morning, the Spanish swashbucklers finally brought their swords ashore.

The fight didn't last long. Only a few Indians lived through the shelling, and almost all the survivors had the measles. They were too weak to retreat. The Calusa knew they had been defeated, but the last thing they wanted was for the pirates to get what they came for – the gold. So the healthiest warrior grabbed their stash (a big bag of doubloons), jumped in his canoe, and paddled like crazy. Gasparilla's men spotted him leaving, and the chase was on.

Now, here's the crazy part, at least as it relates to me. While they battled, a hurricane blew in and nailed Pine Island Sound. Gasparilla didn't care. He just wanted that gold and ordered three of his men to pursue the Indian. They rowed after the warrior in a longboat, chasing him from island to island across the bay. They fired their muskets. They shot their pistols. They howled and screamed. Nothing slowed that Indian down. Then the rain hit, and, dude, it came down *hard*, so thick those pirates couldn't see five feet in front of their boat.

Hurricane rain doesn't last that long, though. It's about the heaviest rain I've ever seen, but, until you get close to the eye of the storm, it comes in a quick wave; then it's gone. By the time the rain had stopped, the Indian had vanished. When they rounded the next clump of mangroves, the Spaniards saw nothing but a big, empty lagoon surrounded by swamp. The pirates slowly rowed their boat up the lagoon as ferocious gale-force winds beat the treetops above.

The lagoon got narrower and narrower. The trees came close. Branches clawed at the men in the wind, and they began to spook. Just then, the Indian surprised them! He jumped out and shot one of Gasparilla's men through the heart with an arrow. The warrior loaded another, took aim, and . . . the pirates blew his head off with a musket ball.

The Calusa's canoe sat in the mangroves not far away. The gold was gone. With no time to waste, the freebooters searched the swamp frantically for the loot, but before long they were forced to row back to Joseffa and ride out the hurricane on high ground.

They cussed the sky. They vowed to return, swearing an oath to find the gold. And after the storm had blown over, they drew up a map while it was fresh in their minds. But, for two hundred years, that big bag of gold was never found.

The Traps

Now fast forward to August 8, 2004. That was a Sunday, the day everything started to happen.

Normally I don't like to work on Sunday. I'm a professional fisherman, and Sunday's are primetime for every amateur boat-owner on the water. Pine Island Sound is a zoo on the weekends. Normally, in the summer when school's out, I work the water on the calmer days, the weekdays. But, I'm a high school kid. I burn through the green. So, Sunday or not, off I went.

I fish for two things, mostly, blue crabs and mullet – not at the same time, though. I catch mullet around November and December, then switch back to crabs.

Catching blue crab is getting tougher and tougher. It's not my fault, as far as I can tell. Blue crabs are on the decline everywhere, and nobody seems to know exactly why. All I know is it's harder to find crabs. That means longer hours on the water if I want to make any cash.

Luckily, my overhead is low. I live at home with Mom in Palmetto Cove – rent free. I don't have a boat payment, and my mom pays my insurance. She's good that way. I give her some cash when I have extra. All I really have to buy is fuel and my fishing license. Oh, and the traps.

I use your basic crab trap that I buy off old timers, cheap. It's pretty much just a box made out of plastic-coated chicken wire. It has a place for the bait and a couple of holes where the crabs get in. At the top, there's a hole just big enough to let smaller crabs swim out. A short rope hooks the whole contraption to a float.

All the floats have my special marking, a red elephant head, so everyone knows they're mine. I painted the elephant heads last summer in honor of the *White Stripes*, because that band totally rocks.

My boat? Well, she may have been built way before I was born, but I always think of her as a rock star, too – even named her the *White Stripe*. What can I say? I like the *White Stripes*. They rock. I got the boat from my dad, well, kind of. He had just let it sit there in the canal behind our trailer since he quit fishing in the nineties. He used to catch boat-loads of mullet back in the day, but that all came to a screeching halt when the State of Florida banned mullet nets in 1995. Since then, the only thing my dad catches is a buzz. Mom divorced him after a few years of that. Now he lives in some dump over in Matlacha. It's not far from my house, but I still don't see him that much – not a whole lot in common, I guess.

For years, the boat just sat there, growing barnacles. I suppose mullet boats weren't worth much after the net ban, or maybe my mom got it in the divorce deal and didn't want to mess with it. I don't know. Anyway, it ended up in her name. When I was twelve, I fixed her up, and suddenly I had my very own boat, twenty-two feet long with an open hull and a Johnson outboard motor way up front towards the bow. I sit over the motor, up on a tower.

So on that fateful Sunday morning in August, I jumped in my boat at about seven to go check traps. As I pulled away from the dock, Hammerhead, my dog, jumped off the seawall onto the bow, wagging his tail. He never misses a trip. Hammerhead's a wicked-smart black lab. That dog can tell where I'm going by the clothes I put on.

I idled by Mr. Henley's trailer and waved. He was sitting on his dock fishing for sheephead. He's old. He's always fishing for sheephead.

"Mornin', Harley," he said. "Gonna bring me back some sweet crabs?" He whistles through his dentures when he talks.

"Yes sir, Mr. Henley. You know I'll save a couple for you."

Mr. Henley was nice for an old guy. He never chased us out of his yard or yelled when we played baseball in the street. Whenever I had a good day, I'd always throw a couple of crabs his way.

"I'll see you at supper time." He whistled the *s*'s in *see* and *supper*.

At the end of the slow zone where the canal meets the bay, I pulled my Tampa Rays cap down real tight and throttled up the *Stripe*. She skipped to the surface faster than a ballyhoo on caffeine, and we were off. Leaning into the wind with his tongue flapping out the side, Hammerhead braced himself against the casting deck in front of the tower. That dog loves going fast.

Boats seem to fly when you're up on plane. Some really do go fast, like the Bajas or Cigarettes. Mine? Well, she could probably do about thirty-five with no load and a tail wind – not so fast. But still, on the water, that feels like you're flying. Maybe the lack of a windshield had something to do with it.

I headed up the channel out of Palmetto Cove for the open water of Pine Island Sound. If you love the water like I do, you'd love Palmetto Cove. It's not fancy, but it's close to everything out on the water, all the good stuff anyway.

Palmetto Cove sits on the west side of Pine Island about halfway down. Pine Island is around fifteen miles long, mostly fields, trees, and swamp. By car, there's only one road to get there. Two lanes of asphalt roll in from Cape Coral and cross a drawbridge in Matlacha. When school is open, I go over that bridge on the bus twice each day. If the weather is good, which is most of the time around here, the view from that bridge makes it twice as hard to concentrate on schoolwork. I'm really not one to be cooped up inside studying, anyways.

But I digress.

On that summer day, the weather was totally beautiful. And school was the last thing on my mind.

My first set of traps waited less than a mile away. I could already see the white Styrofoam floats bobbing in a straight line across the shallow grass flats.

As I mentioned, to run the White Stripe you had to sit up in the tower. That made it hard to control from down on the deck, so I adapted. I ran an electric motor from the stern. It's a little slower, but it's only an arm's length away. Saved on fuel too. Also, I had no automatic trap puller. I did it the old fashioned way, by hand. It was a nice workout too – part of my benefit package.

As the Stripe eased up to the first trap, I killed the motor and hopped down off the tower to lower the electric into the water behind the boat. Just as the boat passed the float, I shoved the tiller to the right as far as it would go. That action spins the boat in a circle to the left. I work on the left, or port, side of the boat and try to be totally done with the trap and have it back in the water in one revolution. Doesn't always work out that way, but that's my little game.

I grabbed my gaff, basically a stick with a large hook on the end, and reached out for the trap line. A couple of seagulls laughed overhead, begging for a handout as I worked. Hammerhead barked a few times to run them off. He knows his job. Good dog.

Once I got the line, I chucked the gaff back in a rod holder and hauled up the trap. Only one crab ran around inside the chicken wire, a big one, though, a seven-inch male. We call those jimmies. I opened the trap and dropped him in a 72-quart cooler. Then I grabbed a chunk of mullet from another old cooler, rebaited the trap, and threw it overboard. I know it's not glamorous enough to appear on The Most Dangerous Catch, but to me fishing for blue crabs is one of the best things I can do.

I looked up to get my bearings. The boat was just finishing its first circle. I straightened the tiller and headed for the next float, bright white with a red elephant head on the side. A pelican skidded in behind me using his webbed feet like water skis and paddled along with the boat begging for free breakfast. These bums were everywhere.

I owned about two hundred traps and tried to keep most of them wet all the time. Usually, I set out ten to twenty traps in each line. That's about the limit of my arm strength before I give out and need a serious break. I liked to check a third of my traps each time I went out, which means I pulled anywhere from fifty to seventy traps a day. If I made it out five days a week, like in the summer, each trap got tended twice a week.

I finished up the last trap, shut down the electric, and climbed back up onto the tower.

One of the best things about an office on a crab boat is jamming the tunes. I had a screaming set of wakeboard speakers mounted on the tower – seriously loud. Me and my buds loved to carve the water behind the *Stripe,* and those puppies shot the tunes all the way back to whoever was hanging onto the rope. I plugged in my iPod and put on some old Green Day. Good thing crabs don't have ears.

The Johnson roared and we jammed to the next trap line with Billie Joe Armstrong screaming out the lyrics of Geek Stink Breath. Hammerhead was nose to the wind barking his face off. Guess he was rockin', too. See? This business has its moments.

Ripples across the water let me know the breeze had picked up a little. Clouds were building over the mainland. We'd probably get a thunderstorm later on. That's the typical summertime pattern – nice in the morning, rain in the afternoon, clear by dark.

I brought my old mullet boat off plane as the beginning of the next line got close. A couple of flats boats, guys looking for snook, poled near the shoreline of a mangrove island.

I cut the motor and killed the music. On the weekends, I need to listen for other boat traffic while I've got my face stuck in a crab trap. If I don't, I'm liable to get run over by some German tourist who's never driven a boat before.

A few motors droned in the distance, and I figured I'd better check their positions before I got started. A couple were way off to the west running the Intracoastal Waterway. Another looked like he was headed towards Captiva, a resort island north of Sanibel full of big houses and hotels. And one boat was coming in from the south, straight up my line and headed right at me. Looked like another flats boat.

Flats boats are common around here. Sleek, low, and fast, they're like a saltwater version of a bass boat, built for speed, stealth, and shallow water. Most of them have a platform on the back over the outboard. It gives the guy a place to stand while he's slowly pushing the thing across the flats with a long pole. It's a good way to sneak up on fish.

Many flats boats are pimped out with all kinds of obnoxious colors and logos. This was one of those, and, as it got closer, I recognized the driver, Dustin Majors, a real pain in the butt. He's my age, and grew up here, like me. I've known him my whole life. He's always been a pain.

His dad's rich. He set Dustin up with that boat last summer. Pretty slick ride, though, I have to admit – a twenty-four foot Pathfinder with a Yamaha 250 four-stroke on the back. Trim tabs, jack plate, power pole, and three electrics – two in the back, one in the front. Oh yeah, and the custom pimp wrap.

His old man set him up in business, too. His daddy's got some big, international company, so he flies in all his clients, and Dustin takes them out fishing. Easy money. His dad's company pays him three hundred bucks a trip. Believe me, I know. The little dill weed brags about it all the time.

And, of course, with all that jack and the hotrod boat, he gets the chicks, at least until they figure him out. That usually doesn't take long.

He knew it was me by the tower on my boat. Not many mullet boats around any more. He kept coming right at me anyway. When he got about halfway up the trap line, I spotted his current hood ornament sitting in front of the console.

Now, I've just got to say, Eden Baker is smokin' hot. I've known her since I was two. Some girls start out like the ugly duckling, then turn out beautiful. Not Eden. She was born hot – hot to the bone!

Eden lives with her folks on a canal not far from me. She's a sweetheart too, knows how to be cool, how to treat people, how to be real. How she ended up with a jerk like Dustin I'll never know. But it was just a matter of time. She'd learn the score. Ditch him. And when she did . . . let's just say I've had my eye on her for a while.

I whipped off my AC/DC T-shirt when they were about fifty yards away and reached for the gaff. By the time they were on me, I was hauling up the trap, hand over hand, doing a great job flexing every single muscle from the waist up. Crabbing, the way I do, is a workout with results. Might as well let Eden see the goods.

Dustin swerved the Pathfinder around me at the last second like I knew he would. As he roared by, he looked at me with one hand on the wheel and his other on his forehead making an L out of his thumb and first finger. Dork. He's the real loser.

His client, his daddy's client I should say, looked a little freaked in the face. He lunged for a handle on the console to keep from falling out.

And there was Eden, sitting on the front seat in nothing but a string bikini. Man, she was so hot! She threw me one of those cutesy, little girl waves – you know, the kind where they hold their hand close to their body and wiggle their fingers. And she flashed me a big, gleaming smile to match. Boy, for a couple of slow-motion seconds, the gates of heaven cracked open just wide enough to grant me a glimpse inside. And then, she was gone.

That's when the spray from Dustin's wake totally splattered me and Hammerhead. Not cool.

Sweet Trade

Out on the water, it's a different world. I can see why pirates liked it so much. The rules are different. The sea is in charge. She lays down the law. And when she does, you'd better listen. No second chances for foolish swabs and scallywags. Arrrgh!

No roads either. Just cruise wherever you like, whenever you like.

The bay is my backyard. I grew up in it. Before I had a boat, I had a kayak, and I've explored every drop. Hammerhead's been going out with me ever since he was a pup. I'd open the front compartment of the kayak and set him in there, and away we'd go – me paddling my butt off and him just sitting there with his tongue hanging out, all happy.

We searched for treasure even before Salt started telling me all his diddies. I just knew pirates had been to the Sound. You can almost hear their sails flap when the wind blows through one of her islands.

The way I see it, pirates liked secrets as much as loot. They secretly attacked ships with no warning and secretly buried the gold and treasure. They made secret maps, sailed secret ships, used secret names, and they even lived in secret hideouts. And there are a *million* secret places all over Pine Island Sound – it's perfect for pirates.

According to Salt, pirates had a secret way of asking a man if he was a pirate. A career in pirating was called working in the "sweet trade." If a man mentioned that was his job, he was in. Of course, as Salt also said, all that secrecy can confuse a man.

He told me once that Gasparilla used Tampa as a source of information and a place to recruit sailors. In those days Tampa was still controlled by the Spanish. Gasparilla's face was too well known for him to show it in town, so he'd send a well trusted man like Long John MacBlane, a Scotsman who'd been with him forever.

Long John knew Tampa well, but Tampa never got to know him. That's because Long John was a master of disguise. He not only changed his looks, but he could also change his voice and appear as a different stranger every time.

In the autumn of 1783, he sailed a sloop into Tampa Bay flying the British flag. Pretending to be unskilled with the anchor, Long John kept sailing his vessel directly in front of oncoming ships. The harbor-master became so exasperated with the bumbling Brit that he allowed him to tie up next to a great, grand brigantine from Puerto Rico just to get him out of the way.

That is exactly where Long John wanted to be.

Begging a thousand pardons, Long John disembarked his vessel and immediately paid the harbor-master a tidy sum of gold to win the man over. As he stuffed the coins into his pocket, the master's grumbles turned to roses. And, the man was more than happy to gossip about the other new arrivals to boot. He colorfully described the Puerto Ricans to Long John and pointed him to a nearby tavern to meet them. Once inside the disguised pirate found the capatin of the brigantine sitting with his men drinking rum.

Long John walked up to the table and, in his thickest English accent, said, "I say, my good fellow, I'm afraid I've just arrived in this jolly port quite alone. My crew took ill with the scurvy, and I had to maroon them in Havana to recover. Would you mind terribly if I joined your table?"

The Puerto Rican, having been in the tavern for some time, was feeling quite jolly himself and, in broken English, replied, "Sit. Drink. Brothers of the sea, we are, no? Juan Ponce de Coronado at your service."

Long John gladly accepted the man's hand and the chair he had pulled out. He explained to his new Spanish friends that he had sailed from London to Portugal to spend a few weeks in Lisboa. He told them that while there he had heard something of the "sweet trade" in Florida and had decided to cross the Atlantic to see if there was any profit to be made.

"Ah, mi amigo, true brothers we are," said Coronado happily. "You have found the sweet trade here with us!"

Coronado went on to explain that he and his men had been in the sweet trade for years and that they had amassed a fortune because of it. Long John's eyes gleamed with delight as he learned that these men were not only pirates, but wealthy ones as well. A few rums later, Coronado mentioned that he planned to sail south soon and bury some of his treasure in a spot near the Florida coast, a place he had scouted on the way up from Puerto Rico.

Long John couldn't believe his good fortune. He had been in Tampa less than one afternoon, and he had already accomplished his goals. He would follow Coronado to his secret spot, kill him, take his gold, and deliver his men to Gasparilla. Long John spent the next couple of days cavorting around Tampa without a care in the world.

On the morning of the third day in port, he arose to find Coronado's crew preparing the ship for departure. Long John sipped a cup of Earl Grey tea as he bid Coronado farewell and wished him a happy voyage. Once the ship was out to sea, Long John rounded up the few men he had recruited to help him with the job and set off after Coronado. He soon spotted the brigantine, and slowed his sloop so that she lagged behind just far enough to keep only the Puerto Rican's masts in sight.

True to his word, after sailing south for a day, Coronado anchored his ship off a pass between two islands. Through his spyglass, Long John watched as a small group of sailors rowed

Coronado through the pass. Long John hastily sailed his boat around the backside of the nearest island and slipped up the bay to intercept the Puerto Ricans. After a while, he spotted their long boat on the sands of the mainland. Out on a nearby plain of palmetto and grass, Coronado and his men opened the earth with picks and shovels. Next to them sat a large, wooden chest.

Staying low and out of sight, Long John and his free-booters anchored the sloop and waded to shore. When they got close enough to hear Spanish, they drew their swords. Long John didn't take any chances. He also carried a blunderbuss, a short, stumpy gun with a bell shaped end crammed full of rusted nails, broken glass, and a pile of gunpowder.

Long John and his men burst out from behind the brush catching Coronado by surprise. The Spanish men didn't even have time to draw their swords. After disarming the furious Coronado and his men, Long John demanded that they open the chest and show him the gold. A smirking Coronado ordered one of the men to do so.

Now, it was Long John's turn to be surprised. The chest contained no gold at all. Instead, short pieces of plant stalk filled it to the brim. Coronado was a sugar cane baron. He had come to Florida to plant new fields for his "sweet trade."

So mad he could barely speak, Long John had the men tied up and loaded into his sloop. He sailed it back to Coronado's ship and, holding the blunderbuss on their captain, forced all the crew down below, then locked them away.

As for Coronado, Long John bound the baron's hands to a length of rope and threw him off his own ship to ride the waves all the way back to Gasparilla's secret headquarters on Charlotte Harbor. Without water skis or any flotation devices, the good Coronado didn't keep his head above the briny sea for very long.

Maybe that's what I should have done to Dustin. He deserved a taste of the sweet trade.

Anyway, ever since my kayaking days, I always had one eye looking for signs of treasure whenever I was out on the water. People laughed, but I knew it was out there. Pirates couldn't take it with them when they died, especially if it was hidden in a secret location and somebody whacked them with no warning. All that gold and silver was just waiting, only a matter of time.

Plus, I've always thought that being a crabber is a lot like being a pirate. Both happen on the water, and both involve taking stuff that you don't have to pay for, right? And both definitely have their secrets. Crabbers think like pirates, which helps if you're looking for gold.

I finished up with the last trap in the line and checked my treasure chest, the old cooler where I keep the crabs. All their claws snapped up when I opened the lid. Looked like about thirty or so. Luckily, most of them were big jimmies, what they call number ones and number twos. Maybe I'd bring in a bushel, about seventy-five crabs. One time I caught two bushels in a single haul. That's my personal record.

You won't get rich fishing for crab. They're not exactly worth their weight in gold. People, like my mom, are always railing on me about getting another job, one that pays more. But, man, look at what's available to a kid my age. MegaMart? McDonalds? Seriously? Plus, who would trade an office with this kind of view for a job bussing tables at some corporate owned barf box? Flash – not this guy. I mean, seriously dude, I'd rather wade around out here checking traps on foot with a cooler tied to my butt than do that.

Hammerhead got his nose out of the way as I closed the lid on my treasure chest.

"Three more lines to go, boy."

He just licked his chops and gave me that *what's for dinner* look. Sometimes I have to net a mullet if he starts driving me crazy. Makes a big mess, though, when he tears into it: fish guts everywhere. Still, it's better than the constant whining and his cold, sweaty nose always poking me in the back of the knee.

I climbed up in the tower and fired up the *Stripe*. I cranked the tunes and gunned the motor. In less than five seconds, we were blasting across the top of the water headed to the next line. Not bad for an old mullet boat.

The view from the tower when I'm running on the Sound is seriously awesome – even better when you wear polarized sunglasses like I do. The water is shallow and clear enough to see everything. Fish shoot out of the way when they feel me coming. Big, fat stingrays can just suddenly leap out and get three or four feet of air. Oh, and we have manatee too. Some people call them sea cows, kind of like a walrus but without the tusks. I have to look out for them because they stay near the surface and swim pretty slow.

As I zipped along, halfway to the next set of traps, I spotted one. It's pretty easy to see a manatee on the water if you know what to look for and keep your eyes peeled. They are truly massive animals, all blubber and muscle, about 800 or 1000 pounds. Instead of hind flippers, manatees have a huge, round tail. When they kick that thing, it pushes up columns of water every few yards. That push is what I saw first.

I grabbed the throttle and slowly pulled it back. The motor got softer, and the music got louder. I wonder if manatees like to rock? Didn't seem to bother this one. After a few seconds, she emerged ahead of that push I was talking about and lifted her nose up into the air. I say she because a moment later her calf came up beside her. Cute little bugger – for a manatee – all gray and wrinkly like an elephant. The mom had three long, white prop scars across her back. She had probably dove down to get away from some boat and barely made it. Most of the adult manatees have those scars. It's sad. I do my best to look out for them. Never hit one yet. Shows what you can do if you pay attention.

Mom dove back under, but the baby kept his head up a little longer to peek at Hammerhead. The mutt definitely saw the little manatee as well. Oh yes. Saw him and wanted him.

Before I could stop him, Hammerhead launched directly at that poor, little thing. Now, I learned something about manatees that day. They can move when they have to. That guy ducked his wrinkly little head back under and took off like a seal before Hammerhead got his first paw wet. Because the water was so clear that day, I saw him shoot past his mom for the open bay.

Hammerhead splashed down behind the bigger manatee, and she didn't take too kindly to it. She lifted that enormous tail out of the water and brought it back down like a whale – about two inches from Hammerhead's nose. Dude, that would have hurt! Talk about hammerhead. That would have been the last hammer to ever hit his head.

He did the smart thing, turned around and swam back to the boat. Lucky for him Labradors have webbed feet. He's fast. He made it back to the boat before she could fire another shot. I climbed down and pulled his soaking butt back onboard. He thanked me by shaking saltwater all over my freshly dried shorts. Man's best friend? Ha. Some dog.

So a couple of minutes later, we pulled up to the next line, and I started my routine. Hammerhead stretched out on the deck in the sun to dry out. He can truly be one lazy first mate.

The first trap contained two crabs. Both were shorts, a crab that isn't wide enough across the shell between the two points. I can't legally keep them if they don't measure at least five inches across. Back into the bay they went.

"Fatten up guys."

Maybe I should consider giving them steroid injections. I heard it works with cattle down in Argentina. Too bad I hate needles. I don't think I could work up the nerve to give a crab a shot.

With the electric motor, I nudged the *White Stripe* up to the next float, shoved the tiller over, and grabbed my gaff. When the trap broke the surface, I thought I had a big jimmie. Then I saw that it was just some trash – an old bottle. I find stuff like that sometimes. Found an old flip-flop once. How it works its way through the hole in the side of the chicken wire, I don't have a clue. Storm maybe?

With the boat spinning around, I dumped the bottle out on the deck and rebaited the trap. The chicken wire box splashed back to the bottom just as the boat circled back around to the line. Perfect. I grabbed the tiller and straightened her up.

The bottle tumbled across the deck and clunked into the back of the boat. Not wanting the glass to break, I reached for it as I guided the *Stripe* to the next red elephant head float. Something rolled around inside the bottle. I let go of the tiller.

The long bottle looked old, I mean ancient, older than AC/DC even. The label had worn off, if it ever had one, and the glass was clear, like a liquor bottle. It had some scum on it, so I grabbed my T-shirt and wiped it off. I looked hard at the thing inside. It appeared to be a rolled up sheet of paper. *No freakin' way.* I felt my heart take off, and I started hardcore tripping.

The small end of the bottle was plugged, maybe a cork, not sticking out far enough to grab. I looked around for something. The gaff point might work. I poked the point of the hook directly into the center of the black plug and pushed. It was hard. Didn't have much give to it. I kept working it. After a while I got the whole thing through. The plug didn't give up and fall apart or anything. It held together pretty well. I pushed the hook further until the barb popped through, then spun it around so it would catch on the underside of the plug. I yanked straight up and the whole thing came flying out.

I tilted the bottle and carefully slid the paper out. It was yellow and old, like pictures I'd seen of the original Declaration of Independence. Slowly, so it wouldn't rip, I unrolled the paper. I knew right away – it was a map.

Dude. My heart was going ninety miles an hour.

It looked like islands in the water. Some of the islands had words next to them, but I couldn't read any of that. And, there were some numbers. Maybe it was Spanish. It had a lot of vowels and some *de*'s and *la*'s. And right in the middle of one of those islands was a big, fat *X*. *No freakin' way!* I was holding a pirate's treasure map!

I tried to think, but my brain had stopped working. I just stared at that paper. Maybe that's what they call shock. I don't know. Looking back on it, I guess everything in my head just sort of floated away. I heard the water lapping on the side of the boat, and I heard an outboard cruising by somewhere, but those things were like a million miles away. The only thing that snapped me out of it was Hammerhead doing that cold, wet nose thing into the back of my knee.

I studied the layout and the shape of the islands, but you know how ancient maps are. Everything's a little distorted since they didn't have airplanes or satellites to see what it really looked like from above. It definitely looked different from anything I was used to. It could be anywhere. If only I knew Spanish.

Salt. His name just popped into my head. He knows some Spanish, he knows the water, and he sure knows pirates. Plus, he's one of the few people I could trust with a thing like this. He lived all alone on a remote island. He didn't even have a cell phone. Who was he going to tell? Anyway, the old man could keep a secret. If Salt could do anything, he could keep a secret.

The Crabby Pelican

Since Salt didn't have a phone out on Cayo Costa, about the only way to reach him was to go to the island and hope he was home. I must have set all kinds of speed records for a mullet boat on the way over. Hammerhead bailed on his front seat and headed for the back of the boat after I smacked a couple of wakes pretty good with the bow. After a bumpy forty minute ride, we eased into Pelican Bay and idled towards Salt's canal.

Most of Cayo Costa is a state park run by the Florida Park Service. The only way to get to the island is to take a boat or swim, and I wouldn't recommend swimming since Boca Grande Pass is full of sharks. Lots of folks sail over and spend the night in their sailboats in Pelican Bay next to the ranger station. For that reason, and because of the manatees, the whole bay is a slow speed, no wake zone.

That just about killed me.

It felt like we'd never get to Salt's canal. After a year of idling, I steered the *Stripe* into the cut between the mangroves. It's a couple of hundred yards long; then it doglegs to the left and runs another fifty to Salt's place. I kept idling the boat past all the branches and roots, occasionally spooking out redfish. A great blue heron sprang off a branch and squawked away over the trees. I could tell from all the wildlife that no one had been down the canal recently. Since it was a Sunday, Salt was probably still at home, sleeping.

I rounded the dogleg and stared at a very disappointing sight – the empty, dead end of Salt's canal. No boat at the dock.

I kept going anyway, figuring I'd leave a note on his door, not that I knew what it would say. He can't call me. He doesn't have a phone. And e-mail's out of the question. I realized I still wasn't thinking very clearly. I just needed to pull over and take a break. Slow down a little. Maybe ole Hammerhead had to pee. I drifted to the dock and tied up the boat.

Hammerhead immediately jumped off and trotted down the wooden dock to take care of business. I pulled the map out of the bottle once more and looked it over. Some of the scribblings were faded; some stood out a little better. Words were written by hand in script, and, to make things worse, a lot were written upside down. I had to turn the map around several times to even guess at the Spanish.

I could understand just one phrase: "*Golfo de Mexico*." The Gulf of Mexico. At least this was a map of the Gulf coast, but which part? I needed Salt.

Hammerhead came panting back to stand on the dock next to the boat, happy and relieved.

"Okay, boy. Let's go leave Mr. Salt a note."

Salt lived in the oddest house, even for Florida, and we have a lot of odd houses down here. It stood on short, fat pilings in the middle of an old oak forest, completely surrounded on three sides by piles of stone crab traps. The season was closed for a couple more months, so they were in his yard instead of in the Gulf.

The oak trees were seriously enormous. I mean these trees were huge, with massive trunks. I could barely see the sky through the leaves. When oaks grow this big and this close to the sea, the wind kind of stunts the tops at a certain point, and they just spread out instead of growing taller.

The small forest of oaks sat up on a little, sandy hill. My guess is that it's maybe ten or fifteen feet above sea level. That may sound low, but it's actually pretty high for the islands out here. My house is no more than five feet above sea level, a little scary during hurricane season when a storm surge can easily top ten.

The house itself was dark green and so old I've never been able to tell if the green comes from paint or moss. All kinds of moss grew everywhere, like a big moss fest, moss-a-fa-looza. Spanish moss grew all over the trees and the house in long, gray beards. Slick, bright-green moss patches spread over other boards. And, wiry black stuff, that could've been Mr. Henley's nose hair, sprouted out of knotholes. The place should've fallen down years ago. That's the way it looks, but if you pound on it, watch your knuckles. It's rock solid. I'll never make that mistake again.

But, the oddest thing about it is the shape. It's round, completely round, like one of those old hat boxes in your grandma's closet. Salt says the place has been in his family for generations, and they built it round so the hurricane winds could never get a grip. Maybe that's why the slick moss is plastered all over, too. Makes it even more slippery.

Hammerhead and I walked up the steps to the porch, and, just because I'm polite, I knocked on the door. Nothing. I knocked again.

"Who is it?"

I knew that squawk, and it wouldn't be answering the door either. It was Salt's roommate and sole companion, Aruba, a colorful Amazon parrot. He was named for Salt's favorite island down in the Caribbean, the place he always threatened to sail away and retire to whenever fishing for stones got bad.

"Hey, Aruba. It's me, Harley." I looked at him through the window. "Don't get up. I'm just going to leave a note for Salt."

"Raaaaaaawk!"

Luckily I had found a pen on the boat, but no paper. I checked out Salt's porch. Nothing. I didn't want to just write on the wood. Then I spotted a dried up sea grape leaf lying on the porch. They're big, like, about the size of your hand. I picked it up and pressed it against the door.

Salt, I found something. Gotta talk soon. Going to the Crabby Pelican. Harley.

I wedged the leaf into the crack between the door and the jamb and stepped over to the window.

"Take it easy, Aruba. See ya."

The bird just sat on his perch staring at me kind of sideways with one of those beady little bird eyes.

"Ready, boy?"

Hammerhead looked up at me and wagged his tail. That dog's happy 95 percent of the time, even in a situation like this. Unbelievable.

We jumped off the porch into the sand and dead oak leaves, and walked past the crab traps back down the hill to the dock. On a Sunday, if Salt isn't home, chances are he's at the Crabby Pelican.

At the canal, I could see the sky starting to cloud up a little. I checked the tree tops. Maybe the wind had started to shift. An afternoon thunderstorm was a definite possibility. Oh well. For a mission like this, I was fully prepared to get a little wet. Wouldn't be the first time that day.

Hammerhead jumped into the boat before I did and worked his way over to the crab cooler.

"Get your nose out of there. We're going to the Pelican. You know I'll get you something."

He reluctantly backed off, licking his chops and looking a little ashamed of himself the way dogs can do.

I unhitched the Stripe, climbed the tower, and started her up. Soon, but not soon enough, we were flying across the flats again, dodging sand bars, oyster beds, and mangroves on the way to The Crabby Pelican. It's a good haul south in a small town called St. James City at the southern tip of Pine Island. I took every shortcut I knew, but the ride still took almost an hour dock to dock.

As we idled up the canal to the restaurant, I could smell the burgers. Even with all kinds of seafood on the menu, the Pelican probably sold more burgers and fries than anything else.

The dock was packed, as I knew it would be on a Sunday at lunch. There wasn't an open slip in sight. My eyes floated over every boat until – BAM! – there it was, Salt's boat. He has a bigger boat than mine, made for the open sea and the stone crabs that live under it. He had docked towards the far end in one of the larger slips. The crab boat stood out pretty well because of the flat top. Nearby, on the end of the dock, I saw my friend Bill's boat, a 26-foot Angler open fisherman. Actually it was his dad's boat, but he took it out more than his old man.

I'd run out of dock so I tied up alongside the Angler. Bill wouldn't mind. I threw a couple of rubber fenders over the side so I wouldn't mess up his dad's pretty paint job and hitched my ropes on the cleats sticking up from the Angler's gunnels.

Hammerhead hopped over into Bill's boat without me saying a word. He smelled the burgers, too. I threw on my T-shirt and flip-flops and followed him.

The Pelican sits slam up to the edge of the canal with an outside deck leaning over it. There's plenty of tables along that deck with umbrellas to keep the sun off and those little sprayer things shooting out mist everywhere to cool folks down. Hammerhead and I walked up the steps and threaded around the tables. The deck was jammed with people, which meant my dog enjoyed a sea of adoring hands. He even got treated to a couple of appetizers. Everybody loves a happy dog, and he played them to a tee.

From up on the deck the view included the dock, the boats and people's back yards across the canal. The Pelican backed up to a neighborhood built on canals, fancier than Palmetto Cove, so the yards are a little easier on the eyes. One house even has a little windmill spinning under the coconut trees.

"Go on," I told Hammerhead. "Go lay down by the door, and I'll get you something."

Hammerhead knew the routine. He shuffled over to the kitchen door at the end of the deck all sad and lonely because he couldn't come inside. He slowly spun around three times and laid down with his chin on his paws, so he could stare at me with those pitiful eyes. Well trained actor, he was.

"That's it. Now stay."

I walked back to the regular back door, the one with the porthole for a window. The place is old as dirt, been there forever, so has the crazy back door. It weighs a ton, like a bank vault. If anything happened to the restaurant, I guarantee you that door would still be standing. I threw my weight back and heaved it open. An old couple shuffled out to the deck as I fought to keep the thing from swinging back and ending their lives.

"Thanks, sonny."

My friend, Bill, sat at a table inside making noise with some other guys from school. His back was to me, so naturally I wet my finger in a glass of ice water and planted it inside his ear. He jerked away and yelped like a little kid.

"Dude! Wet Willie's are so immature!" He sounded well irritated. "Grow up."

"Not half as immature as you, dude," I laughed. "You just sounded like a pre-schooler!" I watched him dry out his ear with a napkin. "By the way, Hammerhead left you a hot, steamy surprise in your boat. Sorry. He's been on the water for a while."

"Dude!" He jumped up from his chair and looked out the window at his dad's boat. "Seriously, dude, that's not funny."

"Relax, man. He's got more home training than you do. He left it in your cast net bucket. You can rinse that out." I winked at the other guys and pulled Bill's cap down over his face as I walked away.

The Crabby Pelican has two rooms inside for customers – the dining room and the bar. The dining room holds, like, fifteen tables or so. It's not fancy. They put big sheets of white paper down on the table tops and give crayons to the kids. If the pictures are good enough, they get stapled to the wood on the ceiling. Those pictures cover the place like fish scales to the point where you can't see much of the wood anymore.

The bar is around the corner, off by itself, longer than it is wide, and darker than the dining room since it has windows on only one side instead of three. And, those windows have bushes growing over them outside. The bar itself is wooden with little nautical knick-knacks frozen under clear epoxy. Salt sat at the far end sipping an ice tea.

Like a horse with blinders, I made a beeline towards him and didn't even notice the waitress rushing out of the kitchen with a tray of coleslaw. In a move only a waitress or an NFL tailback could pull off, she changed direction and jogged around me at the last instant.

"Harley Davidsen Cooper! Are you trying to dance with me? I don't get off 'til six, boy. You need to make an appointment if you want me to put on my dancing shoes!"

That's right. My full name is Harley Davidsen Cooper. Most people think my dad named me after the motorcycle because he rides one now, even though he screwed up the spelling on the birth certificate. I don't tell folks any differently either because the real reason's too embarrassing. My mom named me after one of her soap opera stars – one of her *female* soap opera stars.

The Crabby Pelican's waitresses have always thought I was named after the bike. And they've been there as long as the Crabby Pelican. So it's been years of good press for me.

I had nearly plowed into Verna. I always get her and her sister mixed up. They both work at the Pelican and both look so similar that the only way I can tell them apart is to look at their ears. Verna has way too many earrings in hers, like ten in each one.

Honestly though, it really doesn't matter if I keep them straight or not. They both always give me a hard time. That's okay. It's embarrassing, but it's never dull.

"Sorry, Verna. Didn't see you."

Everybody in the bar was staring at us now.

"Well, you're lucky you weren't dancing with this cole slaw. You better look out, boy. It's liable to think you're being fresh and jump right off this tray to give you a kiss."

She hustled out to the dining room – thank God.

Salt was smiling down at his tea. He wasn't looking at me, but I knew he'd seen the whole thing. I sat on the empty barstool next to him.

"Dude. Am I glad to see you. Disregard the note on your door." I lowered my voice. "Listen. I found something today. Something you're gonna like."

"That so?" He squinted at me under the bill of his Matlacha Seafood Company cap. That old hat was as sea beaten as his face and as tattered as his gray hair. He had a cup of some kind of chowder full of oyster crackers in front of him. He went back to it. "Must be pretty important to track me down here."

"Salt, I think it's a map," I said and then lowered my voice even more to where no one but Salt could possibly hear. "A treasure map." I looked around to make sure no one was listening in. They all seemed to be minding their business.

"Harley!" boomed a voice from the other side of the bar.

The voice startled me, and I jumped.

It was Big Frank, the cook. "Got anything for me?"

It took a second to remember his name, even though he had worked there longer than Verna.

"Uh, yeah, Frank. As a matter of fact I do. A couple dozen jimmies. Ones and twos."

"Well, alright then! Let's get 'em in here out of the sun." He turned to Verna's sister Gladiolus and barked loud enough for the whole place to hear. "Hey! Gladdy! Got a new special tonight! Blue Crab! Write it down on the board!" Then he rang that stupid bell twice. So much for being inconspicuous. "Want me to put it towards your account, Harley?"

"Uh, yeah. That's fine. Hey, Frank. Mind throwing Hammerhead some scraps?"

"Way ahead of you, crab dude. He's on the second course already."

"Thanks." I turned back to Salt. "Hey Salt, how about giving me a hand with those crabs?" I winked at him.

"Man, you're wound up tighter than a school of bait," he laughed. "Can I finish my soup first? Why don't you go to the john and relax a little?"

He was right. I had completely barged in on his lunch.

"Oh, sorry. Okay. Be right back."

I slid off the stool and went around the corner into the tiny hall that led to the men's room. Just before I passed the lady's room, the door opened and this enormous woman squeezed out. I don't mean fat. I mean tall, as in Amazon. Now, this hall was so small it looked like it belonged inside a boat. When she camc out, I saw there was no way it could hold us both. But before I could stop, her enormous body pinned me to the wall of that tiny hall. An awkward moment to say the least.

"Me, excuse. No did I see you," she said in a thick Russian accent.

Her name was Ivana Rovich, my neighbor, the only wealthy resident of Palmetto Cove. Everyone knew her story. She moved here from Russia about five years ago. Her husband passed away a couple of years later, after he had built her a gigantic mansion overlooking the Sound. He was some kind of vodka maker.

She pressed against me not moving, just smiling down at me. I'm sure she knew who I was, too. Palmetto Cove's not that big.

"That's okay, Mrs. Rovich…if…I could…just," I said between grunts as I tried to wiggle out.

She didn't budge an inch. She just smiled. I got nervous. If anyone saw us that close to each other I'd never live it down. The lady was old enough to be my grandmother.

"Hey, I'm sorry. Maybe I could ask you to step back into the restroom for a second, Mrs. Rovich?"

She stepped forward instead, shoving my face into her chest.

"I sorry. No understand English much very good."

She understood English just fine. And, she knew exactly what she was doing. She was enjoying it.

All of a sudden someone busted out laughing. I didn't even have to look. It was Bill, my friend from the dining room.

"Dude. That's funny!" he said.

His remark didn't make things any better. Then he made the situation even worse by wetting his finger and sticking it into my ear. I tried to grab his arm, but I just couldn't get my hand around the Russian lady. She should've been a professional wrestler. She was smothering me...and slaughtering my reputation!

Mrs. Rovich just kept smiling through the whole thing. And now, with Bill's finger in my ear, the whole thing was getting a little weird.

"Move...back...please, Mrs. Rovich," I said, barely able to breathe.

She stuck a business card between my teeth.

"You need work? You call me. I have big, big . . . yard. It need big, strong man. Man like you. Strong like bull!"

Luckily, right after that, let me go. But, the ancient lady winked at me as she walked away. I felt queasy.

Bill was still twisting his finger in my ear. I punched him in the gut.

"Ow, man! I was just getting you back." He couldn't stop laughing, despite the fist to his belly. "Guess you're a just little miffed cause I snuck up on you and your girlfriend, huh?"

I just ignored him and walked into the tiny bathroom, using the tiny hook to lock the tiny door. Unbelievable. That story won't go away anytime soon. It would just get bigger and more ridiculous every time someone told it. Great.

The bathroom was so small I could barely turn around. A closet with a urinal, a toilet and a sink all crammed in between walls covered with hot chick, beer posters. I looked in the grimy mirror, took off my Rays ball cap, wet my hands, and ran them through my hair. It's dirty blond, in case you were wondering. Curly and shaggy, the way I like it. Keeps the bugs away.

Then, I splashed my face to get the salt crust off. With a couple of paper towels, I dried off and replaced my cap. I took a whiz, zipped up, and shook my shoulders a little to relax them. Okay, I felt better. I unhooked the door and opened it, ready to face the humiliation once more.

Bill was still there, snickering into his hand.

"Laugh it up, hotshot," I said. "Laugh it up."

I walked back down the hall and around the corner to the bar. Salt's stool was empty. I looked around the bar and didn't see him, so I headed for the dining room and the back door.

"Getting those jimmies, Harley?"

"Yeah. I'll be right back, Big Frank."

I walked down the crowded bar and through the congested dining room careful to avoid Verna and Gladiolus. Wasn't easy, but I made it to the door without bumping into either one. I brought my shades down over my eyes just before I shoved the porthole door open.

Dustin, his client, and Eden were coming up the deck. Dustin spotted me. Wonderful.

"Well, well, well. Crab-boy. Still got the crabs?"

He could be such a dork.

"Another day in paradise, Dustin. Excuse me."

"Whoa, whoa, whoa. What's the rush?" he said stepping into my path. "Don't you want to meet my guest?"

"Hi. How are you?" I said as cordially as the circumstances allowed.

The man looked Indian, or something. You know, Hindu, not American. Probably didn't speak a lick of English.

"Harley here's a regular expert on crustaceans, aren't you Harley? Big business down here in Florida. Tell him how much you clear a year, Harley. Go ahead, tell him."

"Well, it's not quite as good as it used to be, but it's a living," I said politely.

The man just nodded and smiled, as if he understood everything.

"Awww. That's too bad, crab-boy," said Dustin. "Maybe it's time to scrap that garbage barge and get a real job. Maybe you could run down to MegaMart and bag groceries for your mom."

The dork usually didn't get to me, but that last comment turned off my politeness like a switch. I could take his insults, but there's no reason to bring my mom into it. Yes, she's a cashier at MegaMart. Not her first choice in life, I'm sure, but she works hard for everything we have. We can't all be rich, corporate execs like Dustin's dad.

"Yeah, I wanted a cushy job like you, Dustin, but your daddy said the professional block head position was already taken." I stared at him while my blood pressure rose.

"Ooooo. Touchy, touchy. Come on, guys. Smells like low tide out here."

He brushed past me making sure to slam his shoulder into mine as he did. The Hindu looked nervous. He just tipped his head and followed.

Eden caught my eye and mouthed the words *I'm so sorry* as she went. She also brushed up against me, smelling like flowers on the beach. I didn't mind that part at all.

At the end of the deck. Hammerhead was still chowing down, so I left him there and walked the other way, towards the stairs leading down to the dock. Salt was standing in front of my boat working his teeth over with a toothpick.

"You better come onboard," I said when I got within earshot.

Salt stuck the toothpick into his shirt pocket and stepped down into Bill's boat. He wore a long sleeves shirt and matching pants. Both tan. Salt always dressed like that, no matter how hot it was. Personally, I don't know how people can stand to dress that way, especially in August.

"Well?" said Salt after he had crossed all the way over to my boat. He stood there on the bow, arms folded over his chest, looking mean.

"Hang on," I said.

I moved around him to the very tip of the bow. The boat has a small casting deck there. Under that fiberglass deck is the anchor compartment. I reached in and dug my hand under the anchor line. The bottle was just where I left it.

We went around the tower to the back of the boat where I had a couple of seats, away from the dock and prying eyes. In the bright sunlight, I pulled out the paper and handed it to Salt. As he unrolled it, a cloud passed over the sun making the map a little darker. Salt looked like he was studying the paper hard. I couldn't see his eyes because of his sunglasses, but he did at least sound like he was being thoughtful.

"Hmmmm," he said, as if he was a doctor looking at a lab report.

More careful examination.

"Hmmmm."

"Well?"

"Yep."

"What do you mean, *yep*? Is it a map, or what?"

"It's not a *what* so it must be a map."

"You think it's real?"

"It's real, all right. Just feel that paper."

Salt always like to have a little fun with me.

"C'mon, Salt. I know it's real paper. Is the map a real treasure map?"

"Only one way to find out."

"How's that?"

"Find the treasure."

I knew he was still joking, but that actually gave me a glimmer of hope, because somehow he made it sound like finding the treasure was possible.

"I can't understand much of it, Salt. Is that Spanish?"

"Looks like it."

"Well, do you know what it says?"

"Yep."

"Salt, stop fooling around and just tell me!" I suddenly blurted out.

He lowered the map and looked over his glasses at me. He just held that look without saying anything. I wouldn't ever want to be on Salt's bad side. He's never really directed it towards me, but I'm sure he has one. I just hoped I'd never set foot in that territory.

"You didn't say 'Simon says.'"

I breathed a sigh of relief.

"Okay, here's the Gulf," he said in that gruff, sea-going voice of his.

"That's the part I get."

"And these little outlines? They're all islands in a bay."

"And the words?"

"Well, says here, this one's Bird Cay. 'Isla de Joseffa' that's Joseffa Island." He thought about that for a moment. "And this one here? This one's Guana Cay." He stopped pointing at the islands and looked at me over his glasses again. "That means bird poop island. Must've been the birds' privvy." He let out a little chuckle at that one. "And, over here, see that bigger one? That says it belonged to a bunch of Indians, and not the kind that just walked in there with your buddy just now. American Indians. The Spaniards called them Calusa."

"Calusa? The same ones that lived here?"

"Could be."

"So it's a map of Pine Island Sound?"

"Didn't say that. The Calusa ruled this coast from up near Tampa down to the Keys. Lotta territory."

"Well, I found the map in the water *here*."

"Don't mean nothing. Storms come and move everything."

"Why are there little fish symbols all over the lagoon next to the big *X*?"

"Probably fish pens. Calusa had them all over. Long gone, though."

"And the big *X*?"

"That'd be the free-booter's international symbol for buried treasure."

When he said the word *treasure* I could have sworn that I saw Salt's eyes twinkle through the sunglasses. He loved this pirate stuff as much as I did and had to be eating it up on the inside. But, old Salt? He'd never let it show.

"So what kind of treasure is it?"

"Don't say. But I reckon it has to do with these Indians. I do know this one old tale about the Calusa Indians that might fit."

In his rusted voice, he told me the Joseffa legend, the one I re-told at the beginning of this thing. He loved telling stories about pirates and the sea, and can sure tell them a lot better than I can. He's so much more dramatic. Over the years, I'll bet he's told me over a hundred, the same ones a few times. I don't ever stop him, even if I've heard one before. I like to hear them as much as he likes to tell them. It's way better than going to the movies, cheaper, too. But this story I had never heard.

"So all that gold could still be around hcrc," I said when he was done. "Dude, that's totally sick! But when I looked at that map, none of those islands looked familiar. Where's Joseffa Island today?"

"Time don't wait for you to strike gold before it moves on and changes maps. Here's what ya do – take this thing home tonight. Pull it out when there ain't no one around and compare it to some charts. You've got those right?"

"Yeah. There are some old ones laying around. My old man left them."

"The older, the better. There's one date on here. See right there? Says it was the year 1804. That's a long time ago. Those islands aren't going to look the same, not the same shapes. But . . . they'll likely be in about the same position. Connect the dots, and you might have something."

"Does it say anything else useful?"

"No. Not really, though it does have the symbol for a dead man near the treasure. That could mean anything though. Those pirates killed people all the time." He rolled the map up, stuck it in the bottle, and passed it back to me. "You do that, and if anything turns up, find me. I'll help you look for it. But right now, you'd better get those crabs up to Big Frank."

"Awesome, Salt. Thanks, man."

"I'll be out on the island the next couple of days should anything turn up," he told me as he made his way back over Bill's boat.

The Lucky Swab

When I got back up to the deck with the cooler of blue crabs in my arms, Hammerhead was still lying by the kitchen door. No surprise. What shocked me was that Eden Baker was sitting next to him in the plastic chair.

"Hey, Harley."

"Hey, Eden. Watch out. That dog's got fleas." My weak attempt at a joke.

"This sweet thing? He certainly does not."

With his eyes closed, Hammerhead was enjoying the chin scratching Eden offered him. I set the cooler down and sat on it in front of them. She had pulled on a T-shirt and a pair of tight, white shorts, but in my mind I still saw her body in that string bikini.

"Listen, Harley. I just want to…well, apologize for Dustin's rudeness."

"Did he leave you for the Hindu?"

"No, he's in there playing Mr. Big Fisherman for the tourists. I got tired of it. It's just that he doesn't think before he runs his mouth."

"Look, Eden. You don't have to apologize for him. I've known him my whole life. He didn't just start acting like that today. I can handle it."

"I know you can. I just wanted you to know that sometimes even though I'm in the same boat with him, I'm not in the same boat with him. Know what I mean?"

Her hair flowed over her shoulders like silk...*golden* silk. And, her eyes were so blue they put the sky to shame. My temperature must have shot up to a hundred and three just looking at her. I almost forgot to breathe. I tried to maintain my cool, but all I could do was repeat what she had said.

"Yeah. I know what you mean."

She leaned over and put her hand on my knee. It felt as hot as she looked. I thought my heart was going to knock my head off.

"You're a cool guy, Harley Davidsen Cooper. You've got a lot of class."

She stood up and walked past me back to the restaurant, and I didn't say a single word. I couldn't. I couldn't even turn around and watch her go. Didn't want her to see my face while it was still as red as it felt.

Once, I had been at a beach party, just a bunch of kids on the sand. Everyone had stayed together until sunset, and as fate would have it, I found myself standing next to Eden. That evening she taught me the Sunset Game.

"Pick a time," she said as easy as the breeze.

"Say what?" I said.

"Guess how long it takes for the sun to set once it hits the water, dummy."

When I still didn't get it she explained that you have to guess the time it takes for the sun to completely disappear below the horizon once the bottom part touches the water. I had watched a million sunsets, but I had no clue.

"Five minutes," I said.

"Way off," she said giggling at me.

"But if I'm right? What's the prize?"

She blew me a kiss.

"Two and a half," she said, looking at her watch.

I can't even tell you how long it took. I didn't care. Those seconds next to her watching the sun sink into the sea had to be the finest seconds that ever ticked by in my life. Everybody quieted down to watch the sun set, and it was like Eden and I were all alone. No prize, though. Like she said, I was way off.

"Mmmm. Mmmm. Mmph. I remember those days." It was Big Frank in the kitchen door, with one huge hand over his heart.

There is no privacy on the shore. None whatsoever.

"C'mon, loverboy. Hand over those crabs."

I was glad for the change of subject. I handed him the cooler and followed him into the kitchen.

The Crabby Pelican's kitchen is a greasy place. I slipped on a slick spot and almost busted my butt. Luckily, I found a stainless steel table to grab on the way down. Some guy smoking a cigarette and peeling potatoes smirked at me after I had righted myself.

Big Frank dumped the crabs into a large plastic bucket. They skittered around down there for a few seconds before they settled – all those blue claws frozen up in the air daring somebody to reach in and try to grab one of them. It was the end of the line for them, but they weren't going down without a fight.

"Looks good. Looks good. I'll put twenty-five bucks in your account," said Frank. "Couldn't get any more?"

"Only had time to check a couple of lines this morning."

"Got time for a burger?"

"Yessir."

"Sweetheart, get your butt over here and put a plate together for our seafood distributor."

The potato peeler stubbed out his smoke into the side of a garbage can and shuffled over to a stack of white plates. I kept my eye on him the whole time he fixed the food. You never can tell about these shifty potato-peelers that Big Frank brings in. Didn't want any funny business in my lunch.

I guess I shouldn't be so paranoid. They treat me pretty good around here – at least Frank and the waitresses. By law, I'm only supposed to sell crabs to a licensed wholesaler, like Matlacha Seafood. But technically, if Big Frank's giving me food and not cash, I'm not selling to him. Anyway, he's getting a great deal, and he knows it.

I poured myself a Coke and took my plate of burger and fries out to the deck. Hammerhead lifted his black head and swept his tail across the boards like a broom as I took a seat in the plastic chair. Then he stood and eyeballed my lunch after I plopped it down on the cooler.

"Here you go, boy. Thanks for being a chick magnet." I gave him a fry.

The burger was perfect. No hairs or cigarette butts. I left a few fries on the plate and set it down for Hammerhead. He licked it clean, ketchup and all. There's not much that dog won't eat.

I looked up just in time to see Captain Dufuss walk out the back door. He turned the other way towards the dock without spotting me – the Hindu in tow. Eden brought up the rear. Nice choice for caboose, if I do say so myself. She looked over and tossed me another one of those cute, little girly waves. Dude. That's all I can say about it.

I don't know if it's hormones or adrenaline or what that rushes around in your blood when you see a sight like that. All I know is, it's good. Powerful good. They ought to put that feeling in a bottle and sell it.

To avoid further confrontation, I waited until they pulled away from the dock before me and Hammerhead went down to The Stripe. She was still tied up to Bill's Angler. He had probably walked down the street to one of the guy's houses to play video games. Loved his games. I didn't get it, though. How can you stay inside when you have all this adventure out here?

The time was probably getting close to two o'clock. I've gotten to where I can usually guess the time within fifteen minutes if I can see the sky. That's in the day. I'm no good at night. Maybe if I spent more time on the water at night I would be. Maybe I could beat Eden at the Sunset Game, and my prize would be to take her on a nighttime boat ride. I decided to time the next sunset I saw, just in case.

I could see the big, anvil-shaped tops of several thunderstorms sticking up over the houses and trees. If you stare at a storm for a couple of seconds, just stare at it, you can tell which way it's going pretty quick, especially if it's against a structure like a house or a tree. One thunderhead looked like it was going to cross my course back to Palmetto Cove. I decided that if I swung out wide enough I might miss it.

"Let's go Hammerhead."

He quit sniffing around Bill's boat and jumped over into the Stripe. Ten minutes later we were back out on the bay blazing down the channel.

Wind from building storms was starting to rough up the water in patches out on the Sound, and the air felt fifteen degrees cooler as the boat skipped across those little waves. Between us and home, a solid column of water connected the clouds and the bay. I went back to the trap line I'd left after finding the bottle and finished checking it while waiting for the rain to blow by. But, the storm pushed closer and chased me west, so I ended up checking two more lines that lay further away from the lightning and rain.

My arms worked the electric motor and pulled the traps like a robot on auto-pilot. My mind was not on the crabs or even the afternoon storms. I couldn't stop thinking about that map. When I should've seen crabs dropping into the cooler, I saw gold doubloons.

Though I had never actually seen one, I knew exactly what the Spanish coins looked like, thanks to Salt. He described them in almost every pirate story that he told. One tale centered around a boat-load of doubloons off Cuba. I'll try to tell it the way Salt told me.

The seas were mighty on that day, as the Florida Blanca sailed south towards Cuba. The waves rolled by like mountain ranges, peak after peak after peak. Gasparilla rode his ship high to the frothy tops and down deep into the lowly valleys as wind punished the sails and lighting tore through the sky.

The men worried and fretted aplenty, some even prayed, but old Gasparilla kept his eye on the compass and his hand on the wheel. He knew his great, grand three-masted barque had seen worse before. So, he stood tall at the wheel, firmly guiding her through the perilous squall.

All at once, he saw a body in the stormy sea, a man's head bobbing in the surf. The captain had not heard his crew raise the alarm, so he knew this unfortunate soul must have been cast from another vessel. Then he saw the man's arms flail weakly against the waves. The swab was still alive.

"Man overboard!" he yelled through the storm. "Throw a line!"

Against the raging whitecaps, the men wrestled the swab onboard and took him inside to the quartermaster's cabin. Gasparilla gave the wheel to Long John MacBlane and followed them in.

The rescued man seemed barely alive. One of the pirates doused his throat with a bit of rum to revive him. The man sat up and his eyes opened wide as he stared at the cut-throats gathered around.

"Have I died and gone to hell?" he asked.

"Not yet," replied Gasparilla. "But that fate be swift upon ye if ye don't hastily repay our kindness. Pulled you, we did, from the teeth of the storm."

"Thank you, kind sir. I'm forever in your debt." The man checked his wet pockets, but found them empty. "I'm afraid I have nothing to offer you as the sea has taken all that I own."

"Then the sea be taking you back," said Gasparilla, and he motioned for his men to carry the man back outside.

"Wait, wait!" cried the man. "You men appear to belong to the sweet trade. I may have something of use to you."

"Aye. Go on."

"I crew for Spain aboard the Angelina, and we're fresh from Porto Bello homeward bound for Barcelona."

Gasparilla drew his dagger and held it to the man's throat. "And why would a Spanish swab be of any interest to me?"

"Our cargo," the frightened man stammered, "our cargo is a shipment of pure Aztec gold bound for the king."

Gasparilla's eyes sparkled with delight, and he lowered his blade just a bit.

"Doubloons," the man continued. "We're carrying many chests, each requiring the strength of six men to lift them."

Now, Gasparilla was well aware of the operation the Spaniards ran over in Panama, and all over South America for that matter. He knew they had created a very profitable business seizing gold that Indians used for jewelry and ceremonial pieces. The conquistadors melted it all down and stamped it into coins covered with the images of their royalty and religion, like crosses, or Latin phrases, or coats of arms. Each coin, or doubloon, had a value worth two months' pay for each of his men.

"And this Angelina, where be the galleon now?" asked Gasparilla.

"Sailing against the storm to the safety of Havana," the man said. "I fell from the rigging in the gale, and they left me for dead."

"And dead you be if your tale prove false! How many days do they lay in Havana?"

"As soon as the weather's clear they sail for Spain. The king demands his due."

"What be your name, swab?"

"Sebastian de Rupit."

"Well, Sebastian, you've bought yourself a little time. We'll see about this ship and then we'll see about you."

Under Gasparilla's steady hand, the Florida Blanca continued towards the coast of Cuba and wandered the seas east of Havana after the storm cleared. They drifted many days waiting for the galleon that never came. Supplies ran low and the buccaneers had to dine on hard tack, a stale biscuit best eaten in the dark, so the sight of the bugs inside wouldn't turn the stomach. The men were getting restless, but none more so than Gasparilla himself. He had let several promising ships pass as he held out for the treasure laden Angelina.

Just as he was about give Sebastian back to the sea, a call came down from the crow's nest.

"Spanish galleon off the port bow!"

Gasparilla raised his spyglass and did indeed lay eyes on a galleon flying the flag of Spain. He handed the glass to Sebastian.

"Take a look, swab, and tell me true. That be me ship?"

Sebastian aimed the glass. "Yes, Captain. You're staring down the Angelina."

Gasparilla ordered the cannons ready as he turned the barque towards his prey. The men scurried across the deck while the Florida Blanca angled up behind the royal ship. One man hoisted the Spanish flag to make the pirate boat look friendly. As they drew near, the freebooters saw the galleon riding low in the water, a sure sign that she carried a heavy load. Gasparilla lifted his spyglass once more and read the name on the back of the ship to himself – Angelina.

Taking no chances, the Spanish galleon turned to run, but the swift barque proved too fast. The Blanca's phony Spanish flag came down, and they raised the jolly roger, a sight that caused many ships to give up without a fight. Gasparilla had designed his flag himself, simple, yet convincing – black cloth with a single white skull, holes for eyes. It was the eyes that struck fear in men. The light that blazed through the eye holes made the skull gaze down like a vengeful spirit, still very much alive.

But, the stakes were too high for the Angelina to surrender that easily. Gasparilla fired a warning shot across her bow. The galleon responded with a shot of her own, and the fight was on. The two ships traded fire as the pirates drew near. The Florida Blanca took a hit that ripped through several sails and, by the time the buccaneers were close enough to throw their grappling hooks, the Angelina had a hole at her waterline, and the sea had begun to sink her.

Gasparilla and his men pulled the ships together and took to fighting hand to hand. The battle was a bloody one as the Spaniards fought to the last to defend their gold. Cutlasses sliced through arms and severed legs. Flintlock pistols blasted the air as their fiery balls ripped heads and hearts. When the smoke had cleared, most of Gasparilla's men still stood, but they knew they were running out of time as the sea flooded the lower decks.

At the tip of his cutlass, the pirate captain forced Sebastian to lead them to the loot. As he had foretold, the treasure room held many a chest. The men managed to haul all but two onto the deck of the Florida Blanca before the sea claimed the rest for her own, and the Angelina sunk out of sight into the depths below.

"Well, Sebastian, your luck be grand so far," Gasparilla said to his captive as one of the men pounded on an iron lock with a hammer and chisel. "We'll soon see if it holds."

The lock gave way, and the sailor threw open the oaken chest. A pile of fresh doubloons shimmered in the sun like they had been kissed by King Midas himself. Gasparilla knelt on one knee and ran a hand under the flashing coins. His arm sunk to his elbow in gold, and the widest smile spread across his face.

"May your days be your own as long as ye live them," he said to Sebastian. "One lucky swab ye be!"

True to his word, Gasparilla let the man live. He even gave him the choice to join his crew or be released to the shores of Cuba. Sebastian chose his family over the sweet trade and the pirates dropped him off on a remote spot to make his way back to Havana and board a ship for Spain. Before he bid his former captive a fond farewell, Gasparilla instructed his quartermaster to give Sebastian a cut of the booty, the same share enjoyed by each of his men. Sebastian de Rupit lived the rest of his days in Spain with his family a happy, and wealthy, man.

A tailing redfish snapped me back to reality.

Redfish tails break the water when it's shallow and they're feeding on small crabs in the grass. I used the electric motor to sneak over and hooked him on a chunk of cut mullet. He went into the bait cooler for dinner.

After the last trap line, we had run out of room to dodge the storm. It was on us, a nasty one too, so black it looked purple. Lightning blasted down every ten seconds, and the wind started to whip up a pretty serious batch of whitecaps. The White Stripe is a decently sea worthy vessel, but she's made for the calmer waters of the back bay. A summertime squall can turn that calm water into a raging mess, and fast. I'm talking three footers breaking all over the place – not to mention the lightning and rain. Unprotected in an open boat tower is not the best place to be.

The sea is the boss, so I ducked the boat into a nearby tidal creek to ride it out. I tied the boat to a tree and put on my rain jacket just as the first big drops started to fall. Hammerhead looked worried.

"Sorry, Hammerdog. I only have one raincoat."

I pulled the anchor line out from under the casting deck and put the bottle in a cooler. Hammerhead crawled under the deck as the rain began to pour.

Well, I got wet. That storm pounded us. About the only thing you can do in a boat like mine is hunker down. I pulled my hood over and sat in the back of the boat as far under a mangrove tree as possible. And that's how it was for two hours.

Man, that had to be the longest storm in history. Usually those things blow through in less than a half hour. This one just went on and on and on. By the time it was over, the sky was already getting dark.

I pulled out my cell phone to call Mom. I was way over due. But the battery was completely dead. It wouldn't even turn on. Bummer. I was probably twenty or thirty minutes away from Palmetto Cove. My seafood buyer would be closed. Mom would be furious. I was up a creek in more ways than one. Oh well. I'd figure it out.

I fired up the boat and gunned it down the creek. Tree limbs beat the hull as we turned the corner into the open bay.

Air has got to be the most breathable immediately after a storm. I just wanted to suck in as much as I could. Mangroves have a woody, earthy smell. Some people think they stink. I love it, though. When we cleared those trees, Mother Nature gave us another sweet surprise. That musky mangrove air said goodbye and a fresh blast from the open gulf said hello. Ahhhhh. Hammerhead stuck his nose in it all the way home.

By the time I got back to our canal, it was almost completely dark. I idled past Mr. Henley's yard and cut the motor as I crossed our property line. Sometimes stealth is the best policy when you know you're going to get chewed out. Maybe mom was out or had gone to bed already. I drifted up to the dock quiet as a mouse and tied her off.

A single light burned in the trailer's kitchen window. She was waiting.

The crabs couldn't live out of water all night. For situations like this, I had constructed a holding tank from an old, seventy-five gallon aquarium. Instead of using a filtration system, I just pumped raw sea water in from the canal. A drainpipe takes the overflow back, and a tin cover keeps the raccoons out. I slid the cover off and dumped the crabs out of the cooler into the tank.

"Sleep tight, guys. I'll pick you up in the morning."

I set the cooler down and walked in to face the music. Mom was sitting at the table in the kitchen with a nearly empty glass of tea in front off her. Not good. She had been waiting.

"Do you have any idea what time it is?"

"I'm gonna say nine?"

"Nine fifteen." She stared me down. "What's our rule?"

"Call if I'm going to be later than 6:30 or sundown, whichever comes first."

"Let me see your hands."

I held up my fingers knowing what was coming.

"They don't look broken to me. You mind explaining why you didn't call?"

"Mom, I got caught in that storm. Had to ride it out way over by Cabbage Key. Then, my phone was completely dead."

"You're going to be completely dead when I'm through with you. Do you have any idea what it feels like to wait for your kid during a storm like that, and he doesn't even call? I can't keep doing this, Harley. I can't take it anymore."

"Mom, it hasn't happened since June."

"Twice in one summer is two times too many. If it ever happens again, that's it! I mean it, Harley. No more boat. No more crabbing. Nothing."

"Yes ma'am," I said head down, as remorseful as possible.

"Come here."

She laid one of those big, *squeeze you to death* momma hugs on me.

"I was so worried, Harley."

I knew the worst was over. The financial lecture was coming next. It always did.

"How'd you do, anyway?" she asked.

"Got nearly a bushel and a half."

"Got the money? We could sure use it."

"They're closed. I threw the crabs in the tank. I'll get it in the morning."

"Harley, listen. I know how much you love crabbing. I really do. But, honey, it's unpredictable. And even on a good day, it isn't that much. If you got a steady job, a real job, you'd have money left over, and you could still go out in the boat for fun. I mean, we've got taxes coming up, all the bills, your grandma's rent at the home, groceries. There's no reserves. If something were to happen...well, I don't know what we'd do. I want you to really think about it. You could get something near school. I could pick you up on the way home. Okay?"

I decided to take a chance.

"Mom, I found something pretty cool today."

"You're not even listening."

"No. Wait. This could definitely help."

She let out a sigh and reached for her tea.

"While I was checking a line, I found a bottle. Really old. When I looked inside it, I found a map."

"Harley."

"No, Mom. I pulled out the map, and it was ancient. In Spanish and everything. Mom . . . it's a treasure map."

"Oh, for God's sakes, Harley. When are you going to grow out of this pirate thing."

"No, no, no. I took it to Salt. And he . . .

"Salt?! That hermit's a lunatic! I told you to stay away from that man. He's dangerous. Do you know he's done time? Do you?! God knows what goes on out there in that cabin."

"Mom, Salt knows Spanish. I needed someone to help me read it. Plus, he knows the waters. If anybody could figure this thing out, he could."

"Yeah, well, if this was some sort of treasure map, that old man would figure it out alright. How to get the loot into his pocket."

"He's really not like that, Mom."

"And you're old enough to know everything, are you? Harley, I'm telling you – you need to give up this fantasy land you've been living in and get your head in the real world. You've got less than two weeks before school. By the time school starts, you need to have a real job lined up, either in Cape Coral, Matlacha, or close by on Pine Island. That's it. End of discussion."

She got up and poured the rest of her tea into the sink. I knew there was no use saying another word at that point. My mom is a determined woman. I don't hold it against her. She's had to be, raising two kids by herself.

But still, hearing her talk like that, especially about Salt, hurt me inside. Made me a little angry, too. I didn't want to say anything I'd regret, so I just turned around and walked back outside.

The night air was thick and humid, but being out of the trailer felt good. The space felt good. I slowly walked past the crab tank. The crabs were all piled on top of each other, looking peaceful enough. A coconut had fallen off our tree. I kicked it like a soccer ball into the canal. Felt good to kick something. Then I just walked down to the boat, connected the battery charger, and sat on the seawall.

Sounds from a couple of TV's floated in on the air. I heard canned laughter on one of them. It always sounded so cheap. The crickets and other night insects seemed to be working really hard to drown out the buzz of air conditioner compressors. I felt like going for a boat ride, but I'd already burned enough fuel for one day. So instead, I grabbed the redfish out of the cooler and started to clean it.

Times are tough all over. Isn't that what they used to say in the Great Depression? That's the way it felt. Mom needed the money. I can understand that. But I just can't possibly imagine myself working retail. Wearing a name tag. Putting on polyester uniforms.

I don't know. Maybe there was a job out there that would be tolerable. But I guarantee you, nothing could come close to crabbing.

After a while I heard my mom walking down the trailer to her bedroom at the end. Once she went in there she probably wasn't coming out. That was my cue. I grabbed the redfish fillets and stuck them in the cooler with the bottle.

As I carried it all back to the trailer, headlights turned into our driveway, and a car pulled up behind Mom's old Corolla. My sister Tori was home, not in her own car. She doesn't have one. Some guy brought her home, as usual. They'd sit out there for at least an hour before she made it in. I could already hear her laughing before the motor cut off.

She wasn't supposed to be drinking. She was only eighteen. But I would've bet my last crab that she couldn't pass a breathalyzer test. Because she had failed the tenth grade, she was still in high school. She didn't hang out with those kids, though. According to her, she ran with an older crowd that was more her type. Derelicts, I'd say. Bunch of drunk, jobless freaks.

Tori and Mom fought all the time. Tori started complaining that she didn't see enough of Dad. She also accused Mom of keeping him away. That's a complete load. Dad didn't care about us. He never called or came around – unless he wanted something. Even so, she started to go over to Dad's place in Matlacha to "spend the night." It was just an excuse. She wasn't staying there. But, I think Mom knew it and let her go anyway. I figure she just got tired of fighting.

Without looking over at the car, I opened the front door and went in. Hammerhead was lying on the floor in the living room. He started to beat his tail on the carpet when he saw me. In the kitchen I dropped the redfish into a plastic container and threw it in the fridge. I wasn't hungry anymore.

"Come on, boy."

I patted the side of my leg, and he jumped up to follow me into my room. I shut the door and locked it once he was in.

My room's slightly larger than the men's room at the Pelican. Single-wide trailers aren't the most spacious homes. I had four drawers built into the wall on one side with a small closet next to it, a window, and a single bed. The walls were made of brown paneling from the 1980's. I bet my fist would go right through if I hit it hard enough. Many times I've been tempted to try. Kind of felt like it on that night.

Hammerhead laid down in his corner, while I plugged my phone in to charge. I rummaged around in my closet and found the old charts, which I threw on the bed next to the bottle. I found some notebook paper and a pencil, too. Carefully, I slipped the map out of the bottle and unrolled it. Then I laid a sheet of paper on top and held the two layers up to the light. Using the pencil, I traced outlines of all the islands onto the paper, making sure to put an *X* on the same spot the pirates had. Very carefully once again, I returned the map to its bottle and stuck the bottle under my jeans in the bottom drawer.

I looked at the paper. It wasn't a Xerox copy, but it was close enough. I wrote the word *Gulf* where the Gulf of Mexico was. The rest of the water appeared to be a back bay, but which one? It showed a bunch of small islands, like twenty or so, scattered around the water. They all had names, Spanish names. By the time navigation charts came out, most of the names had probably changed.

I unrolled a chart that covered the whole southwest Florida coast. It wasn't that old, just from 1972, and it wasn't that detailed since it covered such a large area. As I studied the chart, it became obvious that about the only bay that could hold a big spread of twenty or more islands from Tampa south, was Pine Island Sound. Maybe, Estero Bay, which is the next bay south. But that was a big maybe. Estero bay is very small compared to the Sound. The next body of water that had any potential was the area around the Ten Thousand Islands south of Naples. Forget that. Way too far, I don't care how many storms tossed that bottle around. No, the best bet was Pine Island Sound, especially since it's a known fact that the pirate Gasparilla had lived in a fortified mansion on the north end of it.

The next chart I opened up was from 1929 showing Pine Island Sound. I studied the layout of the islands. Some were a little off. Some sand bars were shown in the wrong places. North Captiva Island was cut in half. They called the lower half the *South Banks* on that chart. It was tough. The low lying mangrove islands shift around all the time as the trees grow and die. Oysters will take root on a sand bar, then a little mangrove sprout comes floating along, gets stuck, starts growing and – BAM – before you know it, a new island is born. Ten years later, a hurricane blows through, kills all the trees, and it's back to being a sand bar.

I looked at the paper I had traced from the map trying to memorize the pattern of islands. I looked over at the chart. Back to the paper. Back to the chart. Paper. Chart. Paper. Chart. Nothing fit. I didn't see anything that looked similar. I needed another approach.

Besides the map, the only other thing I had to go on was Salt's Calusa story. If they really did have a town around here, it must've been on something more permanent than a low mangrove island. In Pineland, a small community north of Palmetto Cove, the Indians had built shell mounds. We went there on a field trip back in middle school. The mounds were big, maybe twenty feet high, like small hills made of dirt and conch shells. They said the Calusa built houses and temples on top to keep them from getting flooded.

Only two islands in the middle of Pine Island Sound had that kind of elevation – Cabbage Key and Useppa Island. They were both privately owned. Cabbage Key had a restaurant open to the public up on top of the tallest mound. It's an old place. Built a hundred years ago. Today it has dollar bills stapled all over the walls and ceiling. People say it's the spot

Jimmy Buffet wrote "Cheese Burger in Paradise" about. They also say there's over $70,000 stapled to those walls. That's a treasure in itself.

Useppa is a private club. They only let members on the island. I went there once on a field trip, too. My whole class went over on this jungle boat called the *Tropic Star*. We toured all the trails and old buildings. Big mounds there too. The island sits across from Cabbage Key and it's larger. I remember going through an old museum out there. I didn't really pay attention to anything though. Wish I had.

Then it hit me. That museum was where I needed to go. It had all the stories and maps and information I was looking for. Somehow I needed to get on that private island, and very soon.

I kept looking over the charts until, after a while, it started to rain. Nothing put me to sleep quicker than the sound of rain hitting the metal roof of our mobile home. My eyes got heavy. I looked over at Hammerhead. He was already snoring. I put everything away on top of the dresser and turned off the light. My room wasn't dark, though. The streetlight outside the window makes it bright as day. I could read by it if I wanted to.

I put my head down on the pillow and thought about the day. The bottle. The map. Salt's story about the Calusa's gold. Eden. Oh, man. That girl is so fine.

I wondered if I was doomed to be a swab at sea, always treading water. Or would my luck change? Before I could come up with any answers, my ship sailed away to Slumber Island.

Heaven

On Monday morning, Hammerhead's nose woke me up. He rubbed the thing all over my cheek like a cold, wet magic marker. Sure enough, the glare in my window had brightened just a little from streetlight to sunlight. I looked outside. Mom's car was gone. That meant she was at work, and, since Tori never gets up before noon, it also meant the bathroom was mine.

I let Hammerhead out the back door and took care of my business while he took care of his. The charts and the map went into a bag. A handful of fig Newtons went into my pocket. And, I was out the door with all that and a little water.

Onboard the *Stripe*, I shoved the bag under the casting deck for safe keeping and took the battery off the charger. Then, I walked back to the crab tank.

"Rise and shine, fellas. Time to take a ride."

Hammerhead was already snoozing under the aquarium and refused to budge until all the crabs were in the cooler. When he sensed I was ready to go, he yawned, stretched and followed me down to the boat.

The outboard chugged the boat slowly down the canal while Hammerhead curled up on the deck and stuck his nose under his tail for the second time that morning.

"Poor thing. Do you need an earlier bedtime?"

Old Mr. Henley sat in his usual lawn chair on his dock with a fishing line in the water.

"How they biting, Mr. Henley?"

"Hook's been setting itself this morning. They just jump right on."

He showed me a stringer that held three, large sheephead, a kind of pan fish that's striped like a zebra, black and white. They look a little odd because they have these big goat teeth. I guess they nibble the barnacles off the dock pilings with them.

I eased up to his dock and reversed the motor for a second to stop the boat.

"Let me give you a little something to go along with those, Mr. Henley."

I opened the cooler and carefully pulled out a big jimmie.

"Oh, my. He looks delicious." He licked his lips. "Drop him in my gunny sack."

He had an old cloth bag under his chair. I dropped the crab inside as he held it open, then gave him two more. He grinned through his dentures like an ancient, but very happy, trick-or-treater.

"Bless you, Harley," he whistled. "You want to come inside for a popsicle or something?"

"No. I'm good, Mr. Henley. Enjoy the surf and, uh . . . surf."

"Oh, I will. Succulent seafood for supper!" he whistled. "Simply sensational!"

A few minutes later, I eased up to Smitty's dock and tied off in front of the gas pump.

The full name is Smitty's Bait and Seafood Emporium, but everybody forgets the last part and just call's it Smitty's. Smitty himself is hard to forget, though. That's because there's so much of him to remember. He's huge. Probably goes about 350 or 375, at least.

"Need gas, Harley?" Smitty looked down from the dock holding a cup of coffee in one hand and a dripping jelly donut in the other.

"Yep. Twenty-four gallons. And I've got about a bushel here."

"What happened? Get caught in that rain last night?" He set his cup on the pump and helped himself to another enormous mouthful of donut before handing the nozzle to me.

"Yeah. Had to tie up and ride it out. You were already closed by the time I made it back."

"Did you hear Bonnie formed off the tip of Cuba?"

"No. Didn't watch the news. Tropical storm or hurricane?"

In addition to selling almost everything in his store, Smitty bought all my crabs. He was Palmetto Cove's only licensed seafood wholesaler. And like me, he loved to talk about the weather.

Weather was our main topic of conversation, especially in the summer months when hurricanes were flying around. Always good to find fellow weather geek. Most people look at you funny when you start talking about cumulus clouds or wind shear. Not Smitty. I could always count on him.

"It's just a tropical storm," he said through a mouthful of donut.

"Which way's it headed?"

"Panhandle. Got a lot of sheer on it, though. They don't think it's gonna do much."

Bits of donut and jelly dropped by my head as I pumped the gas. Minnows rushed in to nab the free breakfast.

"Got another depression coming into the Caribbean around Barbados. Say it has a good chance of developing," he said with his mouth full again. "It'll be Charley, if it does."

"They ought to start naming the thunderstorms around here when they get like that one yesterday. I'd call that one Pain-In-The-Butt."

He laughed at my lame joke. Didn't take much. He was naturally jolly and laughed a lot. Another reason we got along.

"Otis!" he laughed out loud. "Get over here and take these crabs! Pain in the butt! Ha, ha, haaaaa!" His whole belly shook.

Otis, his dock hand, didn't do anything fast. Guess he was on island time. I stopped the pump at twenty-four gallons, gave the nozzle back to Smitty, dumped in two quarts of two-cycle oil and slid the cooler up on the dock before Otis even got to the boat.

I'm almost positive his name wasn't really Otis, but when you worked for Smitty, you got what you got. And, in Otis's case, that was a new name.

I jumped up on the dock and started for the store. Hammerhead looked up briefly and then put his head back down. Tough life.

Smitty's was old. Looked like it belonged out west or somewhere. Somebody had cut the timbers out of local pine trees. I knew it was pine because the bark still stuck to it in places. And it had to be local because no self-respecting sawmill would let wood out of its doors that had been mutilated so badly. Out of all the columns that held up the porch and all the rafters that held the roof, not a single one was straight. Looked like Dr. Suess had built the place himself.

A tin roof kept the rain off the main building and its two porches, back and front. Wormwood wrapped the exterior. Wormwood is a type of cypress siding with holes through it like Swiss cheese. How that keeps the weather out I'll never know. But they say nothing, not even termites, can eat it or rot it.

Behind the cash register, sitting on a tall stool, sat Smitty's wife, Okra – short for Okralia. Though not nearly as large as Smitty, she was a big woman, and as dark as Smitty was pale. And ever since I could remember, since I was a little kid, she was always trying to get me to go with her. I didn't take it personally. Miss Okra tried to get a date with almost every man, or boy, that walked through the door.

"Well, look at you. Coming up in here all shaggy blonde and tan. You better not get any darker. Folks gonna start thinking we're related. Then when they see us making out at the movies, don't you know they going to talk!"

"Morning, Miss Okra." I hoped no one else noticed my face getting red.

"You hungry this morning, honey? Miss Okra's running a special on peanut butter cookies today. They fill you up! And good? Oh, Lord. Stick some of that cookie up on your forehead and your tongue's gonna beat your brains out trying to get to it." She laughed so hard she bounced on the stool.

"Okay. I'll get a cookie and the gas."

Miss Okra's peanut butter cookies were a legend around here. They're sick. Huge as a dinner plate. And, they tasted better than your favorite dessert – I don't care what it is.

Otis shuffled in and handed Miss Okra a small sheet of paper.

"He say you got just under a bushel." She leaned towards me and put a hand up to her mouth so no one else would hear; although, except for me and her, the store was empty. "But, sugar, just cause you so mmmmm, mmm sweet, I'm gonna let you slide."

She gave me $65 for a full bushel, subtracted $48 for the gas, and threw in the cookie for free. Then she reached into the cash register and handed me my pay – a ten, a five and two ones. Some paycheck.

"Now you got enough to take me out someplace. Don't need nothing fancy. You got all the fancy business I want," she said, looking down from her stool with those big, bulgy eyes. "I get off at five. Don't be late."

"I don't think your husband would like it too much, Miss Okra."

"You let me handle him. Besides, I know his nap schedule. We'll sneak off while he's sleeping and be back before he knows a thing."

"Have a good day, Miss Okra." I made a break for the door.

"Go buy those movie tickets, Harley Cooper! I get off at five, you hear?"

Walking out the door, I counted my money just to keep my head low. But, I almost dropped it in the water when I looked up and saw Eden Baker scratching my dog's head down on the dock.

"I'm beginning to think this dog's deprived," she said, flashing her eyes at me. "He acts like no one ever pets him."

Hammerhead was totally getting into it. If he was a cat, he would've been purring. I would've, too. Lucky dog.

I surprised myself by stringing enough words together to make two complete sentences.

"That mutt's playing you like a fiddle. No dog ever had it so good," I said. What was she doing here?

"I doubt that," Eden said. "You probably work him to death out there on that boat."

"About all he works at is an appetite. I'm the one with the blisters and calluses."

She played the world's smallest violin for me with her thumb and first finger.

"Let me run into Smitty's and buy you a band-aid. Please. I've worked my dad's boat with one arm tied behind my back."

"He's got a trap puller. This is a whole different game."

"Doesn't matter. My point is, it's a piece of cake."

"I'd like to see you try."

"Harley Cooper. Are you inviting me out on your boat?"

No matter how bleak things get the night before – like listening to Mom's *get a job in two weeks* lecture – there's always the next day, and you never know what sunshine might come your way then. A day on the water with Eden Baker? I forgot all about the night before. Score!

Sitting side by side up in the tower with the *White Stripe*'s *De Stijl* CD blasting through the speakers, we roared up the channel into one of the finest days of my life.

On the way to the first line, I spotted a school of mullet by Rat Key. I brought the Stripe down off plane and cut the motor. Momentum carried the boat towards the fish as I got my cast net ready.

People have come up with all kinds of ways to throw a cast net. At twelve feet, mine's on the large side, so I put the rope in my teeth between two weights and flip about five hunks of net over my right elbow. That splits the net in half. Then, I gather the two halves of the net in each hand and get ready. It's really a showing, not a telling. Next time I'll have pictures.

The boat drifted up to the school and they never saw it coming. Once in range, I launched the net. Just before it hit the water, the mullet sensed the shadow and shot away in different directions. Too late. Mullet nets have a large mesh so the water goes through fast and they sink quick.

I hauled the net back to the boat with fifteen, fat mullet inside. Plenty of fish to bait the traps that day.

"Nice one, Harley," said Eden from up on the tower.

"Grab a knife and come on down."

"You want me to cut those fish?"

"Comes with the territory."

She climbed down and pulled a fillet knife out of the scabbard as I emptied the flopping mullet onto the deck. I made it easier for her by grabbing another knife and cutting one up first so she could see how I did it. Using mullet for crab bait was rare.

She didn't even watch. Just jumped right in. We soon had blood, guts, and scales all over the place. To his credit, Hammerhead did help with clean up – a little. By the time we had gotten all the fish chunks into the bait cooler, he had licked a one-foot square area enough to see the gel-coat again.

"See how hard he's working," said Eden. "Poor tongue's gonna fall off."

Hammerhead just grinned and wagged his black tail. That dog will be up for an Academy Award some day.

"Mind filling that bucket up with water?" When I asked the question, I was really only thinking about cleaning up the fish blood before it dried. But, I have to admit, when she leaned over the side to dip the bucket in the bay, I couldn't have paid my eyeballs a million dollars to look anywhere else. And, when she poured that sea water all over the deck, I wasn't looking at how the water washed everything white again. I was admiring her perfect red-polished toes.

"You gonna just sit there all day? Don't you have a rag around here somewhere?" she demanded more than asked.

I quickly grabbed the old deck towel and wiped down the places the water had missed. Eden gave no clue whether I'd been busted or not. By the time I finished the deck and stuffed the cast net back into its bucket, Eden had already climbed the tower. I shimmied up next to her and blasted off to the first trap line.

"Okay, so it works like this," I said once we were back down on the deck. "I'll steer us around with the electric. You hook the line with the gaff and pull the trap. Dump 'em in the cooler and then hold the trap for me to re-bait. Then toss it back." I was glad to talk about business. Crabbing instructions kept my mind off how gorgeous she was and that kept my tongue from swelling up.

"I think I can handle it," she said with a pearly white smile that made the swelling start again.

But, what she did next rattled my concentration even more. She took off her shirt. Now she stood directly in front of me in just her shorts and a bikini top. She said something about not wanting to get her shirt dirty, but chicks time that stuff perfectly, on purpose. I'm convinced. Why didn't she take it off before the mullet? My tongue agreed. It was the size of Texas.

She snagged the line on the first try. Points for Eden. She retrieved the line hand over hand and pulled the chicken-wire trap up on the gunnel with no problem. It held two blue crabs and a catfish.

"Smaller one looks like a female. And watch those barbs on the fish."

"You know. This isn't my first trip in a crab boat, Harley."

She never stopped working while she talked. Like an expert, she dumped the fish overboard and inspected the female to make sure she didn't have eggs. It didn't.

"I usually throw them back anyway," I said. "Did you know they only mate once?"

"That's 'cause they have the brains." She let the female slide back into the water and dropped the jimmie into the cooler. "They know how to work it."

I threw a hunk of mullet into the bait compartment, and Eden flung the trap back into the water just as the boat completed the first revolution. Bravo. The girl could work.

"Nothing to it," she said clapping the slime off her hands.

"Let's see what you have to say after the last line. We're just getting started."

The day was awesome out on Pine Island Sound. Not a ripple on the water, clear sky. And since it was a weekday, I only spotted a couple of boats. Both were far off. We had the water to ourselves. And, I had her. Heaven.

"Pretty nice office you have out here, Mr. Cooper."

"Just thinking the same thing."

"Dad has good years and bad years with stone crabs. How is it with blues?"

"The same, only worse. Dustin's right. I don't make a bunch of money doing this."

"Can we please not mention his name today?"

Wow! That was a really good sign.

"Gladly. Anyway, my mom's always on me to do something else. MegaMart's hiring, of course. But how could I possibly trade this for that?"

We reached the next buoy. Eden worked the gaff like she'd been doing it the whole summer.

"I know. But what about after school? I mean you're gonna have to start making some real money someday, right?"

The trap was empty. She held it for me to bait.

"Yeah, I know." God, she was beautiful. I told myself to stay cool. "I'll figure something out when the time comes. Maybe shrimping or charters. I don't know. I just like the water. You know, they have those gi-normous crabs up in Alaska."

"Yeah, right. Like, you're going to freeze your butt off up there in all that ice. You wouldn't last one minute, Florida boy."

Even though it was pathetic, I did have a plan: strike it rich by finding hidden treasure. She'd probably just laugh at that one, though.

"Well, I do have a treasure map."

Where did that come from?!!! I just blurted it out. Oh my God!

"A what?"

Too late now. Even Hammerhead looked at me like I was some sort of idiot.

"I found this map."

"When?"

"Yesterday. But you can't tell a soul."

"Shut up! Where is it? I want to see it."

She wasn't laughing. I let go of the electric motor and walked up to the bow. Once I had the bottle, I pulled out the cork and let the paper fall into my hand.

"That cork says Robert Mondavi. That's a current day California wine, Harley."

She still wasn't laughing, but she wasn't buying it either. She stared at mc, amused.

"The cork's from my mom. The real one has a hole."

"Open it up!"

She followed me to the chairs at the back of the boat.

"Un-real. It looks so old. And it's in Spanish and everything."

"Yeah. That's part of the problem. I got Salt to help me with it."

"Salt? That old man?" She wasn't smiling anymore. "Harley, that man's been to prison."

"I know. That's what everyone says. He's never mentioned it to me, though, and I've known him for years. And look – I'm still alive. Anyway, he translated some of the words and told me to compare the map to some navigation charts, which I did."

"And?"

"And, nothing fits. But, this map could be over two hundred years old. Things change a lot. This island looks like a main island." I pointed to the bigger one marked *Isla de Joseffa.* "If I could figure out which one that was – what we call it today – the others might fall into place. The Calusa Indians might be involved here too. I was thinking about this museum on Useppa because they've got a bunch of stuff about the Indians."

"Totally. I've been out there. Dus . . . uh, somebody I know's father has a membership there. Maybe we could stop by today after we're done."

"Cool."

"Absolutely cool."

"No. Cool that you're not laughing at this."

"Laughing? Why should I be laughing? Even if this is a fake, it's going to be an adventure. And, there's one thing you should know about me, Harley Davidsen Cooper – I live for adventure."

Useppa

Tending the rest of the lines went well. Eden wasn't lying. The girl knew how to crab. In fact, she only complained once.

That came on the last line when a crab dodged the cooler and landed on the deck. It skittered around with flippers flailing the air, and, before Eden could react, its pincher found her big toe.

As I mentioned before, Eden has perfect toes. She's the only girl I've seen who does. In my opinion, toes on perfect feet should get smaller from the big toe all the way down to the pinkie toe. On most people they don't. Usually, the second toe is just as long as, or slightly longer than, the big toe. Not perfect. Eden Baker could have been a foot model.

My heart sank when that claw latched on to her toe. The day had been so perfect. Then the crab struck. Eden was screaming and dancing around like her hair was on fire. Her fit came on so suddenly that it took me a moment to react. I guess Hammerhead got tired of waiting. He jumped in and clamped his teeth on the crab's shell and shook his head like a pit bull. The crab let go. Its claw did not. The severed pincher refused to give up.

"Hold it! Hold it!" I said trying to get her to calm down long enough to grab the pincher.

I had to grab her leg instead. Then, I pried open the claw and pulled it off. A tiny sliver of blood trickled down the side of her toe from a small cut.

"Looks like I'm the one that's going to have to get you a band-aid," I said as I searched the first-aid kit. I made sure to keep my head bowed far enough to prevent her from seeing the chuckle I felt working its way up my throat like a hiccup.

"That cooler's way too small to hold all those crabs," she said. "I'm surprised the Fishing Department, or whoever regulates you guys, allows you to use it. You need something more professional, Harley."

"Calm down. Let me get this band-aid around it. I'll grab an accident report for you to fill out in a second. You can file for worker's comp. I'm sure crab attack's covered somewhere."

"That's right. Laugh it up. I'm just lucky you have a quick thinking dog aboard. At least somebody jumped up to save me."

At first Eden looked genuinely upset. Then Hammerhead started wagging his tail, and she lightened up. She even laughed with me. Who wouldn't? A crazy crab with a claw hold on the toe? Seriously funny. Come on.

"Eenie, meenie, miney, mo. A mean old crab got Eden's toe!" I laughed.

"Well, I did holler." Then she completely busted out laughing. She could barely speak anymore. "And that…crazy dog…let it go!"

We laughed until tears rolled out. Eden accidentally snorted, and we laughed even more. Hammerhead, who had been silently watching us with his tail wagging, started barking.

"Looks like Santa *Claws* came a little early this year," I said holding out the amputated crab claw.

"Oh, that's lame, dude," she said when she could finally talk again.

My stomach said it was lunchtime. I broke out a big bottle of cold water and we passed it back and forth between bites of

Okra's humongous peanut-butter cookie. I served slightly crushed fig Newtons for dessert.

"Want to run over to Useppa and have a look in that museum?" I asked.

"Sure. But how are you going to get on the island? You're not a member are you?"

"No. But, it's summer. Nobody's around. We can tie up on one of those docks on the back side. Once we're on, how're any of them blue-bloods going to know the difference?"

"Blend in."

"That's right. Lay low like a one armed crab."

"Stop it." She slugged me in the arm before climbing up the tower.

"Hey. I just saved your life."

"Hear that, Hammerhead? Mr. Cooper here's trying to take all the credit. Jump up and bite him in the butt."

Hammerhead just looked at us like we were crazy. He answered Eden by sneezing and turning to something more interesting out on the water. Faithful dog.

The midday breeze had started to kick up a little, but the ride over to Useppa wasn't bad at all. I tied the *Stripe* to an old dock nested in a clump of mangroves out of sight from any of the main buildings.

We took the trail that led from the dock through the mangroves. It turned up a hill towards a bunch of high-dollar homes up on stilts. People call them cracker box houses, though I've never seen a box of crackers with a tin roof. Most of these homes were empty in the summer, only used during the tourist season from November to April. They all had golf carts parked underneath. No bridges to Useppa Island, and the island wasn't big enough for cars.

We hiked right up the hill, like we were official, to the front door of the museum. A woman came out. Unfortunately, she locked the door behind her.

"Oh, I'm sorry, kids. Were you coming to view the exhibits?"

"Uh, yes ma'am," I said. "This is the museum, right?"

"It is. But I'm afraid we're closed for the day."

"Closed? It's only one."

"Yes. I know it must seem odd, but we coincide our hours with the arrival and departure of the ferry from Captiva. Do try and come see us tomorrow, won't you?"

She hopped into a golf cart and drove away, waving good-bye as she went. "Toodle-oo!"

"Well, Indiana Jones, what now?"

"Why don't we poke around and see if there's another way in?"

"Break in?! Harley, are you kidding? What if there's an alarm? What if we get caught?"

"Alarm? Here? Eden look around. We're probably the only ones on this island.

Eden did look around. The croquet course, pool, and tennis courts were all empty. The only thing that stirred was the wind blowing on some dry palm fronds.

"Besides, don't you live for adventure?"

"Adventures outside of jail. We better not get caught."

Hammerhead followed us around to the back of the building into the shade of a big oak. Some of the buildings on Useppa were over a hundred years old. They were all wood frame and bright white. The museum still had its original windows, staring out like big, rectangular eyes. I spotted one with no screen. It slid open with no problem. And, no alarm.

"Lay down and take a nap, boy," I said to Hammerhead.

I looked over at Eden and saw a very worried adventurer.

"Eden. You don't have to go in if you don't want to. Anyways, we're not taking anything except a little information."

"Just keep going before I lose my nerve."

Inside the museum, the air was quiet, cool, and old smelling. The window had led to a closet in the back. I tip-toed over to the door and put my ear to it.

"Sounds like the coast is clear," I whispered.

Careful to make as little noise as possible, I turned the rusted doorknob. It croaked like a frog, a big frog. I froze and waited. No footsteps rushed over. No voices called out.

The door creaked open on equally rusty hinges. I crept across the carpet. Eden followed doing the same. Every once in a while, a board moaned under the carpet padding, but, other than that, the place was ghost-quiet. I felt relatively sure we were alone.

The museum showed the history of Useppa Island in chronological order, from prehistoric times up to current day. Judging from the seventies mustaches and haircuts around us, I figured we had popped in somewhere towards the end.

"We need to backtrack towards the front. Follow me," I whispered, feeling like a pirate sneaking towards a treasure room.

As we crept around the cases and dioramas, I couldn't help wondering if any of Gasparilla's men had ever done the same thing on the same spot. Not in the building, of course, but on this island, perhaps secretly searching for the Calusa's gold while they were asleep.

The further up the hall we went, the older the pictures got on the wall.

"We're going back in time," I whispered as we made our way to the front of the building.

At least that got a tiny smile out of her. Since we had climbed in the window, Eden had seemed a little grim.

A set of keys rattled outside the front door.

"Hide!" I whispered almost out loud.

We looked all around for a door, a hiding place – anything. The only thing big enough was a large glass case that held a scale model of some sea battle fought during the Civil War. The case sat on top of a solid oak pillar. We dove under that just as the front door swung open.

The overhead lights came on.

"I know they're in here somewhere," said a man's voice.

"Me, too. They had to have come in on that boat," said another man's voice.

Eden and I were crammed close together. I felt her nerves start to shiver. I put my arm around her shoulders to calm her down.

"Shhhhhh," I whispered. "It's gonna be fine. They'll never look back here."

I suddenly felt awful for putting her in this situation.

"Help me look, would ya? If we don't find them, the boss man's really going to come down on me," the first man said.

They started to tear something apart. We heard ruffling and shuffling and what sounded like cardboard boxes getting shoved around.

"Don't see 'em in there?"

"Nope."

"Well, follow me to the back."

Heavy footsteps passed by less than ten feet away. They kept going to the back. It sounded like they went straight to that closet with the window. A few seconds later, we heard the door creak open.

One of the men cursed. I won't repeat what he said exactly, though it did involve the open window. And, then the window slammed down.

"A-hah!" said one of them.

"Find 'em?"

"Yep! Right here."

"Well, thank God. You'd think he was going to have a fit if he didn't get these brochures instantly."

"He's gonna have a fit when I tell him that Barbara's still leaving the windows open. Who knows what kind of varmints have slithered in here. And, you know who'll have to get 'em out!"

"Got that right."

"Come on. Let's bring the whole box so 'His Royal Highness' doesn't have a heart attack."

Although I played it cool for Eden, I thought I was the one next in line for cardiac arrest. My heart rate dropped considerably once they left and re-locked the front door.

After they had gone, we waited, huddled in the dark, my arm still around her shoulders. To tell you the truth, I really didn't want to move it. And, she wasn't asking me to move it, kind of nice, under the circumstances, of course.

"You can either move your arm," she said, "or, you can kiss me." She wasn't shaking anymore. She was looking dead at me.

My heart went from zero to sixty for the second time in the last ten minutes. She felt so good under my arm. Smelled so good – even after crabbing for half a day. How do girls do that?

I didn't know if she was joking or what, but I didn't miss the opportunity. I kissed her. And you know what? She kissed me back. In fact, she started to lay one on me so hard, that I lost my balance. I shifted my weight and had to rise up a little to keep from falling. I didn't fall, but I did conk my head right into the bottom of that big glass case. And, let me tell you, I hit it hard. Oh yeah, with a big clunk, too.

Eden busted out laughing. I didn't know whether to check my scalp for blood or tell her to be quiet. The men couldn't have gotten that far.

"I'm sorry. I'm sorry," she said while still laughing. "If you could've seen your face!" She brought a hand up to cover her mouth. "Boing!" More laughter. "Right into the case!" Even more laughter.

"I know. I know," I said as I rubbed my head. "It's funny. Laugh a little softer, would ya?"

"Sorry…sorry." She gradually got a hold of herself.

Needless to say, the mood was totally shot. Oh, well. A door had swung open and I had taken a step inside.

"Come on. Let's finish this and get out of here," I said and crawled out into the open, making sure to keep my head low.

Eden came out grinning like a Chinese monkey.

"You remember that time we played the sunset game on the beach?" she asked me.

"Yeah."

"I wanted to do that then."

"What?"

"Kiss you."

She put her arms around me and kissed me again. Man oh man.

"More where that came from," she said. "But not here. We got to go."

We moved past yellow photographs of people standing next to huge tarpon. Then, the pictures led to drawings and we found ourselves in the pre-historic Calusa section. In between the two time periods, there had been zero mention of pirates.

I scanned the walls for anything that looked like Indians with gold, or Indians standing next to the Spanish.

"Over here," said Eden.

I crossed the room to the small plaque she was pointing at. It hung on the wall next to a drawing of people outside drying a bunch of fish in the trees.

"Joseffa Key", a fishing rancho
was established on Useppa between
the years of 1784 and 1794.

"No way!"

"Harley, this island could be it."

" Isla de Joseffa. Joseffa Island. Useppa Island."

"Over the years they began pronouncing it differently."

"It shifted – just like the sand bars and islands," I said. "The date's a little off, but dates probably shift around, too."

"Aaarrrggg, matey! I smell me gold!" she said with one eye winked shut.

"Let's get out of here before they make us walk the plank."

We tore through the museum to the closet in back. The window had been shut and locked. I opened it and jumped out so fast, Hammerhead barely had time to move. I closed it behind Eden, and we both ran down the trail as fast as we could back to the *White Stripe*.

I half expected the boat to be gone when we popped through the mangroves, but there she was, waiting for us. I fired that motor up, and we took off.

Gigantic thunderstorms had formed over the mainland. I knew it was only a matter of time before they marched to the sea.

"I've got to get back before those things are on us," I said above the roar of the motor and wind.

"You're not afraid of getting wet, are you?" She poked me in the ribs.

"More like I'm afraid of my mom. I got stuck out here yesterday, and she blew a gasket. Threatened to take the boat away and everything. We can come back out tomorrow if you like?"

"Gotta go in to town with my mom in the morning. Back to school stuff. Maybe later?"

The tide was up, so I flew across some skinny flats and oyster bars to save time. We made it back to the Palmetto Cove channel around two o'clock. The last thing I wanted to do was drop her off, but I needed to take the crabs to Smitty's, clean up the boat and get things ready for tomorrow before the rain hit. I had to force myself to turn the *Stripe* left towards her place, instead of right, towards mine, when we got to the tee in the canal.

The boat coasted to a stop at her dock under the shade of the Baker's tall Australian Pines. There was just enough room for me to tie up behind her dad's crab boat.

"Well, skipper, I had a fabulous time as your first-mate today. I am your first mate, right?"

She spoke as easy as a song, with none of the awkwardness that I was feeling.

"Uh, yeah. Of course. And, you did pretty good for a girl."

"Say what?!"

"Sorry. You did great for anybody."

"That's more like it."

Before I knew what hit me, she planted another kiss right on the lips. A big wet one. It was getting good, too.

"What the hell are you doing, girl?!!!"

It was her father, Jake Baker. He stood on his boat, right in front of mine, looking every bit as big as Smitty. Except Mr. Baker was solid muscle, and he was nothing like Smitty. The man almost never laughed.

"Get away from her, boy!"

Thank God there was five feet of water between our boats. I think he'd have jumped over if it was any less. He looked like an angry Rottweiler.

"Daddy, stop it."

"You're that Cooper kid, aren't you? You better get the hell off my property before I break you in half – you good for nothing . . . your dad's a worthless scumbag, and so are you!"

"Daddy, you have no right . . ."

"Girl, you better git your happy butt up in that trailer, or you're gonna find out all about my rights. NOW!"

It hurt more to see Eden so upset than it did to listen to her old man put me down. His words didn't have much effect on me. I was already used to it. I had lots of training. Mr. Baker is a drunk, like my dad. The only difference is he's a functioning alcoholic. He can still go out in his boat most days.

Eden looked at me with tears in her eyes. She mouthed the words *call me* and ran up the steps to their mobile home.

"Let me tell you something, boy. Man to man. She's already got a boyfriend. And, unlike you, he's worth something. Gonna give us all a bright future some day."

I stared at him with my teeth grinding together.

"I don't think he's gonna take to kindly to it when he finds out you've been messing around with his girl. In fact, I know he won't. And, I'll tell you something else – I don't either."

He reached down and picked up a short two-by-four.

"Now, get the hell off my property before I come over there and do something the law's gonna make me regret."

I didn't say a word. I just took my time, calmly unhitched my boat, and backed away from his dock. Eden had disappeared into their trailer. Mr. Baker just stood there glaring at me until I was halfway down the canal.

Salt always says life is full of good and bad. Can't have one without the other. That day had been one of the best I'd ever had. Mr. Baker had definitely just ended it. I rounded the turn out of their canal wondering how bad the night was going to be.

Bull Riding

When I dropped the crabs off at Smitty's, Okra didn't hassle me about taking her out on a date. Maybe she was too busy. Maybe she forgot. Or maybe she sensed my sour mood. In any case, I was relieved she left it alone.

Thunder rumbled in the distance as I walked back into daylight on my way to the *Stripe*. They had paid me for a half bushel, $32.50. I figured that's about what it was. It was fair, but getting the tiny paycheck didn't help much.

I shouldn't have let Eden's dad get to me, but he got to me. His whole scene at the dock put a damper on what had been one rockin' afternoon. Is everybody's life like that? Is that the way it is? On top of the world one moment and a scumbag the next? One big rollercoaster? I felt like a lowly swab again.

The fact that he didn't want me to see his daughter wasn't what bugged me. The fact that he didn't want me to see his daughter because I was worthless did. Of course Eden's used to a guy with a lot of green. She's dating Dustin Majors, or was. Anyway, he's rich, and I'm not. Maybe that's why she was asking me when I was going to get a real job.

At that exact moment, as I was stuffing $32 into my wallet, a strange thing happened. Ivana Rovich's business card fell out of my wallet onto the dock and stared at me, face up.

I picked up the card. It looked harmless enough. So I started thinking. I still had plenty of daylight left. The afternoon storm looked like it might slide to the north and miss us. Maybe I'd see what Mrs. Rovich was willing to pay for a man who's strong-like-bull to do a little yard work. Why not? Her house was just a couple of minutes up the canal past Eden's canal, and I could use the money.

I opened my cell phone and punched in the number.

"Hello?"

It was her. Even with only one word to work with, her Russian accent poured through the phone.

"Uh, Mrs. Rovich. It's me, Harley Cooper."

"Darlink. Please, call me Ivana."

I pictured her face from the day before when she had cornered me in the hall at the restaurant. Her eyeliner was way too thick.

"Okay. Miss Ivana, you gave me your card yesterday at the Pelican?"

"Yes. You need work, no?"

"Yes I do."

"I have much big yard here. It grow like weed."

"Well, I have some time today . . ."

"Today good day. When you come?"

"In a few minutes? But, uh, how much work do you have, and what do you pay?"

"If you good boy, hard work boy, maybe four hour. I pay you $100, cash, no?"

"Okay. Sounds fine. I'll be right over."

As I motored by Eden's canal, I had to look down it. Her dad's boat was gone. Good for Eden. At least she didn't have to deal with the ogre for a while. It was well known around the Cove how badly he treated Eden and her mom. Trailers have thin walls.

Soon, I saw the top floor of Mrs. Rovich's house rising above the trees. I guess I should call it an estate. That's how big it looks. Takes up the entire cul-de-sac at the end of her street. I'm sure she had a lawn service, but those guys just cut grass. They don't touch the weeds, trees or bushes.

The Rovich dock was big enough to park a super tanker, or at least a large sport fisherman. It felt like I was driving a dinghy when I pulled up to it.

Her yard had so much room that Mr. Rovich, may he rest in peace, put the pool next to the tennis court in one of the adjoining lots, over to the side. That's where I heard her voice calling to me, from the pool.

I needed some back-up, so I told Hammerhead to follow me as I jumped off the boat. Instead, he found a shady spot under the tower and curled up on the deck. Some dog.

"Harrrr-leeeeey!"

"Coming Mrs. R-, Miss Ivana!"

I trotted up the pavers to the pool deck, but didn't see her anywhere.

"Miss Ivana?"

"Over here, strong man, over here."

I looked to my right and spotted her lying face down on an expensive lounger. She was so long, her ankles and feet hung off the end.

"Good. Yes. I work on my tan. You help, no? I need more cocoa butter. You put here, please." She tapped a long, red fingernail on her shoulder blade.

She was wearing a one-piece swimsuit that dipped low in the back. A lot of skin showed, greasy, dark with age spots from too much sun. The sight of it made my throat convulse like I was going to hurl.

"Please. I no can reach."

Reluctantly, I picked up the plastic tube and squeezed some cream on her back.

"Ooooohhh. So cold! Delicious. Now rub."

I started smearing the stuff on her skin. My eyes were closed. My brain did its best to picture a one hundred dollar bill.

"Mrs. Rovich, I really came here to do yard work."

"Ivana, darlink," she corrected. "I know. We get to that. But you don't want see me with lopsided tan, yes?"

I didn't want to see her at all. The lady was at least four times my age! She could probably be my grandmother. When that thought hit me, that vomit, or bile, hot and nasty, suddenly rose high enough in my throat to taste it. I swallowed hard.

"Good. You good worker. Maybe you go to Mother Russia. Become comrade. Get all over back, please. Work in with fingers, nice and slow. Mmmmmmm."

To make things worse, she had been drinking vodka. People think you can't smell that stuff. Well, I can smell it, and she reeked.

"Lower."

I opened my eyes accidently. The bile came up again.

"Mrs. Rovich -"

"Ivana."

"Miss Ivana, I really need to get started. I've got to be home by dark."

She rolled over and I came face to face with a nightmare situation. She had some kind of gross, white cream plastered all over her face. I jumped up and shielded my eyes with one very slimy hand while fighting off the urge to puke.

"Mrs. Rovich!"

"Come now. Don't tell me you never see beautiful woman before…Oh, I forget. Okay, okay. I wipe off face."

She stood up. Her huge body in that one-piece suit made her look like some kind of amazon wrestler. But, her ridiculous face reminded me of a circus clown that had just been in a whipped cream pie fight. I started backing away.

"On Russian beach, all take care of face while tan. Natural thing, no? Now, lotion on front, please." She stuck out her chest and kept coming at me.

I doubted Russia even had a beach. But, I had no time for that discussion. Mrs. Rovich had backed me all the way to the edge of the pool.

"Mrs. Rovich, I don't think this is such a good idea."

Suddenly, she stopped, lowering her creamy face to the ground with a big sigh.

"Okay, okay." Her voice lost its pep. "I too old woman for boy. Girl can dream, no? Okay. Just do shoulders. Please finish job. Then I show yard."

So there we stood by the edge of the pool. I swallowed hard again, reached up and rubbed the rest of the lotion onto her shoulders.

I had no escape route if she came at me again. Behind me was the pool, then some low bushes, then the street. I guess I could swim across, hurdle the plants, and sprint down the street if I had to. I knew I could outrun her.

What I didn't know was that someone else was already running down the street. Someone named Eden Baker. Great timing, huh?

When Eden's dad left in his boat, she took the opportunity to go for a jog. She's a pretty devoted runner. One of the reasons her body is so fit. Anyway, she was coming around the cul-de-sac just as Mrs. Rovich was putting her move on me. I guess she stopped and watched the whole thing, then ran off without a word.

I was in more trouble than I even knew.

Luckily, Mrs. Rovich gave up her plan, for the moment, and showed me the yard work that she needed. She told me I could take off my shirt if the sun got too hot, but I decided it was best if I left it on.

I worked like a farm animal for five hours, picking weeds, sawing palm fronds, trimming hedges, hauling debris – you name it. The woman didn't lie about the amount of work she had. And, as promised, she handed me a one-hundred-dollar bill just as the daylight started to fade.

"You must be hungry. You take shower. I cook dinner."

"Thanks, but I need to get going, Miss Ivana."

"Beef stroganoff?"

"Thanks anyway, Mrs. – Miss Ivana."

"Okay. I take rain check. You come back soon, okay?"

I thanked her and headed to the boat. I asked Hammerhead if he needed to go to the can. He just sat there. He's pretty good about taking care of himself, and sneaky. I'm sure he snuck off to pee more than once.

When I got home, I had just enough light left to clean the boat. Mom wasn't there. She had left a message on my phone that she was working some extra hours at MegaMart. Before I carried the charts and the map bottle to my room, I left Mrs. Rovich's c-note on the kitchen table for Mom. She needed a nice surprise when she came home. I stuck a note on top that said: Love, Harley.

I figured I'd shower off, get something to eat and get down to the business of figuring out the map. That all changed in about ten seconds, because when I was done with the shower, Bill called.

"Hey, dude. Wassup?"

"Nothing. Just got done with the boat and I was going to grab something to eat."

"Stop right there, dude. I'm coming by to pick you up."

"I don't know, Bill. I kinda got things to do."

"Dude. Summer is almost over. Let's go down to the Hut. Our sweet freedom's toast in a couple of weeks, especially on a Monday night. Plus, it'll be crawling with chicks."

"Bill, why do you do this to me?"

"Cause you know you love it. I'll be there in five."

The Burger Hut was in Matlacha. They did have the fattest, juiciest, tastiest burgers around – even better than the Pelican. It was kind of like the Pelican, only smaller, if that's possible, dining room with a bar to the side. Only, it wasn't wood frame, and it wasn't on the water. The Hut had been built in the fifties, or so, back when the art deco thing was big in Miami. The place looked like something that belonged on South Beach.

Even though Bill was just fifteen and only had a learners permit, his parents let him drive if he stayed on the island. He picked me up, and we drove along Pine Island Road in his beat up 1987 Chevrolet Chevette. Bill had found the car behind a neighbor's house stuck in the middle of a backyard pile of junk. They had given it to him for free, and he had been nursing it back to life ever since. That piece of junk was his pride and joy.

"When you gonna do something about the smell in this thing, man?"

"That's rats, dude. A family of them was living under your seat when I got the 'Vette."

Oh, yeah. He always called it a 'Vette. That way, people who didn't know any better thought he drove a *Cor*-vette, not a *Che*-vette. But everyone knew.

"Takes a while for rat pee to work its way out. Check out the new tunes."

The car had the original 8-track in the dash. Bill had located one store in Cape Coral called Rainbow Records that still sold a few of them. Most was awful stuff by bands I had never heard of.

"AC/DC, dude."

"Cool," I said. At lcast it was a decent group.

We jammed the rest of the way to *Back In Black*. It was more distortion than music. The speakers were falling apart. But, it got my mind off the rat pee, and Mrs. Rovich.

The parking lot was fairly full outside the Hut. The sign outside always cracked me up. It simply said, "Eat-Burgers-Fries." Nothing like getting to the point.

There was one table left in the tiny dining room. We grabbed it. The place was loud, probably because of the plaster walls and the small size. But, mostly, it was because the folks in the bar were being loud and obnoxious. Two more guys from school, Tim Burken and Matt Ryan, saw us from the lunch counter. They came over and sat down.

"Score, dude," said Tim. "We heard all about what you did today."

My stomach sank. I knew news traveled fast on Pine Island, but how did these guys find out about Mrs. Rovich that fast? I was the only one there.

"Just needed a little extra work," I said trying to discourage anymore discussion.

"What are you talking about?" said Matt, his mouth stretched ear to ear. "Sounds like the only thing you were working on was getting a ticket to hop on the Eden express!"

"Choo! Choooo!," Tim chimed in. "Chugga! Chugga! Chooooo!"

"I think I can. I think I can. I think I can," Matt added, cracking even more wise.

Great. If *they* knew, the whole world knew. Well, at least the Rovich incident was cool.

"Yeah, dude. Way to go." Tim lifted his hand for a high-five. "Don't leave me hangin'."

I slapped it half-heartedly.

"Look guys," I said, "it was really nothing. She just wanted to prove she could pull traps as well as I can."

"Yeah, well, you better tell that to Dustin," said Tim. "I hear he's pretty ticked."

Wonderful. More icing on the cake.

Fortunately, the waitress came around and took our order. I changed the subject.

"What's the team like this year, Matt? You guys gonna actually win a game?"

"Bite me, Cooper! You know…you ought to go out for the team, Cooper. With your size you could play line."

"Or, *tight* end," Tim added laughing.

"Too busy working to be playing."

"I hear you," said Matt. "Dad says I got a shot at a scholarship, so I don't have a choice. I gotta play. Rather be out on the water like you."

We talked about football, fishing, and which wicked teachers we'd be stuck with when school started, until our food was served. Each time the conversation started to veer back towards girls, which was about once every five seconds, I steered it another way. Meanwhile, the noise in the bar grew louder and louder. On top of the ruckus, some girl was woo-hoo-ing at the top of her lungs like a Texas cowgirl.

"Speaking of chicks. What's up with Mrs. Rovich?" said Bill. "I heard she started taking wrestling lessons." He looked over at me. "Got a mean take down move."

That one cracked up Matt so bad, he laughed out a chunk of burger. These guys had been talking, a sure sign the entire island knew about the hallway incident. Wonderful.

"I'm talking smack-down city, dude," Bill continued. "Man, that granny totally had you pinned!"

I just rolled my eyes and changed the subject again.

"What's up with those nuts in the bar? Sounds like a rodeo in there," I said.

"Dude," said Tim, "That's your sister in there."

Oh my God, he was right! I recognized the hysterical laughter. I shoved back from the table and walked around to the bar. There was Tori, the center of attention, hooting and hollering in the middle of a circle of plastered dudes - riding the back of some guy running around on all fours! He was trying to buck her off like a wild horse. She was barefoot in her shortest shorts, wearing a tank-top and somebody's cowboy hat. Money changed hands in the crowd as people bet on whether he'd throw her off or not. And, Tori was clearly hammered.

I cupped my hands and shouted as loud as I could. "*Toooor-iiii!*"

The whole bar hushed and most folks turned to see where that came from.

"Tori, get out of here!" I was fuming. "You don't belong in here and you know it."

I started pushing my way through the crowd to get to her.

"C'mon, don't be a party pooper," somebody said. "She's just riding a bull." They all laughed.

A dude grabbed my arm. I shrugged it off. Tori's mount had stopped bucking. He just stood there on hands and knees, looking at me with blood-shot eyes, my sister still on his back.

"Oh my God," said Tori. "You little *dweeb*. Get trout of my face. You're not the boss of me! Nobody's the boss of me!"

She slurred her words as she yelled at me. It must have sapped the rest of her energy because she started to slide off her horse, face first. No one close reacted. I leapt passed the last couple of guys and caught her just before her nose hit the concrete.

Minus the cowboy hat, she slumped into my arms for a second, not for long, though. The alcohol kicked in again and I had an angry manatee by the tail.

"Get your hands off me! I…am…an…adr-ult!"

"You're not acting like one," I said.

"I has rights!"

"Drinking isn't one of them."

"Mind your own bl-izness! Let me glow!"

But, I didn't let her go. I dragged her, kicking and screaming, through that crowd of losers and into the dining room. She gradually lost her steam and passed out again.

Bill, Matt and Tim were standing at the edge of the dining room. I shifted Tori's weight to one side and reached around to get my wallet.

"Tim, here. Take this to the waitress for me and Bill." I gave him thirty bucks. "Bill, pull you're car around front so I can load her in. Just pop the hatch and we can lay her down."

Tori started to wake up again. In a couple of seconds, we were wrestling once more, blocking the front door. Bill couldn't even get out. I wrapped an arm around Tori's waist and let her slap my back. My other hand found the door.

With Tori doing her best imitation of a rabid chimpanzee, I pushed the door open and stepped outside.

Dustin Major's right fist landed squarely on my jaw.

The punch staggered me. I dropped Tori and tumbled sideways into a bush. When I tried to regain my footing and figure out what was going on, he hit me again.

"Take my girl out on your boat, huh?!"

He punched me in the face a third time. I felt something warm run down my chin.

"I'm gonna kick your butt, Cooper!"

And he started to do just that. I felt a little dizzy and disoriented as he turned me into a human punching bag. I could barely pull my arms up to protect myself. Finally, the bricks stopped falling.

Matt had Dustin in a bear hug from behind. Lucky for me, my friend out-weighed the dork by fifty pounds.

"I'm going to destroy you, Cooper!"

I put a little distance between us and looked around for Tori. She was slumped over on Tim.

"Bill. Please get the car," I managed to say between gasps.

"Cooper! I'm not done with you yet!" Dustin spit, looking more pit bull than human at that point.

I wiped the blood off my chin. "Shut it, Dustin. You're done," I said. "And why don't you talk to Eden? I think she's done, too."

"Oh, I did! And, she is done! She's done with *you*, jerkwad! She saw the whole thing between you and your Russian sugar-mama! You pervert!"

Perfect. Everybody knows your business on the mainland.

"Russian sugar-mama?"

"Not now, Tim. Just help me get Tori in the car."

"That's right. Run away, crab-boy. I will hunt you down! Mock my words, Cooper!"

"That would be '*mark* my words,' jack-face," Matt said chuckling, and still applying the bear hug.

Bill rolled up in the 'Vette, and we put sleeping beauty in the back. On the way home, Bill played some old Paul McCartney, *Band on the Run* I think. For some reason, McCartney's music always sounded so depressing. Of course, it could have been my situation that was bringing me down that night.

Mom was home when Bill pulled into our yard. I really hated to upset her like this, but I couldn't see any other way around it. I had to get my sister in bed before she puked all over Bill's beloved car and made it smell worse than rat pee.

We managed to wake her up enough to have her walk between us with her arms spread over our shoulders.

"You can handle it from here, right dude?" Bill was saying.

"Don't worry, man. My mom's not gonna be mad at us. We rescued her."

"Why should I be mad?" Mom said as she opened the trailer's front door. "Oh, my Lord! What happened to her?"

"A little too much fun," I said.

My mom quickly understood what that meant.

"Girl? Have you been drinking again? Huh? Answer me!"

"Mom, she's barely conscious. You're wasting your breath. Let's just get her to bed, and you can deal with it when she wakes up."

"Where was she? Where'd you find her? Were you boys drinking with her?"

"Mom. C'mon. You know I don't drink. We were getting something to eat at the Hut. Tori was causing a scene. We brought her home."

"Is that blood on you, Harley?"

"I got into a little scuffle on the way out. Separate issue."

"He got into it with Dustin Majors! It was awesome!"

"Bill." I gave him an unmistakable *shut your mouth* look.

"I am just going to lay down and die," Mom said. "You kids have finally killed me."

"It's not as bad as you think, Mom. The thing with Dustin was only a couple of punches. And we got Tori out before she did anything really stupid."

Mom wanted more details. But, news of her daughter riding bareback on a bucking drunk man twice her age might have sent her over the edge. I didn't share that part with her.

Anyway, Tori unconsciously helped herself. She puked all over her own feet. That put my mom's curiosity on a shelf for a little while.

"Good Lord," Mom said "Well, let's get her in the shower. She's starting to stink up the yard."

Bill helped me get her inside; then he took off like a big, fat chicken. I changed shirts and washed my face off in the kitchen sink. My nose hurt, but I didn't think it was broken.

While Mom was busy with Tori in the bathroom, I fed Hammerhead outside. As he chomped away, I recalled what pea-brain had said about my Russian sugar-mama. If Eden had witnessed any of that crazy scene, she had probably drawn all the wrong conclusions. She needed to hear my side of the story – the real side of the story.

I punched her number into my phone and hit the button. It rang four times before her outgoing message picked up.

"Hey, it's Harley. I just needed to explain a few things to you. Please call me back."

I sent her a text, too, and put the phone away. Couldn't blame her if she was mad, I guess. I'd probably feel the same way if I spotted her greasing up some guy in a Speedo. Would I call her back? I didn't know.

Thunder rumbled somewhere, and I looked up into the sky. Hammerhead came over in the dark and stuck his nose under my hand. I scratched his furry ears. A lot of things can go screwy on you in life, but you can always count on your dog.

The Gunshot

Somebody banging around in the trailer woke me up at seven. I reached over and checked my phone. Nothing. Eden hadn't called or texted. Hammerhead grinned, thumping his tail on the floor. I stretched under the covers, but when his nose found me, I reluctantly got up and let him out.

Mom was in the kitchen cooking something.

"Good, you're up," she said. "I was hoping you'd get up before I left."

"You mean you were banging around to wake me up before you left." My face hurt. My whole body hurt, thanks to Dustin's sneak attack.

"Sorry, Harl. I just wanted to see you. Can I cook you some eggs?"

Usually before my mom got all mushy on me, she'd cook me something. Of course, I said *yes*. It was part of our routine.

"Harley, I want to thank you for what you did last night. For helping Tori, *and* for the money. You didn't have to do either one. You're a good kid. You'd make any mom proud."

Her eyes watered up. I knew what was coming. She walked over to the kitchen table where I was sitting and grabbed my head in her hands, pulling my face to her belly. She squeezed my ears shut, so hard I could barely breathe. As long as she held me that way she sounded like she was speaking to me under a pile of blankets.

"Seems like I don't get to see too much of you these days, honey," she muffled. "Always going in two different directions, I suppose. I just miss you, Harley. I want you to know you'll always be my baby."

She let go and moved back to the stove while I sucked in fresh air. My eyeballs gradually started functioning again.

"So crabbing must have been good yesterday, huh?"

"Yeah. I guess it was." I didn't want to spoil the mood by telling her where the money really came from.

"Must be nice to finally have a good day."

"Yesterday was a great day, Mom." I had a vision of one particular female in my head, and she didn't speak with a Russian accent.

"Listen, I know we talked about this a just couple of nights ago, but something happened at work yesterday. One of the guys in the sporting goods department got a job as a fire fighter and quit."

And, poof, my good mood bolted like a spooked redfish.

"They're looking for a part-time replacement. Sounds perfect for you. You'd have all your fishing stuff around. And we'd get to see each other more."

That was all said facing the window. She turned around to set the hook.

"So. What do you think?"

What did I think? That's a good one. What could I possibly think. I was knee-deep in a mom trap. What could I possibly say that would get me out of it and, simultaneously, keep me out of retail?

"You said I had until school starts to find a job, right?"

"Uh, yeah."

"Well, there's a few other places I'd like to check out before then," I fibbed.

Her eyes narrowed a little like she caught a whiff of my crab bait.

"Yeah? Like where?"

"Well, Smitty's for starters. That way I'd be close to the water and be able to keep up with where the fish are. You know I always do good during the mullet run."

"Okay. Where else?"

I had to think quick. And though I hadn't consulted Bill on this idea, I had at least thought of it before.

"I was thinking about starting a service with Bill."

"What kind of service?"

"Yard service. Odd job service. He's got a car. There's a lot of people out here on Pine Island that need things done. Some of them are willing to pay good money."

She turned to the stove.

"Well, Harley, I need results. And, so do you. You're getting older. You need more responsibility. A steady job would look good on your resume. I want you to think about that sporting good position. MegaMart is about as stable as it gets."

She brought over a plate of eggs and toast.

"Oh, jeez, I'm going to be late. Here you go, honey. Have a good day. Where're you gonna be?"

"Checking lines over near Cayo Costa this morning. I'll be back before any storms."

"You do that," she said pointing a finger at me.

She grabbed her purse, gave me a peck on the cheek, and almost tripped over Hammerhead as she ran out the door. I ate the breakfast while it was hot with the mutt drooling onto my foot.

I had gone over the map again the night before using Useppa Island as a reference point. It still didn't make much sense, though. An island that could have been Cabbage Key appeared in the right spot in relation to Isla de Joseffa, today's Useppa, although it had a different name and the shape was whacked. That's about all that really looked close to my chart. Instead of the lone island of Cayo Costa sitting next to Cabbage Key like it does today, there were three long islands between Cabbage and the Golfo de Mexico. Maybe they had merged together to form Cayo Costa later? Who knew?

The pirate's big international symbol for treasure was stamped smack in the middle of one of those islands – the middle one. *X* marked the spot at the end of an oval lagoon, supposedly where the Indian had stashed the gold in Salt's story.

I had a thought. I gulped down the last bite of egg and tossed Hammerhead the rest of my toast. Then, I went down the hall to my room and pulled out the map bottle and charts. I laid the chart showing Cayo Costa, Useppa, and Cabbage Key down on the dresser next to the map. On the chart, I spotted the land-locked lagoon that only Hammerhead and me knew about, the one in the middle of Cayo Costa. Over on the treasure map, I used the edge of a piece of paper as a straight edge to lay out a line from Isla de Joseffa to the *X* on the map, making sure to notice the orientation of that line in relation to Cabbage Key and the Gulf. I held the paper to the chart and laid it down between Useppa and my lagoon. The Gulf of Mexico and Cabbage Key maintained their positions along the line.

It was close enough.

Over on Cayo Costa, there's a long cut that feeds in from the bay side, from Murdock Bayou. That bayou looks like it ends at in a clump of mangroves, but to the right, just before the very end, you'll see the tide blowing out of the trees, and you know something's back there. All you have to do is push your kayak past the mangrove's prop roots, and it opens up to a deep creek. That tidal creek keeps going for a long ways, almost to the beach on the Gulf side of the island. Then, it just springs open into a wide, land-locked lagoon with white, sandy beaches.

My head was spinning. If Cayo Costa used to be three separate islands, that lagoon could be sitting on more gold than the end of a rainbow.

I grabbed everything I needed, ran to the *Stripe* and headed out. Hammerhead had to jump off the dock into the boat just to catch up.

Being out on the water again felt great. Each passing moment put distance between me and my problems on shore. The boat transported us like a worm-hole through space. We entered a whole, new world, full of the coolness of the sea and things that make you forget the stupid junk on land.

I plugged my iPod into the amp and cranked the tunes. The Stripe's hull skipped across the water like smooth stone. It felt great to be alive.

The lagoon was pretty close to Salt's place, only ten to fifteen minutes away by boat. If I picked him up, he'd most definitely have insight on the situation that I hadn't thought of. He always did. He said he'd be around on Tuesday, so I decided to stop by.

Exactly thirty-seven minutes later, I was staring at the stern of the Costa Blanca, Salt's stone crab boat. His dock wasn't big enough for two boats at low tide, so I tied off on the side of the Blanca.

A calm day on the island seems even calmer when you go from flying across the bay at top speed to standing on a quiet dock under a bunch of shady oaks. It was cool to be in the calm air and the stillness amplified the *low tide mud stink*, too. I enjoyed that as well. That salt-marsh smell meant I was out on the water, and out of reach.

Salt was behind his house fiddling around with his crab traps. I'm sure he heard me coming a mile away, but he acted like he just noticed I was there.

"Hey, kid. How's life been treatin' ya?"

"Roller coaster, dude. Up. Down. Up. Down."

"Just hope the ride never stops."

"Why not?"

"It only stops when you're dead," he chuckled.

He threw down a trap and walked over to me and Hammerhead. Well, he walked over to me. Hammerhead was running over to meet him. That dog loved Salt, could be because Salt always managed to find something in his pocket for the mutt.

"How's the treasure hunt coming along?" He handed the dog a cracker and kept one for himself.

"Well, that's kinda why I'm here. I stopped by that museum over on Useppa."

"Useppa? Yeah, I heard they had a break in over there."

"What?!" I couldn't believe it. They might as well run my whole life on cable TV like in that old Jim Carey movie.

"Noooo, I didn't. I'm just kiddin' ya. What'd you see over there?"

"I figured out that Useppa Island used to be Joseffa Key. You know – Isla de Joseffa?"

"Oh, I coulda told you that."

"Well, why didn't you?"

"You didn't ask, my man."

"Wasn't it obvious?"

"Not to you."

I hated when he got like that.

"Well, can I ask you something now?"

"Askin's free. It's the answers that cost ya."

"Do you know anything else that might help me find the treasure?"

"Now that's a good, well phrased question. Let me see the map."

I jogged back down to the boat and got him the map.

"Looks like the *X* is at the end of a lagoon on a small island," he said. "How's that?"

"Dude. I know that already. Now check this out. I compared this thing to a chart last night, and I have a theory. Cayo Costa used to be three separate cayos."

"Could be. Could be. Seems feasible. There are some lowlands out here. Could have been underwater at one time."

"And, if that's the case, this lagoon here," I pointed to the map, "could be landlocked now."

"Sure."

"Salt, I know where it is."

"You don't say."

"Oh, I do say. I've been there before."

He looked from me down to the map.

"And have you seen this growing there next to the lagoon?"

I looked at the old, hand-drawn map. Right next to Salt's dirty finger, next to the *X*, I saw a hand-drawn tree. I had never seen it there before.

"A tree?"

"A tree. Looks like a black mangrove. Pirates always put a landmark in the map as reference point if they could. A lot of times there are three reference points nearby. Find them. Make a triangle. And the treasure's in the middle."

"I remember a few black mangroves out there, but this tree would be long gone."

"Probably right."

He rolled up the map and handed it back to me.

"What's your next move?" he asked.

"Ask if you wanted to go there with me and help look for it."

"Why not? Let me grab a hat."

He walked off towards his weird, round house as Hammerhead followed me back down to the dock.

"You said a hurricane hit the coast as the Indian was hiding the treasure, right?" I asked Salt once we were motoring back down his canal to the bay.

"Right. Big one, too. Indians had known all summer it was coming."

"Known all summer? How?"

"No turtle nests. When a storm's gonna hit the beach, the turtles don't bury their eggs within 200 miles of where it's gonna hit."

"How do they know?"

"How does a salmon know which creek to swim up to spawn? The point is – they know. And, because they know, the Indians knew it, too. Too bad nobody pays attention to that stuff anymore."

"Why's that?"

He raised his eyebrows and said, "Ain't no turtle eggs on our beaches this summer."

"Well, if there was a hurricane back then, it could have washed out the gold that day."

"Indians were smarter than that. He would've stashed it someplace safe."

"Safe? In a swamp on a barrier island?"

"There are places."

I fired up the motor and we skimmed along the edge of Cayo Costa towards the south, just out of reach of its mangrove limbs. Every now and then, one would whack the hull. This part of the bay is extremely shallow, and the water gets about a foot or two deeper just before it goes under the mangroves, so I run really close. Hammerhead sat on the bay side of the boat, away from the trees.

In ten minutes, I saw the slough cut off to the right. I turned in and looked down at Salt to check his reaction. He was bent over scratching Hammerhead behind the ear not even paying attention.

I slowed the *Stripe* down and it settled into the dark water in a trough only a couple of feet deep. The surface rippled a foot below the barnacles that clung to the mangrove roots as my wake sloshed in. Those sharp shells marked the high tide line.

Small herons and ibis flew out of the mangroves squawking as the boat drifted further up the slough. At the end, I turned off the motor, jumped down and lowered the anchor into the muck.

The air was hot and still. Except for the occasional bird, the only sounds came from the light surf on the other side of Cayo Costa. We were probably less than fifty yards from the beach. The island got pretty skinny at that spot.

"Spose you want to head up that creek?" Salt said.

"You know about the creek?"

"Son, when you're born and raised out on an island this small, you tend to know every square inch of it." He used the side of the boat to support his weight and hopped in the water. "We call it Love Canal. But, that's a whole nother story."

Hammerhead didn't need any further encouragement. He jumped in behind Salt and started dog paddling until he realized he could walk. I grabbed the map bottle and followed them.

Mangrove limbs hung low completely covering the mouth of the creek. I watched a dead leaf float in under the limbs. The water moved very slowly as the incoming tide gained momentum.

These tidal swamps look kind of creepy, but there's really not a whole lot that can bother you. Maybe a snake – very rare. Only two or three salt water crocodiles left on the whole west coast. And, alligators usually stay in the fresh water. No, the worst things are the oysters and barnacles. They stick to the mangrove limbs and roots, and they'll slice you like a fillet knife if you step on one or even brush up against them hard enough. I always wear shoes.

Salt lifted up a tree branch and let me go in first, so I could lead us to the lagoon. When he pulled that branch up, it was like opening a door. In the shadows under the tree tops, the creek, maybe six feet across, serpentined back around mud banks and tree roots. Little tree crabs, the kind with one big claw, scurried up the tree trunks or down into their mud holes.

The water was about knee-deep in the creek, running in slowly over a hard-packed, sandy bottom. Hammerhead splashed past us to take the lead, terrifying a snook as he went. The fish shot up the creek close to the surface, so close he trailed a v-shaped wake behind him.

All the trees that surrounded us were red mangroves, the ones that stand on top of exposed prop roots. These roots tangled and intertwined as far as I could see to the left and right, looking like somebody had washed away all the dirt and left the forest high and dry.

Up ahead, the island rose a few inches. This small change in elevation brought in a different kind of mangrove – the black mangrove. They can live in saltwater like the reds, but their black bark is rougher, and their trunks thicker. And black mangroves don't have prop roots. They grow straight out of the mud with an unusual root system of their own. Their roots spread out under the swamp and then grow up instead of down, about six inches into the air.

The black mangroves spread these roots out in all directions under their branches. If it's a big, old tree, the diameter of roots can be like fifty or sixty feet. Looks weird, like hundreds of gnarly zombie fingers sticking up from the grave. I've always wanted to make a horror movie in a black mangrove forest.

Little by little, these black mangroves started to outnumber the red mangroves as we splashed further up the creek. Before long, daylight began to show through the trees ahead of us. The lagoon was getting close.

I looked back at Salt. His face had zero expression, as usual. I could never tell what he was thinking. Sometimes it seemed like he thought about nothing at all. But, I knew different. He took in everything. And that brain of his worked it over like a calculator.

"Better watch where you're going. Liable to step on something," he said.

I turned back around and wondered – had Salt really been to prison? If so, what for?

Hammerhead started barking somewhere up ahead, maybe at the lagoon. It wasn't a friendly bark either. He was warning something to back off.

I picked up the pace and sloshed my way into the clearing past the trees. Hammerhead stood on the left shore of the lagoon woofing at a raccoon. The coon's hair was all puffed up to make it look big, and its teeth were bared. The teeth aren't for show. Coons can do a number on a dog if they want to.

"Hammerhead! Stop!" I yelled.

The coon didn't want to give up whatever it had found in the sand and stood its ground, growling. Hammerhead barked more viciously. I looked for something to throw. There aren't any rocks in this part of Florida, but hopefully I could find a shell. I spotted a bleached out whelk shell that would work just fine.

I'd have to be careful. If the raccoon turned and ran, Hammerhead might try to chase him down. I needed to drop that baby between both of them, so they'd back away from each other. As I bent over to pick up the shell, a bolt of lightning must have hit the ground behind me because thunder almost knocked me down.

I whipped around. Salt stood there with a smoking pistol in his hand. I looked back at Hammerhead and the raccoon. Only Hammerhead was standing. The coon lay on the ground dead.

"What did you do that for?!" I didn't even know he carried a gun.

"Lookin' out for your dog." He put the pistol back under his shirt.

"Well, you didn't have to kill it. I could have scared it away."

"You would have stirred things up. You ever see what a coon can do to a dog?"

Hammerhead walked over and sniffed the raccoon, wagging his tail like he had whipped its butt.

"Since when do you carry a gun?"

"Since I started living on a remote island with no law enforcement."

My ears were ringing. That was one loud gun.

"Just let me know if you're going to do that again, okay? Scared the crap out of me."

Salt's lips parted just a little, his version of a smile. "Oh, quit your bellyaching. Let's find that treasure."

Like I said, I wouldn't ever want to be on Salt's bad side.

I walked up to the dead coon on the beach. Its body still twitched and shivered. Hammerhead looked up at me, tongue hanging out, panting, tail wagging.

"You got him, boy. Good job." I patted his head.

Mother of Pearl

"Pull out the map and let's see what's what," said Salt.

I uncorked the bottle and dumped the map into his hand. He unrolled it for both of us to see.

"Okay. If this is the same lagoon, then this *X* would be right over there." He pointed to a spot in the mangroves to the right of the end of the lagoon.

"Then this tree on the map, was over there, to the right of that," I said.

"And look what we got."

"A bunch of black mangroves."

He started walking up the beach towards the end of the lagoon.

"Now, these Indians were tricky," he said. "Tricky and clever. They knew a storm was coming."

"When the pirate was chasing him?"

"Long before that. They knew 'cause of the turtles."

He stopped and turned to face me.

"Here's what they did, see?" he said in a low, raspy voice like he didn't want anyone else to hear. "They didn't have much to make tools out of – no rocks. Just bones, teeth and shell, along with wood. They'd collect big shells whenever they found them." He looked over at the forest across the lagoon. "Sometimes they'd find more than they could carry and stash 'em away."

"Where? On the beach above the tide line?"

"No. Not in a summer when a storm was coming. They knew how high a hurricane pushed the water. No, they'd stick 'em up in a tree."

"That's stupid. The wind would just knock them down."

"In a knothole inside the tree."

"What kind of tree has knotholes out here?"

"Black mangrove."

He started up the beach again.

"If it was me," he continued, "running from a bunch of drunk, out of shape pirates, I'd put the gold in a place they weren't likely to reach. A place I'd been going to all summer to stash shells or any other treasure I found on the ground – my mangrove hidey hole."

A layer of scum covered the black water at the end of the lagoon. A needlefish swam just below it. Our shadows chased it away to the far side as we passed.

"But, again, that tree would be long gone, rotted away."

"Maybe. Maybe not completely. Anyway, shells don't rot like wood. Not as fast. And gold, it don't never rot."

We had reached the edge of the forest. Salt walked on top of the finger roots into the shade. About every twenty feet, tree trunks rose to the single canopy of leaves that filtered the sun. It felt fifteen degrees cooler under the branches.

Salt took one more look at the map and handed it back. I opened it up. In relation to the water, it looked like we were very close to where the tree had been drawn on the map. The *X* was a little further. I felt my heart beating in my neck. We were close.

Salt scanned the forest very slowly from left to right. In this part of the swamp, the black mangrove was king. Nothing else grew, not a single tree, bush, or weed. Just black mangrove branches high over head, dark trunks and thousands of creepy fingers sticking up in the mud flat.

"What do you see?" Salt asked.

"A big swamp. We're looking for a needle in a haystack, dude."

"Look harder."

I heard the scree-ka-ka-screech of a bald eagle calling out high in the sky.

"What am I looking for?"

"Treasure, knucklehead. You forget?"

"Salt."

"Many times, these forests get a foothold thanks to the efforts of one tree. That tree will take root, and she will just keep growing, straight up, and tower over everything else, which in this case would have been red mangroves, most likely."

He wiped the sweat off his forehead with the back of his hand.

"That first tree will choke off the sunlight from above with its limbs, and choke out the mud below with its roots. It's the kind of tree big enough and different enough to stand out against the other trees to a pirate trying to remember the details of that day."

I looked at the tree on the map. It really did look like a black mangrove, that or an oak, but the ground was too low and wet for an oak.

"It would also be the kind of tree an Indian could easily spot or tell others about. And, it would be tall enough to have a big, ol' knothole way up it."

"But it's gone."

"Not completely. Look. See any peculiar patterns out there?"

I imitated Salt, scanning the trees from left to right, looking for anything weird. Only two things seemed to stand out – the trees on the edge of the forest seemed larger, the ones in the middle, smaller. I told Salt.

"Exactly," he shot back like that was supposed to explain everything.

"Exactly…what?"

After letting out a sigh he said, "I would make a great nanny. Patient. Caring. Always explaining everything."

I rolled my eyes.

"Okay. Look," he said. "When mama tree was here, she had a bunch of baby trees. They lived all around her, the next trees of the forest. When mama tree died, baby trees were all grown up. They had babies of their own. Some of them are dancing on granny's grave."

"Okay. I get it. The bigger ones on the edge are second generation, and the smaller ones there in the center are the grandkids."

"Bingo, Sherlock."

"Now what?"

"Which way does the wind blow?"

I thought about that. I really didn't want him to have to explain anything else. It didn't make any sense, though. The wind could blow in any direction.

He didn't wait for me. "The wind generally blows hardest from the sea. Even in a hurricane, the worst stuff comes off the water."

"So, the tree could have fallen that way," I said pointing through the forest to the east.

"Now you're starting to think like an old pirate," he said and walked off into the middle of the forest.

I followed him out there, trying to step on as few of the creepy fingers as possible. Even though they were kind of rubbery and bounced back, it just never seemed right to walk on them. Hammerhead skillfully picked his way through without dropping a paw on a single one.

Salt stopped in the middle and looked down.

There it was – the dark outline of an ancient stump. The middle had rotted away. The ring of old wood that had survived rose up about an inch in some places and disappeared below the mud in others. A new black mangrove sapling sprouted in its center.

"Granny," said Salt.

"She was big! That trunk is three feet across."

"Need a big tree to start a big forest."

"Well?"

"Get your shovel and start diggin'."

"Shovel?"

"Oh, for Pete's sake! You didn't bring a shovel?"

"Didn't think about it."

"You call yourself a pirate?"

"No. I don't call myself that."

"Well, you are. Probably the last. Now, start acting like it! What have you got on the boat?"

"Uh, the gaff. A bucket. The anchor."

"Well, you better go get them. Otherwise you're gonna wear the ends of your fingers off. Once you start digging, you won't be able to stop."

I left him there in the black mangrove forest. I wasn't looking forward to slogging all the way back to the boat and then carrying all the gear back up the creek, but, he was right. And there was no other way around it. Hammerhead came along to keep me company. The whole trip took about thirty minutes. When I got back, Salt was gone. Maybe he'd walked over to the beach.

I laid all the stuff down next to the stump circle and looked at the ground east of where the tree had stood. The forest floor looked big. Finger roots grew out of the mud as far as I could see. Even though we had narrowed it down, I still felt like I was searching for a needle. But, I had to start somewhere, so I picked up the anchor, walked east about fifteen paces, and slammed the anchor blade into the muck.

The ground was soft, but all those roots made digging difficult. They got wrapped around the anchor and tried to hold it down. I couldn't flip the blades straight up and out. I had to twist and wiggle the shaft to get it out, then chip off black mud that stuck to the anchor like moist, gooey brownies.

I started swinging the anchor over my shoulder like a pick axe to drive it deep. It was hard work – and slow. The ground began to look like a bunch of hogs had come in and rooted around. So much sweat poured off my head, I had to wipe it every five seconds.

I had been just kind of digging at random, a little here, a little there, and I felt like I was getting nowhere. Then I remembered that when the Coast Guard searched for someone lost at sea, they used a systematic grid. That's what I needed. My search was way too messed up. It needed some kind of order.

I stood up, looked at the area, and visualized a big square on the ground. Using the bucket, gaff, and map bottle, I marked three corners of the square. I had to walk back to the lagoon and grab the old whelk shell to mark the fourth corner. When I came back to the stump, Salt was standing there.

"Where'd you come from?" I asked, surprised to see him appear out of thin air.

"My mother."

"More recently."

"I went shopping. Bought you a present." He held out a long, straight stick. "It's Australian pine. Dried by the sun. Plenty hard."

"Thanks, but I don't need a fishing pole right now."

"Oh, but I think you do. You see, pirates weren't the only ones who buried gold." He leaned against a tree. "Others had their reasons for hiding it, too. Take the Cubans, for instance. The Spanish had outposts down there that served as depots or collection points for gold that came up from the south and the west. They'd pile it up at these outposts and, when the pile got big enough, they'd ship it home to Spain."

When Salt's voice turned all dramatic and mystical, like it was doing then, I knew a story was coming. So, I sat down on the bucket and took a break.

"Now, old Gasparilla knew all about this practice. And when merchant ships got scarce on the Gulf, he'd head down south a couple of hundred miles and hit the Cubans.

He was so bold he kept a log book of each separate plunder.

Well, the Spanish got wise. Storing their riches above ground became a liability, so they took it down below. They buried the stuff, and only a few people at each outpost knew precisely where.

One hot summer, Long John had overheard a conversation in Tampa between two Spanish sailors who claimed Fort

Cordero's vaults were full and awaiting a galleon that was to arrive in three weeks. Upon receiving the news, Gasparilla gathered thirty men and sailed down to the Cuban coast to attack the small outpost. The winds were favorable, and they made the voyage in a couple of days.

Just after midnight, Gasparilla ordered all the lights aboard the Florida Blanca to be doused. Under the cover of darkness, he floated the vessel as close to shore as he dared and the men lowered the long boats. They rowed to shore in silence landing well away from the docks and the fort, so they could travel inland and slip in behind the soldiers from the mainland side. Gasparilla assumed the Spanish would not defend their flank as heavily.

His guess proved correct. Only four men opposed them on that side of the fort and not a single cannon. The pirates slipped in and, one by one, they killed the soldiers without a sound. Gasparilla led them to the commanding officer's home where they found him unguarded, asleep in his bed. Rather rudely, with a bucket of fresh pig manure, they roused him from his slumber and held a cutlass to his throat.

'Open ye eyes, commander, and lay them on the man who now owns ye very life,' growled Gasparilla.

The man wiped the foulness from his face and glared back at the pirate.

'My life is still very much my own, you insolent fool,' the officer said. 'By what right do you wake me?'

'By all that's right,' said Gasparilla. 'We be here for the gold your kingdom has stolen from the Southern Indians. Save your skin and give it to us now. Be a fool, and you will die this very night in a most painful way.'

'You are too late, privateer. That ship has sailed two days prior. I'm afraid our vaults are empty.'

The commander's words sent a fury through Gasparilla.

'Then show them to us at once! Or, ye will be tasting me steel soon enough!'

They took the commander outside and, on pain of death, forced his subordinates into the stockade where the freebooters locked them away behind bars of steel. The commander, alone, led the pirates to Fort Cordero's armored vaults and swung the doors wide. All the rooms were empty like he said.

Gasparilla was not convinced. He smelled a trick. So, he led the poor commander back to the courtyard where he had seen a dunking chair. They filled the tank with waste water and strapped the military man firmly in the seat.

'Now commander, I will ask you once, and one time only. Whar be the gold?'

'Haven't you seen for yourself? It's not here!'

Gasparilla signaled his man, and the big pole lowered the chair toward the nasty water. The top of the commander's head dropped below the surface, and they let him soak. Two minutes later, bubbles began to rise. When the bubbles stopped, they pulled the chair up.

With his lungs about to burst, the Spanish captain spat out water and gasped for air.

'I'm telling you the truth! Why won't you believe me?!' he pleaded.

Gasparilla motioned down with his thumb.

'No! No! I . . .'

But, the water cut him off. This time the bubbles came sooner, and the pirates left him down longer after they ceased. Finally, when they raised the dunking chair, the poor man choked and gagged as he fought to rid his lungs of the filthy water.

'You know, commander,' said Gasparilla beneath the man, 'this can go on and on until ye can't expel the water from ye chest. Why not tell the truth?'

By the light of the torches, the commander looked exhausted as he tried to speak. The rest of the pirates had to lean in to hear his voice.

'By Holy God . . . I . . . I've told . . . you. The . . . gold . . . is gone.'

Gasparilla had but to glance at his man and the chair began another slow decent.

'Wait,' croaked the commander.

'What's that, swab? Something in your throat?'

'Wait . . . I'll . . . show you . . . where it is,' he said finally.

'Good boy, commander. You won't regret it.'

They cut him down and allowed the military man to stagger back to his house. The cut-throats watched him with wary eyes and followed his steps closely. At the side of his house, the commander lifted a long stick off the ground. A stick that looked very similar to this."

Salt twirled the stick around in his hand like a baton.

"Tehn, the commander walked back to the courtyard, to a sandy area past the dunking chair. He began to test the ground."

Salt took the stick, which was about as big around as a broom handle on one end and tapered to a point on the other, and stuck it deep into the mud. The stick sunk down easily.

"It wasn't long before the Florida freebooters heard the stick strike something solid, just a foot or two below the sand.

Get the idea?"

I stood up and took the stick from him. "Thanks, Salt."

Honest to God, the guy was a walking pirate encyclopedia. You'd think he'd been hunting treasure all his life.

"Now you might hit the mother lode with that thing," he said, "or you might happen into bits and pieces of old conch shells. That feels more subtle. Stay on your toes."

Using the stick to feel around in the ground was definitely faster than the break-your-back-with-an-anchor method. I worked my original grid using the stick about every foot. A half hour later I hit something hard.

"Salt, there's something here!"

"Well, grab that fancy shovel of yours and dig it up," he said from his seat at the base of a tree trunk.

I stabbed the ground with the anchor blade, scraped off the gooey brownies, then rammed it into the earth again.

"Easy now," said Salt. "Don't break whatever's down there."

I used the stick to probe in the hole I'd dug. The object seemed to be about six inches further down. The ground was soft enough to use my hands. I dug around until I felt something hard with my fingertips. Feeling along the edges, I was able to work my fingers under the object a little. It felt smooth.

I tried pulling up. The mud sucked around it as the object pulled free. I held it up in front of me and saw an old bottle covered in grime.

"Whatcha got there?"

"Oh…just an old bottle." I was disappointed.

My arms sore and my heart defeated, I walked back over to the lagoon and held the bottle under the water to wash it off. The muck came off, except for a few places where the glass was stained, and, after rinsing out the inside, was looking at a clear bottle almost identical to the one that contained the map. This bottle, however, was empty.

I walked back to the dig site and handed it to Salt. He sniffed the open end.

"Smells like 200-year-old rum," he joked. "Looks like your other bottle. I guess those fellows liked this brand. Appears they might have been scratching around this spot as well."

Upon hearing that, a little adrenaline shot into my blood. My heart started thumping again, and I started probing the ground faster than ever. Another hour later, though, things were different. The adrenaline and my enthusiasm had run out. I had to keep switching hands and holding the stick differently because of blisters popping up on my skin. Salt just sat there by that tree.

We talked a little while I worked. I told him about Eden, Mrs. Rovich, and the problems I was having. He was a good listener, but he didn't offer any great suggestions. I think he may have nodded off a time or two. Oh, well. It felt good to let my frustrations out and it definitely made the time go faster.

After a while, I was so thirsty I got cotton-mouth. I bet Hammerhead did too. As much as I hated to do it, I walked back around the lagoon and down the creek to the boat to get a jug of water. The tide had risen half a foot, so the trip was more difficult. The saltwater cooled me down, though, and for that I was grateful.

At the boat, I heard that bald eagle again. I looked up and saw him circling in from the Gulf, probably checking the Bayou for a fish. They are big birds. Sometimes they'll fly up to an osprey and fight the smaller bird for their fish. I've even seen an osprey drop its fish in flight and the eagle swoop down and snatch it mid-air before the fish hits the water. This eagle just kept calling and soaring over me in a lazy arc.

With the gallon jug in my hand, I headed back up the creek under the mangroves to Salt and Hammerhead. This time I splashed along with the flow. When I got back to the stump, Salt had slumped over asleep.

"Salt," I said to wake him up.

He lifted his head and opened his eyes.

"I've poked around this whole area. Do you think it could be further east?"

"Could be anywhere," he mumbled.

I poured some of the water into the bucket for Hammerhead.

"Want some water, Salt?"

"Sure."

He took it from me and swallowed down a few gulps. I looked at the ground on the west side of the old stump, towards the lagoon. Zombie fingers stuck up all over the place.

"Could be over there, as well," said Salt. "Tree could have fallen the other way."

He didn't sound very sure of himself. My arms were so tired, about to fall off, but I sucked it up, marked out a grid on the west side of the stump and began searching the ground every foot with the stick.

An hour and a half later my arms did fall off. Not really, but if I had poked the ground with that stick one more time, they would have. I collapsed on the mud across from Salt. Hammerhead came up and licked my face.

"That sweat taste good, boy?"

He wagged his tail.

"Salt, this could go on forever."

"Been two hundred years and counting."

"That doesn't help."

"Look, kid. You can't just snap your fingers and find this stuff. It takes elbow grease."

"Can't we hire migrants or something?"

"Listen, and listen good. I know you're joking around, but let me tell you something. When it comes to a situation like this, don't trust anybody. I mean no one. Gold has a way of turning even your closest friend against you. I could tell you stories you wouldn't believe."

A crazy image of Salt in a sword fight on a pile of gold jumped into my head.

"Salt? Can I ask you something?"

"Askin's free."

"Some people say you've been to prison."

"Some people ought to mind their own business," he said, scowling.

He stood up. I could tell I'd touched a nerve.

"Sorry, Salt. I…I don't know. It doesn't matter either way to me. I just -"

"Look, son. You said it before. Life has its ups and downs. Gives 'em to every single person whether they admit it or not. My advice to you is to keep your head pointed in the right direction no matter what. And if you *do* happen to make a mistake, do all you can to set it right until you think you've done enough. Then do some more. Live it that a way, and things usually work themselves out." He started walking off. "I gotta take a whiz."

I sat there until Salt had walked past the lagoon and over the rise to the beach. The eagle cried again somewhere above. He sounded close, like he was hovering just over the treetops.

I looked up just in time to see a fish come flying down through the branches. It crashed down in front of me, square in the middle of the old stump and flopped around.

The fish was a big trout, and his gills still working the air. I picked him up. The eagle's talons had punctured his side. He was bleeding a little. I ran him over to the edge of the lagoon and lowered him into the water. Holding his tail, I worked him back and forth a little to get some water through his gills. But, he didn't want any help. With a flick of his tail, he splashed out of my hand and swam off into the depths of the lagoon.

I heard the eagle again and looked up into the clear sky. He still cut circles over the black mangrove forest. Weird.

I washed the fish slime off my hands and walked back to the site. Hammerhead gave me a strange look.

"Your guess is as good as mine, Hammer-dude."

The eagle circled and screeched. It seemed like he was screeching at me. Using my everything-happens-for-a-reason policy, I decided to attempt the impossible, or at least, the highly improbable, as Mr. Johnson, my old math teacher, would say.

I picked up the stick and walked over to the old stump. Its gnarly outline rimmed the dark ground like a miniature volcano. The little sapling in the middle was bent by the fish now, and even had a little slime on it. I shoved the stick into the mud next to the sapling and pushed on it hard. It went down about a foot and a half, and then ran into something that felt like a rock.

I probed around it, thinking that I had connected with the bottom core of the old tree. The stick sunk down almost three feet in several places.

I pulled the young mangrove out of the mud. All its roots came out intact, so I stuck it in a nearby anchor hole and shoved dirt around it with my hands. I'm all about trees.

Back at the stump, I started digging at the center, throwing handfuls of mud to the side. I must've looked pretty excited because Hammerhead came up and started sniffing my face to see what was going on.

In a couple of minutes, I had pulled out a pile of muck. In a couple more, I had my hand down into whatever the stick had hit. Under the mud, things slid around under my finger tips, coin-sized things. I eased one out, pinching it between two fingers.

The small object felt solid, like metal, but my hands were so dirty they only smeared the mud that covered it.

I stood up and ran it over to the lagoon, sat in the water, and washed it off between my legs. When all the mud was gone, it still had a thin coat of scum, so I pulled out my pocket knife and scraped the disk with the blade to expose its true color – bright, shiny gold!

My heart raced so fast I could hardly breathe. The water and sand around me started to go dark. I thought I was going to pass out. Then I realized it was Salt's shadow. I looked up over my shoulder at him, still unable to form words. The midday sun silhouetted his body against the sky.

"Whatcha got, kid?"

"S-S-Salt! I f-f-found it!! I found it! Goooooold!!!"

I handed him the doubloon.

Salt squinted as he rolled it over in his fingers. "Mother of pearl."

We're Rich

Salt bent down to hand the coin back to me. As he did, his gun fell out of his pants and landed in the sand.

He scooped it up and gave me a weird look, then stared at the pistol in his hand.

"Salt? The gold?"

"Is that what it is?"

I thought I'd kept him out in the heat too long. He acted kind of out of it.

"Sorry, kid. Just thinking about when I was your age…After you found that gold piece, did you plop down in the water so I wouldn't see you'd wet your pants?" He laughed a little, which was odd for him.

"Dude, you're weird. I'm excited, but I'm not a first grader."

"So, where'd you find it?" His eyes were glazed over.

"Man, the strangest thing happened with this eagle." I told him what had happened. When I looked into the sky to point the bird out, it had gone.

I looked back at Salt. The glaze had become more of a gleam. I had seen it before a time or two when he told me pirate tales, a far away sparkle.

"Let's go find the rest," he said.

We tromped back across the black mangrove roots to the stump. Using my hands, I scooped up big hunks of swamp mud and plopped them in the bucket. I could see more doubloons. The mud was filled with them the way cookie dough is filled with chocolate chips. Sweet! I couldn't dig fast enough. I have no idea how long it took, but I didn't stop until there was no mud left, just a hollowed out bowl of petrified mangrove stump.

It took two hands to carry the bucket back to the lagoon. I took off my T-shirt and knotted the sleeves shut. Then, handful by handful, Salt loaded the shirt with muck while I held the neck hole closed. The water did the rest. Holding both ends tight, I rocked the shirt back and forth under the surface. The mud dissolved and the coins sank into the middle.

After letting the black water drain out the holes, I shook the doubloons out into Salt's hat. When his hat filled up, we used mine. We had two pretty large piles of gold when the process was over. Some of the coins had come clean and shined as bright as the sun. Dude, I couldn't believe my eyes!

"Treasure," Salt said. "So, the old legend was true."

"Salt, I want to split it with you fifty-fifty."

"Tree must have been hollow all the way down. Or, hollowed itself out later."

"Salt? Do you hear me?"

"All those years. No one thought to look in the stump." His voice trailed away. "…sitting there in plain sight."

"Salt."

"That old Indian . . . *stumped* . . . everybody." He started laughing.

And, he didn't stop.

Now, old Salt might crack a smile every once in a while, usually at one of his own jokes, but I had never, ever seen him cut loose. That day, he closed his eyes, doubled over, and just let it go. It kind of creeped me out. I scooted over a little to give him room. He finally plopped down on the sand holding his gut. It took him a long time to wind down. He was lying flat out on his belly, face down on his arms. When his body stopped shaking, he became as still as the dead raccoon down the beach. I thought maybe he passed out or something. Or, went to sleep.

"Salt, did you hear me? I want to split it with you. I would never have found it if not for you."

I think he heard me that time because he rolled over and looked at me. He still didn't look right. His eyes were all squinty and mean. The butt of his pistol stuck out from under his shirt. The whole thing made me nervous.

"*Split* it with me?"

"Yeah. You deserve half."

"*Half?*"

"Yeah, half, man. What's wrong with you?"

"Kid." He sat up and took a long, deep breath, shook his head. It took him a few seconds to say anything. Then he relaxed and didn't look so mean anymore. "That gold is yours. You found it fair and square."

"But, you've done so much for me. I want you to share it."

"Old man like me? That stuff would just cause problems. It's yours, kid. You're the one with your whole life in front of you."

"But, Salt."

"You got family. You got needs. Me? I got all I ever wanted already. I'm set. Even got a place picked out in Aruba."

Aruba? He was kidding himself with that pipe dream. I thought about his old, round house, his beat up crab boat.

"What about a new roof? Or a new coat of paint?"

"Roof's fine. And I like the color."

"How about your boat? I bet you'd like a new one of those?"

"Like the boat the way it is. Comfortable. No, my mind's made up. Quit wasting your breath trying to change it. Not gonna happen."

When Salt made up his mind, it's easier to remove a hook from a thrashing shark than to change it. I let it go – for the moment.

I transferred the coins back to the clean bucket. We counted seven hundred and one. I couldn't believe what was happening. It felt like a movie. Salt grabbed the rest of the stuff, and we headed for the boat.

As we walked back down the beach along the lagoon, I couldn't take my eyes off the big pile of coins in that bucket. So beautiful. So much gold. I was rich! We were all rich. Not just me, but Mom, too. And Tori, I guess. And, even Salt. He was just being noble. I'd make him take some eventually. Our lives were going to change – big time! And just because we'd found a bunch of shiny metal. Funny how the world works.

I should have been watching the ground, though, because I stepped right on that dead raccoon. Scared the crap out of me. Big, black flies buzzed up all around my foot. Some gas, or something, hissed out of its guts, and I jumped like it was a snake. The bucket weighed me down so much that I staggered and fell. Luckily, I had the presence of mind to keep the bucket upright. Nothing spilled out.

Salt didn't say a word, just kept going right past me. I stood up and followed him to the creek. As we splashed along under the shady mangroves, I started thinking. I wondered how our lives would change. I thought about new cars and a new home. I thought about Mom quitting her job, and Tori wanting to spend it all on clothes. Maybe I'd find a new boat. All good things, except Tori's clothes, but something wasn't right. Something felt out of place. I realized I was worried about how it would change the way people looked at us. What would Eden say? Would she think I'm just another Dustin?

Most of the folks in Palmetto Cove were poor, like us. It kind of pulled us together, though. And when a rich person, like Mrs. Rovich, came along we all made jokes. We trusted our own and helped each other out. Would that change? Would people start jokes about us?

I was probably just tired. My muscles hurt. The thrill was wearing off a little. Maybe stepping on that coon did something to me. I was just a little worried.

When we got back to the boat, Salt must have read my mind.

"Listen, son. What you've got in that bucket there is powerful medicine. It can do a lot of good. And, it can do a lot of bad."

I set the bucket in the boat and hauled Hammerhead over the side. Salt grabbed my shoulder and turned me around to face him.

"Let me give you some advice. Use it to pay for things that you need. Just things that you *truly* need. Put the rest in the bank. Otherwise, keep living your life just the way you are now. And I wasn't kidding back there. Be very, very selective about who you tell. Your mom needs to know. Outside of that, I'm not sure it's anyone's business."

I jumped in the boat and gave Salt a hand up.

"There's a lot of good-hearted, kind people in this world. And, Harley, believe me, you're one of them. But there's also a bunch of worthless, no-goods. And, this is just the kind of thing that brings out their worst." He slid his sunglasses onto his nose. His speech was done.

As I drove the boat back to Salt's place, I asked him what I should do with the gold. He said to hide it in a safe place and, when the time was right, tell my mom. He gave me the name of a guy in Cape Coral, a treasure hunter, who could help turn some of the gold into cash. Salt said he'd contact him for me to keep things anonymous.

"How much you think he'll be able to get for it?" I asked.

He pulled down his sunglasses and looked at me for a moment before he said, "Harley. You're holding well over a million dollars in that bucket."

I almost did wet my pants when I heard that.

I shoved the throttle forward and the *White Stripe* jumped up on plane. We beat the bushes all the way to Salt's dock. I forgot to idle across Pelican Bay. Salt had to tap my leg to remind me to slow down after we made the turn into his canal.

"Maybe I ought to leave it out here with you, Salt," I said as he got off the boat.

He thought about it for a second. "No. Better take it with you. No law out here. And I'm not always around. Just squirrel it away safe somewhere." He waved and headed up the dock. "Act normal. Go check your traps. I'll find you in a day or so."

I turned the boat around and idled down the canal. As soon as I rounded the dogleg, though, I gunned the outboard and roared away to the bay.

When the *Stripe* burst free from the island, the sky seemed brighter than usual, more colorful. The water looked clearer, and the air smelled fresher. I was king of the world!

I just started screaming at the top of my lungs. I felt like a wild man, so alive! I cut the boat hard to the left, then hard to the right, leaving a big *S* pattern on the water. Then I just drove it around in a circle. Dude, I was hard-core trippin'.

I wanted to share it with somebody so bad. I throttled down the motor, and the boat bobbed around in its own wake. Hammerhead licked both sides of his black muzzle and panted. He must have thought I'd flipped out.

"We're rich, buddy!"

I found my phone and punched in Eden's number. Her voice mail picked up immediately. Bummer.

"Hey, Eden. It's Harley. Call me back, okay? I've got some big news!"

Salt wouldn't like me telling her, but I couldn't help it. Anyway, Eden could keep a secret. And, besides, she already knew about the map. This was just what I needed to get her over the Mrs. Rovich thing.

I climbed down the tower and picked up the bucket of gold. If these were the coins that Indian had carried, he must've been one strong dude. I didn't know if I could have carried it up a tree, let alone in a hurricane.

I dumped all the doubloons into my wet t-shirt and tied both ends tight, then hid the bundle and the map bottle under the casting deck as far as I could shove them. I covered them with the anchor rope, tied one end of the rope back on the anchor, and set the anchor on top of the pile.

Afternoon clouds were just beginning to pop up over Pine Island on the far side of the Sound. The sun hung at about one o'clock, and the boat sat halfway between Cayo Costa and

Useppa. The first float in one of my trap lines bobbed in the water about a half-mile away. It was tough, but I swallowed down my excitement and headed for the line in a massive effort to appear normal.

Even the fishing was better that day. I checked fifty traps and pulled out at least a bushel and a half of blue crab. Nice ones, too. By four, I was running back to Palmetto Cove with plenty of time to dump them off at Smitty's.

When I slowed the boat into the Palmetto Cove channel, it felt like I was sailing into a dream, like I was an actor in a movie. Now that I had the gold I was just going through the motions. How long could I keep up the act before folks found out? I had to quit smiling so much.

People waved from their yards as I motored by. I waved back, but they seemed to stare a little too long, like they suspected something. No secrets on shore. Paranoid? I don't know.

Okra stood watching me with her hands on her hips as I docked the boat at Smitty's.

"Well, there you are, boy! Where you been? Thought we had a date!" she said laughing her eyes shut.

"Uh, hi, Miss Okra. Just out working. You know . . . as usual."

"Got your shirt off working on that tan, I see. What'd you bring me today, sugar?"

"About a bushel and a half, I think."

"Well, I better go find that slow, no-good Otis to haul 'em in for you." She turned back to the store and cupped her hands around her mouth. "Otis! Get down here and get these crabs!" She turned back to me. "He be back directly. I better get my butt back to the cash register before Smitty finds out. That fat boy liable to fire me on the spot. I see you later, honey. Otis! Where are you!"

I rinsed out my bucket with the hose on the dock and put some fresh water down for Hammerhead. Otis finally shuffled out and took the crabs to the processing room. I waited around on the dock for a few minutes to give him time to relay the total to Okra.

As I stood there trying to appear calm, collected and ordinary, Smitty came waddling over.

"Well, it's official," he said. "They named it Charley this morning."

"Charley?"

"Yep. Tropical Storm Charley. Headed towards Jamaica. Though, if you ask me, it really doesn't look that impressive. They showed it on the news today."

"Where's it headed after Jamaica," I asked.

Smitty guzzled the last of a Coke, wiped his mouth and burped.

"Oh, too far out to tell, really. Headed west-northwest right now. They expect it to turn, though. And intensify."

"Which way."

"To the north. Gulf eventually. I went online and checked out the probabilities. Right now we have a whopping two percent chance of getting hit here in Palmetto Cove."

I remembered Salt's theory about the turtles.

"Think we ought to be worried?" I asked.

"Naw. It's really no chance at all. Besides, we haven't seen a hurricane in our neck of the woods since Donna in 1960. You know how it is. With Cuba blocking everything from the south and the state of Florida from the east, it's got to be a very peculiar scenario for anything to wind up here."

"Where do you think it will go?"

"Me?" He pulled a pack of peanut butter crackers out of his pocket. "I think it'll fly over the west tip of Cuba and zip up to Texas or the Florida panhandle like they all do."

Okra walked out of the store with my money in her hand.

"Here you go, sugar," she said as she handed me the cash. "Don't go blowin' it on any of those cute little girls you run around with. Save it for somebody special." She winked at me, then swiped a cracker from Smitty. "You better look out," she told him. "Those things gonna make you fat!" She laughed at that one as she went back in.

Smitty hung his head down towards me and cupped his mouth with a hand.

"She's one to talk," he said.

"I heard that!" she shouted back from the porch.

He lowered his voice a little more.

"I got her a treadmill for Christmas. You know what she did? Got rid of my easy chair in front of the TV. Put that treadmill in its place. Told me I didn't need a chair. That if I was gonna watch TV all the time, I should be exercising while I watched."

"Women," I commiserated.

"I heard that, too! You better watch yo' mouth, Harley Davidsen Cooper. You know I love you, but I'll knock yo' butt into next week!"

"We better stick to the weather, Smitty."

"Agreed. Hot one today, huh?"

"Hot one everyday," I said.

Back on the boat, I decided to cruise by Eden's place before I went home and just see if her dad's boat was out back. Sure she was mad at me. But that was just a misunderstanding. I could clear it up if I could only talk to her.

It seemed very unreal to be running around in my boat with a million dollars under the deck. I wondered if old Gasparilla ever sailed into a port with enough loot on board to buy the whole city. He must have thrown some wild parties.

I slowed down before Eden's canal and peeked around the corner. Her dad's crab boat was gone, so I idled into the canal under the tall Australian pines. The afternoon wind picked up just a bit and whispered a song through their needles. We had one of those trees next to our trailer, and in the winter when it was cool enough to open the windows, I'd listen to that sound at night and imagine I was a million miles out to sea.

I tied off the *Stripe* and hopped onto the Baker's dock. Stepping stones led me through the small yard up to their trailer's door. I knocked.

Mrs. Baker opened the door.

"Hi, Mrs. Baker. I was looking for Eden. She around?"

She frowned at me through the crack in the door. She was a timid woman, and always worried. I would be, too, if I had to live with Eden's dad.

"No," she said. She had a squeaky, little mouse voice. "She went off with Lori Stillmeyer to Cayo Costa. Helping with the scouts."

Lori was a few years older than me. She was a nice girl, but never very popular. Didn't date at all, so she spent a lot of her spare time running the same Girl Scout troop she used to belong to.

"They coming back on the ferry at six?"

"Oh, no. Won't be coming back today," she squeaked. "They're staying out until Saturday, camping."

Figures, I thought. She's mad at me, mad at Dustin, so she took off to avoid us. Probably got her phone turned off, too.

"Thanks, Mrs. Baker. Would you please tell her I stopped by?"

"Oh, I don't know if that's such a good idea." Her squeaking reached a new high. "I heard all about what you did."

"Wha . . . Listen, Mrs. Baker. Nothing happened. That was all . . ."

"I really don't need to hear anymore, Mr. Cooper. Thank you. Good-bye."

She shut the door in my face. Fantastic. So much for a tight-knit community that stuck together. Thanks, Mrs. Rovich.

Except for a few small pieces of property like Salt's, Cayo Costa was mostly owned by the state. They turned it into a park for the public. On the north end, where the island was about a mile wide, the rangers had an office next to a little marina on the bay. The campground was over on the beach side of the island. You could rent a one-room cabin or stay in a tent on a tent site. Pretty cool place to camp since you're right on the beach and there's no cars or buildings or anything.

More than likely, Lori and Eden had set up camp in a bunch of tents, depending on how many girls went on the trip. Maybe tomorrow I would just happen to show up at Cayo Costa State Park. It was a public park, after all.

I unhitched the *Stripe* and drove around through the canals to home. By the time I got there it must've been around five or five thirty. Mom's car was in the driveway. As I lifted the bulging T-shirt back into the bucket, the sheer weight of all that gold washed goose bumps onto my skin. Again, I really wanted to tell someone. I guess that someone was going to be Mom.

How would I break it to her exactly? This was the biggest thing I'd ever shared with her. I wanted to choose the right words, but walking up to the trailer, nothing profound occurred to me.

I opened the front door and held it for Hammerhead. Mom stood over by the sink peeling potatoes.

"Hi, Mom."

"Hey, Harley. How was it out there today?" Then she turned around and saw the bucket in my hands. "Oh, you saved some for dinner? Well, just in time. I was about to open a box of Hamburger Helper."

I decided to be direct, just come right out and say it.

"No, it's not crabs, Mom. I think you need to sit down."

She stopped peeling in mid-potato, and a look came over her. Tiny lines wrinkled her forehead. Mom's can really melt down into worry mode fast. Maybe I had been too dramatic.

Tori came walking down the hall. Great. I didn't want her to know, but I couldn't stop now.

"Mom, you know, you can't ground me away from Dad. I don't even think that's, like, legal," she said to Mom not even noticing I had come home.

The lines across Mom's forehead were met by a pair of hardening eye-brows below as Tori whined her way to the kitchen.

"Anyway," Tori continued, "tonight's, like, the night. And I . . ."

"Tori, could you please be quiet for just a second? You're interrupting Harley. He was about to tell me something."

"He's always telling you something! When do *I* get a chance to say something around here?"

"Tori, be quiet! In a minute. Okay?"

Tori frowned and leaned against the counter, immediately starting to twirl her hair and smack her gum super loud. I really didn't want to say anything in front of Tori, and, in hindsight, I shouldn't have. But I guess I was too excited, and I probably wanted to show Tori up a little, as well. Bad karma, man.

"I found it, Mom," I blurted out.

"You found what?" she said.

"The treasure!"

"The what?" Her eyes blinked open.

"The map. Remember the map on Sunday?"

"Uh-huh."

"Well, we figured it out and ta-daaa – gold!"

I leaned the bucket over so she could see.

"Looks like an old T-shirt to me," said Tori.

"Awww, man!" I took my knife and ripped through the cloth.

A pile of gold appeared, most of it dingy brown, but some just as brilliant as a jewelry store showcase.

My mom's hand came to her mouth. "Oh, my Lord!"

"That's right." I was beaming. "Seven hundred Spanish doubloons."

Tori quit smacking her gum to come take a look.

"Where'd you get it, Harley?" asked Mom.

"Followed the map to a spot on Cayo Costa. Mom, you don't have to work at MegaMart anymore." My voice cracked. I started shaking.

She took my arm and looked up from the bucket to my eyes. "How much is it worth, Harley?"

"Salt says it could be over a million dollars."

"Salt?" She dropped my arm. "Harley, didn't I tell you about that man? Nothing good's gonna come out of messin' with him."

"I'm telling you, Mom, he's different than all that. He helped me find it. I offered to split it with him. And guess what? He turned me down."

Her hands went to her hips.

"Turned you down? How could that worthless old man afford to reject that kind of money? I bet you he doesn't have a penny to his name."

"He turned me down, Mom. I tried and tried. He wouldn't listen. And, he says he knows a treasure hunter over in Cape Coral who can help us sell it."

"I bet he will," she said. "Well, I know people, too, Harley. We'll figure this thing out, just the two of us. We don't need any outside interference."

"We're rich! We're rich! We're rich, rich, RICH!" Tori started yelling. She danced around the kitchen like a jerk in a bad reality show.

"Tori," I said. "That's the last thing we need to be saying. Listen, we need to keep this thing quiet until it's all figured out."

"Who cares?" she said. "We don't have to worry about the trailer trash around here, yo. We's hit the bigtime."

"No, '*we's*' haven't. I have," I said. "And if you want a nickel, you better keep your mouth shut."

"Tori, he's right. Gold diggers will come out of the woodwork if they hear about this."

"You guys suck in the fun department. The first thing you ought to do is go out and buy some fun lessons. Sheesh!"

She stormed down the hall into her room and slammed the door.

"Harley, you're sure this is gold?"

"What else could it be, Mom? Look at it."

"We need to find a safe spot for it until I can make a few calls in the morning."

"I won't let it out of my sight, promise. And, Mom? Salt really is a good guy. You ought to give him a chance."

"Harley, mother's are protective. I'm only looking out for you. You'll understand when you have kids. Now tell me what happened."

I told mom the whole story beginning on Sunday. Under the circumstances, I didn't think she would get upset about anything, even breaking into the museum on Useppa. She didn't. In fact, her eyes lit up and she hung on every word. If anything, confiding to her brought us closer.

When I had gotten her up to speed, she went back to peeling potatoes, and I picked up the bucket to go shower off. Tori came out of her room with an overnight bag in her hand. She pushed by me into the living room.

"Where're you going, young lady?" asked my mom.

"Dad's. And you can't stop me."

"How you getting there?"

"He's picking me up. I called him an hour ago. He's probably almost here."

"Don't tell him anything," I warned her.

"Don't worry. I won't say a stupid word," she said. "You guys get off my back, okay? I won't tell anybody your stupid secret."

"Tori, please keep it quiet for a while, okay?" said Mom.

"I said I wouldn't tell, mother. What more do you want?!"

I walked into the bathroom and shut the door. After I had the water running, I heard my dad's bike pull up outside. He wouldn't expect me to run out and greet him, wouldn't have anything to say if I did. He didn't stick around anyway. The sound of his motorcycle trailed away before I had even set foot in the shower.

When I was a little kid, I used to get upset about my dad not spending any time with me. I missed him after he and mom split up. But now, he's pretty much just another person, not really a family member. If he is around any length of time, it's only because he wants something. And then there's usually trouble.

The Dream

After the shower, I weighed myself on the bathroom scales – 163 lbs. Next, I picked up the bucket and weighed us both – 203 lbs. The gold weighed forty pounds! Minus the bucket, of course, but still, that's a lot of gold. Salt had said that these old doubloons were worth a lot more than their weight in gold, depending on their condition. Though I'm no expert, they looked pretty good to me.

I put on some shorts and went to work on the coins with a box of baking soda and an old towel, trying to get them as shiny as possible. I just sat on the toilet seat and scrubbed each coin in the sink until it sparkled.

I had cleaned about twenty-five when I took a break and looked at them as they dried on a towel on the floor. They shined up absolutely golden, beautiful, and delicious. Details stood out clearly on almost every one. I had scored big-time! Those doubloons would be worth way more than their weight in gold. I felt like screaming again, but that would not have been cool, so I just bottled it up and did a dance on the toilet seat with my arms pumping and my legs kicking. Maybe I had gold fever. Whatever. I couldn't help it. Good thing I wasn't in a reality TV show. Would have been embarrassing.

I picked up one of the doubloons and held it under the light. On one side, the Spanish had stamped a cross in the middle surrounded by a design that resembled a cloverleaf. A ring of dots circled that. One edge of the coin had been clipped into an irregular shape. I could make out a few capital letters around the side that hadn't been clipped – *V*, *M*, *R*, *E* and *X*. I wasn't sure what that meant. Didn't look like a word, though, not even a Spanish word.

The backside of the coin had a symbol that looked like a big *U* with the top closed off. Inside the *U*, more lines divided the shape into quadrants. All kinds of little shapes and symbols filled each of those sections. I had no idea what they were or what they meant, but I knew one thing for sure – I had a pile of official pirate booty worth a fortune. Woo-hoo!

I wrapped the clean coins in a towel and stuck them in the bucket on top of the dirty ones. In my room, Hammerhead watched me from his spot on the floor between my bed and the closet. I slid the closet door back and put the bucket inside in the corner, then grabbed a few dirty clothes off the floor and threw them over the bucket, just to be safe.

Hammerhead followed me into the living room and laid down in front of me after I took a seat on the couch. Mom sat in her chair watching TV. Dinner on the stove smelled great.

"Long time in the bathroom," she said. "Feel okay?"

"Just cleaning the coins," I said, settling back on the couch.

That couch felt more comfortable than ever. In fact, everything felt more comfortable. Welcome to the world of the wealthy, the lap of luxury, where everything exists just for you. Ahhhhhh.

"Bill called while you were in there," Mom said.

I checked my phone. One missed call. I must have been in the shower.

"You ready for dinner?" she asked moving towards the kitchen. "I went ahead and blackened that redfish. We need to celebrate. Mashed some potatoes, too."

"Sounds good. Mind if I flip over to the weather?"

"Sure. Going out in the boat tomorrow?"

"Yeah, thinking about it. I'd like to see what the wind's doing."

"Hey, Harley? I'm thinking we should put all that gold in a safe place."

"Like where?"

"I don't know. Safe deposit box, maybe. I could get one in the morning."

"Mom, I don't want to sound paranoid or anything, but I really don't trust those bank people," I said walking into the kitchen.

"What are you going to do? Carry it around all the time? You can't leave it here."

"Yeah. I'll keep it with me."

"Well, I'm calling the bank in the morning. Then, I'm going to find a dealer."

"Mom. You're probably not going to agree with this, but I'm taking Salt up on his offer. If this guy from Cape Coral has dealt with Spanish treasure before, he might be able to get the best deal."

She rolled her eyes, but didn't fight me. "Well, I'll tell you what, Harley. Let's do both and we can compare the two."

"Okay," I said, but I still trusted Salt more.

I poured some food into Hammerhead's bowl and returned to the couch with a plate. We ate and watched news until the weather came on. The weather guy said that tomorrow was going to be a typical summer day with a calm morning and scattered storms in the afternoon. Then he went to a wide satellite photo of the Caribbean to show Tropical Storm Charley.

"And here's what we're keeping our eye on – Tropical Storm Charley," said the weatherman. "Charley has winds of around sixty-five miles-an-hour now, according to the latest advisory, but we expect some strengthening over the next few days. It's moving very quickly, twenty-six miles-an-hour, to the west-northwest, but that direction will probably change as well, as an approaching ridge of high pressure steers the system more to the north."

He seemed very concerned about the storm. Then again, weathermen in Florida seem very concerned about every storm.

"That puts Jamaica in the cone of uncertainty. The island nation has already begun to prepare itself for the landfall of a possible category one hurricane. We'll be back with sports, right after this."

My mom muted the sound just as an obnoxious car commercial popped on.

"Sounds like a nice morning," she said.

"Yeah. I think I'll head out and clean more of the coins out on the boat. Check some traps, too. Might as well enjoy the day."

I was actually thinking about where I'd look for Eden on Cayo Costa.

"I'm calling in sick," said my mom.

I gave her a look. "Mom, we need to act natural, you know?"

"Just tomorrow, Harley. Just tomorrow. I need to make a bunch of calls. Okay?"

"Mom, I know you haven't had a lot of time to think about it, but . . . do you think we'll move away?"

"From this trailer? Of course we will."

"No. From Palmetto Cove or Pine Island."

"Oh, I wouldn't worry too much about that, Harley. If we did, I'm sure it would be much better than here."

I didn't want to hear that. My friends were here. My life was here. I couldn't imagine living away from the water. But my mom was a dreamer, not a boater, and most of her dreams were pretty far out there. That's okay if you don't have the money to act on them. That was about to change. It would be up to me to keep her on an even keel.

"Can I ask you something, Mom?"

She looked over at me. "Sure, honey. What's up?"

"Can we make any big, you know, major decisions as a family?"

"Of course we will, Harley. Of course we will."

I'd have to keep at it. She was starting to drift. Her mind was working it over. The wheels were turning.

We sat there and watched the rest of the news, then a couple of game shows until I began to drift off.

"Well, it's been a long one, Mom," I yawned.

"Good night, Harl."

"Good night."

I let Hammerhead out for a couple of minutes before going to my room. I was beat. Long day. I don't think it took me more than three minutes to fall asleep. Then I had the weirdest dream.

I was a Calusa Indian living on Useppa in the village that existed there before the pirates came and took it. And, bro, let me tell you, this dream was so real, I still remember every detail like it actually happened.

We were inside this hut, me and my Indian family, huddled up because this storm was coming. My dad was sick, laying over on the floor in one corner. My mom was bent over him, trying to get him to drink something. Wind was whipping around the hut. I heard it in the trees, and I saw the walls moving.

Outside, I heard this really loud boom. At first, I thought it was thunder. Then people started screaming. I stuck my head out the door. Through the rain, I saw folks running up from the water. Then – *BOOM* – another explosion, a cannon.

I found myself standing on a hill, away from our house. You know how you kind of pop around in dreams? That's what happened. Well, I saw a ship flying a black flag with a skull that had glowing eyes. It was anchored up in the cove beyond our canoes on the beach. Most of the men, the warriors, were sick with a fever. They had spots on their bodies. A few had died. Two had not come down with the sickness. They had been dragging the canoes up to higher ground away from the rising water.

I looked down to the beach and saw those men lying still on the ground – dead. Another boom, and another cannon ball flew by and exploded near my house.

My dad wasn't the chief, but he was on the tribal council, so our house sat up high on the hill close to the chief's hut. The chief's place was completely destroyed. I saw his son, my friend, blown out and wrapped around a tree. I ran to him. Too late. He had died.

Screams came from my hut, so I darted inside. My mom held my father in her arms. She was trying to pull a stick out of his side. It had come through the wall with the explosion next door.

"Take it! Take it!"

At first I thought she was talking about the stick, then I realized she was yelling about the gold. My father was the gold keeper for our tribe.

"Take the evil stuff off the island! Take it away!"

My mom had been against the gold from the start. She thought it possessed evil powers and had never wanted it around. The battle had proven it to her, and she wanted it gone.

I left her there holding my father and, with just my bow and arrows over my shoulders, I ran back outside with the heavy bag of gold. The ship had stopped firing its guns. Now, three longboats filled with men rowed to shore.

I ran to the beach and grabbed a canoe. The wind blew in hard from the east, helping me drag it down the beach. Someone from a longboat fired at me.

I threw the canoe in the water and paddled with the wind as fast as I could. Rain beat against my eyes whenever I turned to look back over my shoulder. A boat with three men followed. They had seen the bag. They wanted me dead. They wanted the gold. They had to be pirates.

My arms burned. My hands began to blister. I stabbed the wooden paddle into the rough water again and again. The pirates fired again and missed. I prayed the weather was with me. The gods sent a curtain of rain to hide my canoe.

Under its cover I turned into a lagoon and continued to the end. I dragged the boat up a small creek into the trees and struggled through the swamp on top of the roots with the deerskin of gold slung over my shoulder. Soon, I came to the big tree. It towered over the others with huge branches that howled in the wind.

I hugged the wet trunk and climbed, and didn't stop until I made it to the hole halfway up. A large knothole opened in the side of the trunk to the hollow interior. I stuffed the bag in the hole and hooked one of its deer-hide laces onto a snag on the inside of the trunk.

When I turned to look back over the trees to the water, the rain had begun to slacken. I spotted the pirates' longboat just rounding the end of the island. They would soon make the corner and see the lagoon.

Wasting no time, I jumped out of the great tree into the branches of the smaller trees and rode them down. Across the tangle of roots, I ran to the edge of the lagoon.

The boat came slowly in the storm. There were three of them. I had one arrow for each. I set one against my bow and waited.

When they beached their boat at the water's edge, I let an arrow fly. The man doubled over, screaming. My arrow stuck out his chest. I reached for another arrow as the gun came around. And then –

I woke up. My heart was racing. I was sweaty. I sat up and looked around my room in the glow of the streetlight. Dude, I was never so glad to be in it. In my whole life, I don't think I have ever felt so relieved.

I put my head back down on the pillow and scratched Hammerhead as I tried to calm down. Dreams come for a reason. What was that one trying to tell me? It was vivid, so real.

It kind of made me feel like the gold was tainted, maybe even cursed. When I had heard the original pirate story about Joseffa from Salt, all I could think about was that gold. I really never stopped to consider what it must have been like for those Indians that day. It's funny how the same situation seems so different when you see it through someone else's eyes, when the tables are turned.

I remembered every detail and, as I lay there and went over each one, trying to make sense of them, I felt something watching me from the closet.

It was the gold.

No Day at the Beach

Wednesday morning, I woke up and looked out my window. The day looked calm and clear just like the weather guy had predicted. I heard Mom's shower running. At least she wasn't lying in bed, stuffing chocolate balls in her face like the rich ladies do on her TV shows.

I threw on a pair of shorts and a T-shirt, then walked to the front door to let Hammerhead out. The air hit me like steam from a sauna. Hot, sticky, humid. A typical August morning.

While Hammerhead took care of things outside, I fixed a delicious peanut butter and jelly sandwich. I wondered if rich people ate peanut butter and jelly. Did they buy the peanut butter at the regular grocery store? Or did they order some snooty version that I hadn't heard of?

Back in my room, I found my old backpack in the closet. I hadn't used it in a couple of years and was glad to find the heavy canvas still in good shape. I poured the dirty coins into the backpack and put the towel with the clean ones in on top. Next, I tossed in the baking soda and the old towel.

I tried on the pack. It sagged down around my butt a little, but it felt decently comfortable. I tied my shoes and stepped out into the hall. Mom's shower was off.

"I'm headed out, Mom."

"Okay, dear. What time you coming back?"

"Early afternoon."

"Okay. You got the gold?"

"I got it, mom."

"Harley. Why don't you leave it with me? I'll stick it in the bank."

"Mom."

"It'll be safer."

"Mom. I found it. I'll keep it safe!"

"Okay, okay. Just be careful."

"I will."

Hammerhead met me at the door and followed me down to the Stripe. I hid the bag up under the casting deck. When I lifted the anchor rope up to slide it in, my hand brushed over the map bottle. I figured that should probably stay home now. If I left it in the boat, it would only end up broken.

I grabbed it and ran back up to the trailer. As I worked the bottle into the back of my closet, I heard Dad's motorcycle pull into our yard. My heart sank when the motor shut off.

The front door opened and Tori ran in, making a beeline for her room. I stopped her in the hall.

"What's Dad doing out there?" I asked her.

"I don't know. Get your hands off me!"

I could smell sour liquor from the night before all over her.

"You didn't tell him anything, did you?"

"Mom. Harley's messing with me!" she shouted.

"Harley!"

I remembered the gold sitting in the boat and let her go. I pushed the door open and jumped off the steps to hurry down to the dock. My dad was standing on the bow of the *Stripe*.

"Mornin', boy. You're in a big hurry today," he said while he picked at his teeth with a splinter.

"Got a bunch of traps to check."

"How's that goin' for you? My boat working out?"

He was up to something. He always tried to be clever in situations like this – when he wanted something. He couldn't just be normal and come right out and say it. He had to play a little game instead.

"Yeah, once I spent a few months scrapping off the barnacles and fixing her up."

"Well, she's looking mighty fine now. Catching any crabs?"

He pulled out a cigarette and lit it. As he did, my dad wobbled just enough to let me know he was still drunk from the night before.

"A few, here and there," I said. "Mullet season's better – if you don't mind throwing a net. You know, working at it a little." I couldn't help pointing out what a lazy loser he was.

"Word has it that you've been catching a bit more than crab these days."

Here it came. I knew Tori had told him about the gold.

"A whole lot more. Shall we say, something worth its weight in gold?" He cackled at his own lame joke.

I stood there on the dock just waiting for him to get to the point. Hammerhead came trotting up behind me. He saw my dad on the *Stripe* and growled low, the one he does just before he barks.

"Shhhhhh," I said. "Easy, boy."

"Now, if that were to be the case, I figure it's time you stepped up to the plate, boy." He took a drag off his cigarette, but he didn't take his eyes off of me. "Aww, now don't give me that pitiful look. I know fishin's hard. Gotta haul them traps, bait 'em up, pay for fuel, sell 'em for next to nothing. Ain't nothing I haven't seen. Lived on that planet for years working the mullet. Putting food on your plate."

He looked at the boat.

"Yep, one fine boat. Lotta work, fishin', and not much scratch. That's why I let it go." He turned back to me. "And that's why I haven't pestered you none. My fatherly gift, you might say." He put his hand on his heart. "But, now. My, my, my. How things have changed. I figure it's time you became a real fisherman. And a real fisherman pays for it all."

He stood directly over the gold. That made me nervous. He flicked his cigarette into the canal and stepped up on the dock. Hammerhead barked at him, pretty loud, too.

"Better watch that mutt, boy. Lawyers getting a heap a cash for dog bite these days."

I grabbed Hammerhead's collar and held him next to my leg.

"Yep. I let you off the hook with that free boat. Thought the low overhead'd help you get rolling. Didn't even charge rent. But, now, as your father, I need to urge you to do what's right. You need to buy that boat from me."

"It's not yours to sell."

"Not mine? Who do you think bought it? Who do you think slaved on it for years so you could even come into this god-forsaken world? Huh?"

When he stepped towards me, the stink of tobacco and whatever he had been drinking came in on the air. Hammerhead started to growl again.

"Mom, got it in the divorce." I wasn't sure but I took a stab at it thinking he would have come looking for a handout a long time ago if the boat was really his.

His face got real ugly. "You ungrateful little – "

"Foley!" It was Mom. She was coming down fast from the trailer. "You're not supposed to be here, Foley. You know that."

"Settle down, Sam. Trying to keep me away from my own son, too? I'm just having a little father-son chat, here. Doesn't pertain to you, so butt out."

"Then you need to have it over the phone. Now get out of here before I make a phone call to people you don't want to see."

"Uppity already. My, my, my. How money changes people. I just figured that since you never bothered to compensate me for that boat, maybe this boy here would be man enough to do it."

He poked my mom hard in the chest with his finger on the word *you.* The scene was going downhill fast. Things never ended well when the two of them got together. Besides, however twisted his motives were, maybe he had a point.

"How much do you want, Dad?" I asked him, trying to defuse the bomb that I knew was seconds away from exploding.

"Twenty thousand," he said.

"Twenty thousand dollars!" said my mom. "Have you finally lost your mind? You bought that thing used for eight."

"Well, you got rent, and on top of that you got interest," he said.

"Foley! I'm warning you! You better leave right now, before I call the cops," said Mom. Her eyes were bloodshot, and a vein throbbed in her neck.

Despite my best efforts to maintain order between my parents, they snapped, like they always did. Dad hurled a few choice words at her; then he went for her throat, literally. When he grabbed her, my mom kneed him in the crotch hard enough to take the wind out of his sails. He staggered backwards doubled over, looking like he was going to puke. But before that could happen, he ran out of dock and fell into the canal.

Now, my dad was right about one thing: he *had* spent years out on the water. But, in all that time, he had never bothered to learn how to swim. He sank like an oyster.

Of course, I jumped in after him. However misguided he was, the man was still my father. The canal wasn't that deep, maybe ten feet. I dove down and found his shirt collar. He was kicking like mad, but not making any progress. I got him up high enough one-handed to reach up and hold on to the dock with my other hand.

Thank God water reduces the weight of an object, or in this case, my dad. I pulled his head out of the canal so he could get air. Looked like he had puked after all. It still dribbled out of his mouth as he fought for breath. I pushed him over to the dock so he could do the rest on his own and hauled myself out.

"You okay, Mom?"

She rubbed her throat and nodded. She was tough. She'd be okay.

My old man, however, was a different story. He'd probably never be okay. At the moment, he was dripping like a wet cat as he made his way up the old ladder onto the dock.

He stood there, all matted down, glaring at us. The morning swim had done nothing to lighten his spirits.

"You haven't heard the last of this," he said to one of us or maybe both of us. "What's right is right. You owe me that money!"

Water squished out of his shoes as he walked up the yard to his bike. He didn't waste any time starting it up and driving off with as much thunder as he could create.

"Harley, you don't owe him a cent."

"I figured that, Mom, but for all his screwed up ways, he's still my dad. Maybe I could give him a little something once we get some of these coins converted into cash."

"I'm telling you, he's like a stray cat. Once you give him a taste, he'll be back for more."

"We could tell him up front that he doesn't get anymore. Have him sign a paper or something."

"He'd burn through that money so fast, and on stuff that wouldn't do anybody any good. Just forget about it, Harley. Come on back inside and get out of those wet clothes."

I followed her to the house and changed. I should have felt better that morning. All things considered, I should have felt great. But between my dad and that awful dream, I didn't feel so hot. I felt like I had taken on a burden that seemed to be getting heavier. I guess life's roller coaster doesn't quit just because you dig up a little treasure.

I kissed Mom goodbye and hurried back down to the boat. I didn't want my burden to sit out there by itself too long.

Since I had gotten a late start that morning, Mr. Henley's dock was empty. He was probably back inside his trailer already, taking a nap and dreaming of sheephead. I guess it was about eleven or eleven-thirty before I pulled up to Smitty's for fuel.

"Well, we're in the cone," Smitty said between bites of hotdog.

"Charley?"

"Yep. Already got a Tropical Storm Watch up in the Keys. Say it's going to grow into a hurricane today and brush Jamaica, then the Caymans. Getting kind of crazy. Tropical Storm Bonnie's supposed to hit up around Tallahassee tomorrow."

"What about here?" I took the gas nozzle from his free hand.

"No watches or warnings yet for Charley. Strike probablity's up, though."

"How high?" I asked as he started the pump.

"Well, they say this morning that we have near a 30 percent chance that the storm will pass within 65 nautical miles of us, but Cedar Key's got almost the same chance, and they're way up past Tampa near the panhandle. Just have to keep our eye on it, I guess."

I pumped the gas. "What about Cuba?"

"They'll probably get it no matter what. But, that's the thing. Those mountains'll take all the punch out of it."

"So, we don't have to worry?"

"Just keep our eye on it." He shoved the last chunk of hotdog in his mouth.

"I'll let you know if I see anything out there," I laughed weakly. I had to keep up appearances.

Once I had the *Stripe* back out on Pine Island Sound, I didn't even think about blue crabs. I just booked it towards Cayo Costa. The morning water looked absolutely perfect, and free of boat traffic as well, since it was a Wednesday in the summer. I cut through the channel next to Useppa and cruised into Pelican Bay on the north end near the ranger station.

Only one other boat sat in the water at the dock. I tied up the *Stripe,* fished out my forty-pound backpack of booty, and hit the shore with Hammerhead. Since I was a day visitor to the park, I had to stuff a couple of dollars into the drop box at the tram station. I wondered if they took doubloons.

The State of Florida kept Cayo Costa pretty primitive, so the tram station really wasn't much more than a wide spot at the end of the dirt road that covered the mile or so to the beach on the other side of the island. The tram, a tractor hitched to a long trailer with benches, had been left there parked in the hot sun. I had no idea when it ran, so me and my trusty lab started walking.

The rangers stayed out on the island for a couple of days at a time in a wood-frame house up on stilts. As we walked by the fence that surrounded that house, I could see the small vegetable garden they had planted. The fence probably kept the hogs out.

Cayo Costa was covered with feral hogs. The Spanish had brought hogs with them when they settled in the area hundreds of years ago. Now they just ran around wild.

The dirt road across the island is pretty cool, because just after it leaves the ranger station, it goes through an old oak hammock where the tree limbs completely block out the sky.

When the road took us into the shade of the oak hammock, I saw where the hogs had chewed up the dirt under the trees. Hammerhead smelled them and it drove him crazy. He sniffed the ground where the hogs had been rooting around for grubs and started whining. His head popped up, alert for motion in any direction, and he bounded off a few yards. I let him go. When nothing happened, he decided to come back and move on.

The road led for about a third of a mile through the forest before the oak trees gave way to pine trees and palmetto bushes. Soon, small, grass covered sand dunes rolled around between patches of taller cover. It kind of looked like a rough golf course. Not long after that, I began hearing the surf. I was glad. That pack got heavy.

The campground lay just before the beach. It had a bunch of tent sites and, like, fifteen rustic cabins, just four walls with screened in windows on three sides and a porch in the front. The only water was at the common bath house, and there wasn't any electricity anywhere.

I turned down a trail to the left that led to the campsites. Most were empty. I figured Eden and her friend the scout leader, Lori Stillmeyer, had set up their tents in the last two sites, the ones at the end of the trail with shade. They were also closest to the beach.

I was right. The tents were there with girl clothes hanging all over a makeshift clothesline, but nobody was home. A tiny trail went from their site through the dunes down to the beach. I took it with Hammerhead in single file behind me to keep his paws out of the sand spurs. Before I saw the waves breaking on shore, I spotted Eden. I don't think anyone would have missed that sight.

She stood there with her back to me wearing a bright blue bikini, staring out at the girl scouts as they played in the waves. Man, if I only had a camera. The surf drowned out my footsteps as I walked up behind her.

"Boo," I said.

Eden whipped around. At first she looked surprised, then she recognized me, and a smile lit up her face. It only lasted for a fraction of a second, though, because she quickly remembered she was supposed to be mad.

"What are *you* doing out here?"

"Coming to visit," I said. "Hi, Lori."

Lori laid on a beach towel at Eden's feet. She waved a little, but didn't speak. The cold shoulder. They had been talking this thing over.

"I don't remember inviting anyone," said Eden.

"Surprise."

"Your relationship with that Russian woman is the surprise." Eden Baker did not beat around the bush.

"Eden, I spoke to your mom. I know you saw me and Mrs. Rovich, but, believe me, I can explain."

"You don't need to, Harley. I saw it with my own eyes. I should have recorded it for You Tube. Not every day you see a kid hanging out with someone old enough to be his grandmother!"

"It wasn't like that. I was just over there to do some work."

"Oh, really. I saw what you were working on! You were rubbing her back, Harley. Don't lie to me. If that's work, that makes you a…a…a *gigolo* or something. And how do you explain your little rendezvous with her in the bathroom at the Pelican. More work? I heard about that one too. Disgusting!"

She plopped down on her towel next to Lori and scowled at the water.

"Harley, she's very upset," said Lori in her nasally monotone.

"I can see that, Lori. Listen, Eden, she cornered me in that hall. Maybe she does have the hots for me. I don't know. More likely, she's got the hots for any guy with a pulse. Frankly, the thought of it makes me violently ill. All I know is, she offered me some work around her yard, and I took it. I needed the money, Eden. I didn't even want to go over there, but I needed the cash."

"And so your job was to go over there and smear cocoa butter all over her? Give me a break, Harley. I'm not a complete idiot."

She sat there cross-legged and hung her head down with her hands on either side of her face.

"Just go, Harley. I need some time," she said to the sand. "The other day? On the boat with you? It was so . . . " She cut herself off to sniffle. "I thought . . ." Then she turned her face up to me. She had tears in her eyes. "Then you turned out to be just like all the rest of the losers. Ugggghhh! I just can't think about it right now!!!"

Eden jumped up and ran straight for the water and, without even slowing down, dove into the waves.

"But, I found the treasure!" I shouted.

"Harley, you better leave," said Lori like a congested robot. "Maybe she'll cool off after a few days."

"Lori, I'm honestly telling the truth. I know it sounds like some lame soap opera, but Mrs. Rovich actually did try to force herself on me – *twice!* She set me up."

"Uh-huh. Happens every day, I'm sure."

I wasn't getting anywhere with that one. They were both in the same camp, figuratively and literally. I hope my English teacher is reading this. She'd be proud that I know the difference.

"Okay. I guess I'll get out of here. Look. You guys should know there's a chance of a storm coming around later in the week."

"We'll be fine. The ranger's will keep us posted."

"Okay. Would you please just do me one small favor?"

"What's that?"

"You and Eden? Just stop and consider that there's a possibility I'm telling the truth? That all guys aren't the same?"

I waved goodbye to Eden, even though she was under water, and walked back across the island with my dog.

I had a forty-pound sack of gold on my back, but it didn't help. The lump in my heart felt double the weight.

Pirates

After I left Eden at the beach, Hammerhead and me got back on the Stripe and just let the wind blow us around the water wherever it wanted to. I didn't even feel like cranking the tunes. I didn't feel like doing anything, to tell you the truth. It's odd under the circumstances, but I felt cursed.

When I went out to Cayo Costa, I really thought I could clear everything up with Eden. That didn't happen, and when it didn't, the situation got even worse, at least for me. I didn't know what to do.

So, we drifted. I sat there polishing doubloons until I lost track of what day it was.

I can't even remember if I checked any traps or just went straight home. I remember watching a little news that night. Tropical Storm Bonnie was headed for north Florida, and Charley had become a hurricane off Jamaica.

Mom hadn't had much luck in finding a qualified person to handle the treasure. She did manage to buy a fancy, new computer on credit, though, and get high-speed internet hooked up. Not a good move, in my opinion, waste of money and highly out of character. Of course, she told me she did it so she could more thoroughly research gold dealers. Whatever.

With about as much remorse as a moray eel, Tori admitted telling Dad about the gold. She just flipped me a limp excuse and left with some dude I'd never seen before.

That's about it.

The next morning I didn't even feel like going out in the boat. I thought I might wake up feeling different, but I didn't. I ate a bowl of cereal and went back to bed.

Around lunch, I threw my golden curse sack over my shoulder and walked down to Smitty's because I didn't have anything better to do. Mom still hadn't managed to find a safe deposit box, but she did manage to go out late and sleep until twelve. My phone had about a million calls on it by then. I listened to a few of the messages – all were about the gold – and didn't return any of them. At least among my friends, the word was out. Thanks, Tori. What a big-mouth.

Luckily, the news hadn't reached Smitty's yet. I didn't feel like explaining anything. I just wanted to get something to eat. But, when I got there, nothing looked good. I didn't know what I wanted. I was a head-case.

Smitty told me that, because of Charley, a hurricane warning was in effect from Bonita Beach to the Florida Keys, and that we were in a hurricane watch area that stretched up past Tampa. I only half heard him though. I felt like I was walking around inside some kind of bubble. It was stupid. Are chicks born with the supernatural ability to crush hearts and destroy lives, or do they acquire it over time?

Mom called in sick again and stayed in her room all afternoon clicking away on her new computer. I don't think she was getting much research done though because she kept coming in and giving me weather bulletins while I sat on the couch watching Sponge Bob. Late that afternoon, she burst into the living room all freaked out because they put us under a hurricane warning.

I wasn't too concerned. The storm was kind of small, and the TV weather guys all thought it was going to hit somewhere north of Tampa. Mom, however, had been on the phone making all kinds of evacuation plans with my grandpa in LaBelle, a small town about forty miles inland. Though it was tiny, Grandpa had a strong, brick house. Mom said it was far enough from the coast that we wouldn't drown in the storm surge. Go Mom.

Around dinner time, somebody knocked on the door. It was Bill.

"Dude!" he said. "Where you been hiding? Is it true, man? Did you find a pot of gold?"

He was all amped up. I really didn't want to deal with it, but I let him in anyway deciding I better downplay things before all of Palmetto Cove got itself whipped into some kind of treasure frenzy.

"Just a couple of old Spanish doubloons. Thought I had more, but turned out to be nothing."

"Lemme see!"

One of the coins was in my pants pocket. I pulled it out and handed it to Bill, then collapsed on the couch.

"Dude! That's totally awesome!"

I mouthed the words as he said them.

"How much is it worth?" he asked.

"I don't know. A couple thousand, maybe."

"Let's go party, man. We need to celebrate!"

"You boys going somewhere?" My mom had walked into the living room.

"Hey, Ms. C. Yeah, I was gonna grab Mel Fischer here and take him down to the Pelican or someplace."

My head hit the back of the couch, and I looked up at the ceiling. There was no way I was going to go out and face that crowd at the Pelican or answer a thousand questions.

"Good. He needs to get out. He's been in a funk for two days," Mom said. "I didn't want to leave him here all alone."

"Are you going out?" I asked her.

"Just gonna have a few drinks. I won't be back late."

"Maybe your boss will be there, and you can buy him a drink," I said as sarcastically as I could.

"What's wrong with him?" asked Bill. "He acts sick or something."

"Sick – love sick," Mom said. "He's got the Eden Baker flu."

"Dude. Get up! Chicks are going to crawl all over you now."

I grabbed a pillow and smothered my own face. "Can't a guy stay home and enjoy a little peace and quiet once in a while?" I asked them through the pillow.

Bill snatched it away and slammed it down on my head.

"You can do that when you're dead, man. Let's go," said Bill.

I don't know how, but somehow Bill got me into his *rat pee smelling* car. Mom had followed us out.

"Oh, God! What is that awful smell?" she asked me after I rolled down the window.

"Bill's air freshener," I said. I held the treasure pack on my lap to keep it out of the rat toilet.

"Listen, Harley. That hurricane's coming up the coast tomorrow. We need to go to LaBelle first thing in the morning. Okay?"

"Okay," I mumbled.

"Bill, you guys are getting off the island, right?"

"Yes, ma'am. My grandparents live in LaBelle, too. We're gonna stay with them."

"Okay. You boys be safe. Good night!"

Bill steered the Chevette through the bumpy yard and onto the road.

"So what's up with Eden? Did she really catch you and Mrs. Rovich together?"

"Yes, uh, no. Dude. We weren't together, okay? I just went over there to do yard work."

"And you were kissing her?"

"*What?! No!* Where did that come from? She, forced me to rub a little sunscreen on her back. AND . . . That's all! Eden happened to see the worst part."

"Whatever, dude. Have no fear. Your secret's safe with me."

"What secret?" I felt a tire roll off the road onto the shoulder. "Watch the road, man. Anyway, I don't even want to think about it."

"Why don't you call her?"

"Mrs. Rovich? Are you out of your mind?"

"No, dumb-dumb. Eden."

"Tried. Even talked to her mom. She's out with Lori and the scouts on Cayo Costa. I even went out there today to explain. She blew me off."

"Forget her, dude. You're a total chick magnet now."

Suddenly I wasn't depressed anymore. I was totally panicked. I just realized that a hurricane warning was in effect, and Eden and the girls were out on a barrier island with no bridges. I reached for my phone.

"There you go, man. Dialin' up some sweeties. Alright, bro!"

"No, I'm calling Eden," I said as I flipped open the cell. "Want to see if she knows about the storm."

Her phone immediately went to voicemail. I took a shot and called her house. If her old man picked up I could always end the call. Luckily, her mom answered.

"Mrs. Baker. This is Harley Cooper."

"I told you, Mr. Cooper, Eden's not happy with you right now," a squeaky little voice informed me.

I could hear Mr. Baker growling at her in the background, wanting to know who was calling. "I know, I know. Listen. Are the girls back from Cayo Costa? You know that storm's coming."

"They're fine. Spoke with her this afternoon. The ferry's bringing them back tomorrow morning at eleven. Rangers are getting everyone off the island as a precaution."

"Good."

"We got it all under control, Mr. Cooper. Thank you. Good bye." She hung up.

"She back?" asked Bill.

"Not yet. Ferry's bringing them over in the morning."

"Well, then. Let's rock!"

He cranked up some really lame REO Speedwagon on the 8-track that lasted all the way to the Crabby Pelican. Once we got there, it occurred to me that it probably wouldn't be a good idea to walk in the restaurant with forty pounds of Spanish treasure on my back. Somebody was bound to make the connection between bad posture and the rumors they'd heard. I couldn't just leave it in the car, though. What could I do? At that moment I felt like a paranoid idiot carrying the thing with me everywhere I went. Why didn't I go stick the gold in the bank myself like any sane person would have done?

"Dude, park over there under the streetlight," I said.

"Where?"

"By thc window." At least I could see the car from there. I stashed the bag behind Bill's seat, and we locked the car up tight, not that anyone would ever think to break into that ancient piece of crap.

Inside The Crabby Pelican, the interrogations began before the door slammed shut behind me. About a thousand people asked me about the treasure. I just told them the same story I told Bill and very little else. After whistling low or saying things like "smokin' awesome," they mostly wandered away.

I searched the crowd for Salt, hoping he'd be there, but he wasn't. At least Mrs. Rovich wasn't either, thank God. Dustin Majors sat at a corner table, though, with some of his cronies. He stared at me like a pit bull, but didn't come over or say anything. After a while, I looked back and he was gone. Probably went outside to hide in a bush and wait for me.

Luckily, Hurricane Charley provided a convenient diversion in conversation. Being the resident weather geek, I handled a lot of storm related questions that night. The National Hurricane Center had upgraded our hurricane watch to a hurricane warning late that afternoon. The whole island caught hurricane fever and declared Friday a holiday.

They didn't prepare. They partied, and had fun. No one took the situation very seriously until I gave them a few examples of what storm surge and high winds could do to a coast. Then they'd get real quiet, stare at me, and mutter "huh" or "really?" and drift away to a part of the room that wasn't so serious. Fine with me. It made them leave me alone, no more treasure questions.

Although I didn't feel like the life of the party, by the time we walked out the door I did feel a tiny bit better. That all changed when we walked up to Bill's Chevette.

The back window had been smashed to smithereens. Safety glass covered the ground next to the tire like diamonds in the streetlight. Miniature valves must have opened in my toes because I felt all the blood drain out of my body.

"Why would someone do that to my baby?" asked Bill.

I couldn't speak. I just walked up and looked through the hole. The floor behind Bill's seat was empty – no pack, no gold, no nothing.

I uttered a swear word, maybe more than one. I don't know. The world spun out of control around me, and I lost track of what I said.

"Harley, you don't look so good."

"They broke into your car. Your crappy car!"

"Take it easy, dude. I know it's not a Maserati, but, come on, it is my car. My only car."

"It was just glass! Idiot!!" I smacked myself in the forehead with the palm of my hand repeatedly. "Idiot! Idiot! Idiot!"

It had to be someone who knew. Dustin? Maybe. But he was already rich. Why would he take the chance? Somebody else, but who?

"It's just a window, dude. We can fix it. I never leave anything valuable in there."

"I did!"

"What? Your backpack? Once they find your smelly underwear, they'll throw it out on the side of the road. Relax. We'll spot it on the way home."

"Dude, it wasn't my underwear in there. It was the gold."

"What? No way! You left two grand out here in the parking lot? Dude, you *are* an idiot."

"Is there a word for an idiot who's, like, an idiot times ten?"

"Britney Spears?"

"Bill, there was a lot more than two thousand dollars in there."

"There was?"

"There was."

"How much more?"

"Try a million."

Bill's eyes opened to the size of dinner plates. He tried to speak, but it came out in garbles and stutters. Finally, he calmed down enough for his words to become understandable. They sounded pretty disgusted.

"Dude. Even Britney Spears wouldn't do that."

I called the sheriff's department, and they sent a cruiser an hour later. The deputy acted like he had better places to be. I don't think he believed my story, but he dusted for fingerprints and took notes anyway. He did find the brick that broke the window, hard to miss since it was laying on the back seat. He didn't find any prints on it, though.

"Son, I don't care where you are. Don't leave valuables in a car," said the cop. "Makes it way too easy for them. Got that?"

I nodded my head.

"Now, look. I'm going to file this report, but even if we find something, it's your word against theirs. Buried treasure kind of all looks the same, if you know what I mean. No serial numbers or anything like that."

He handed me his card and left. I opened my phone and looked at the time – 12:01 am. Then I remembered the new date, August 13 – Friday the 13th. Something too dark to see rolled over in the pit of my stomach.

It was a long, quiet ride home. Bill didn't dare turn on the stereo.

Friday, August 13, 2004

You ever notice how people fall into two groups when it comes to Friday the 13th? I'm not talking about the horror movies. I'm talking about the date. Some people are afraid of it and range from a little apprehensive to scared to death.

Others aren't so superstitious. Maybe they don't even notice it at all. Maybe they even laugh at the first bunch of people. For my whole life, up to that day, I was chuckling away in that second group – not any more.

A weight of impending doom pressed down so hard it woke me up. My luck had changed. I felt it, and it scared me. It could not have been any worse if I was holding a black cat under a ladder with one hand while smashing mirror after mirror against a rock with the other. I was too scared to even get out of bed that day.

I pulled the covers over my head and listened to my mom yell at my sister. How in the world was I going to tell her that I lost the gold?

"Tori! Get out of that bathroom! We've got to go!" yelled my mom from the hall.

"Just a freakin' minute, Mom! Jeez! You'd think the sky was falling!" Tori screamed back.

"It will be soon enough! We need to get to LaBelle now!"

Then Mom began banging on my door. I looked at the clock – 6:00 a.m.

"Harley! Let's go!"

"I'm up, Mom."

She didn't know it yet, but I had decided I wasn't going with her and Tori. I wasn't going anywhere until I knew Eden and those girls were back. The only shred of daylight I had left in my life was the chance that I could work things out with her. I needed that. And, I needed to know she was okay.

I put on a T-shirt and some shorts and went out into the living room to see what the weatherman had to say. I really didn't have to go that far. You could hear the news from anywhere in thc trailer. Mom already had the thing loud enough for the whole neighborhood to hear.

"Okay, folks. Here it is," boomed the weatherman's voice. "Hurricane Charley. As of the latest advisory, the storm is still tracking to the north-northwest, but they expect it to turn to the north sometime today. That puts us inside this big red cone. We're over here on the right side. While Charley should make landfall somewhere to the north of us later this evening, this cone means it's possible that it could turn to the east enough to make landfall here in Fort Myers. It's still moving pretty fast at 18 miles-per-hour, and the National Hurricane Center expects Charley to pick up even more speed and some intensity today as well."

Mom ran in with worry scribbles all over her forehead.

"Charley hit Cuba as a category two hurricane last night. The good news is that the terrain of Cuba lessened the storm somewhat. But, folks, don't let your guard down. The wind has already re-intensified to 110 miles-per-hour sustained. Even if it didn't gain anymore strength, that kind of wind can do a lot of damage."

"Harley, are your things packed and ready to go?"

"Relax, Mom. We have plenty of time. Besides, it's probably not even coming here."

"Harley. This is nothing to mess around with. We have a killer storm on our doorstep!"

"Now, let's talk storm surge potentials," the weatherman continued. "We'll look at the worst case scenarios. If Charley strengthened to Category four status and we got a direct hit, here's what we're looking at. Along the coast – Sanibel, Captiva, Cayo Costa, Boca Grande, Fort Myers Beach – you could get a surge of fifteen feet. Areas up the river and on Pine Island, you're talking ten feet. Now this all depends on how fast the storm is moving and exactly where it hits. But if you're in one of these mandatory evacuation zones, you need to leave now. Keep it tuned here for the latest. We'll be back with more right after this."

Worst case scenarios don't help. Mom's face shifted gears, from freaked to hysterically freaked, by the time the weatherman finished.

"Did you hear that, Harley? Did you hear!! Ten feet of water is up to the top of this trailer."

"Mom, I think you need to go ahead and go to Grandpa's with Tori."

"What!? And leave you here?"

"I'll be out later this morning. The storm's not supposed to get close to us until four or five this afternoon. Bill's leaving later, and he said I could ride with him."

"Absolutely not! That old car probably won't even make it to LaBelle, and you'll be stuck in that flood."

I still didn't have the nerve to tell her about last night – about the gold.

"He's not taking his car. His mom's driving. I need to secure the boat and all the stuff in the yard. Plus, Smitty said I could have some plywood if we needed it for the windows."

"Oh, my God! I didn't even think about the boat. Or the windows!" She sighed. "If you can promise me you'll be there no later than noon . . . "

"I'll be there, Mom. You're about to have a heart attack. You need to go to Grandpa's."

She really looked lost. I thought she might even cry. I had never seen her that upset about anything, other than Dad. They ought to have filters on the cable box so you can dial down the news if you want, especially "worst case scenarios." Sometimes newscasters really freak people out.

Tori finally came out of the bathroom.

"Times up," Mom said. "Let's go, young lady."

Tori looked at me on the couch and back at Mom.

"What about him? He just gets to stay here?"

"He's got to tie everything down. He's coming over with Bill's family later. You, on the other hand, I can't let out of my sight. Get your bag!"

My sister stopped arguing. Maybe it was something in my mom's voice, or her face. Both had become pretty intense.

"Work as fast as you can Harley." Mom hugged me tight and kissed my forehead. "Be safe. I love you. I'll see you at Grandpa's."

Tori gave me her middle finger behind Mom's back, and at 6:20 a.m. they were out the door.

Amazing. She was so freaked that she forgot all about the gold. Good, I wasn't looking forward to having to go through all that. I felt awful enough.

Another thing I didn't tell her was that I needed to go out on the water today and bring in as many traps as I could. Regardless of whether the hurricane hit us directly or not, wind was coming. Tropical storm force winds were enough to stir up the bay and scatter my traps. I'd never find half of them if that happened. I'd have to get a job at MegaMart for sure.

After giving Mom ample time to forget something and double back, I headed down the canal in the Stripe. Hammerhead stood on the bow with his front paws up on the casting deck and his black tail wagging away. I guess he sensed excitement in the air. I felt the opposite – nothing but doom and misfortune.

All along the canal, people hurried around outside their mobile homes securing their property. They took lawn furniture inside. Tied down boats on trailers and lifts. Screwed plywood over windows.

Mrs. Halberstadt, a retiree who lived next to Mr. Henley, had a yard full of orchids. Most were in full bloom. She easily had the most colorful yard in the neighborhood. I watched her unhook a few baskets from tree limbs and walk an armful up to her trailer.

"Storm comin', Harley," said Mr. Henley frowning at me from his dock.

"I know, Mr. Henley. I need to grab a few traps before they get lost."

He folded up his lawn chair and walked off.

Smitty's was open, good thing, too. People swarmed around in a panic. They would have broken down the doors to get in if they hadn't been open. I tied off and went up to the back porch. People ran through the aisles inside snatching bottled water, loaves of bread, masking tape, batteries and anything else they could grab off the shelves. Okra's hands literally blurred as she slid items across the scanner and bagged things up for the streaming line of customers. She only paused to wipe her face with a towel when the sweat beads got to be too much for her eyebrows to handle.

"Pandemonium," said Smitty as he hurried past me. He put on the brakes and cupped his mouth with one hand. "Hurricanes are great for business, though. Maybe global warming'll bring some more." He ran off to help a lady reach a cooler.

Out front, someone blew their horn. Through the glass, I saw long lines of cars full of irritated drivers waiting to fill their tanks. I spotted my Mom's car in the middle of them.

"Shoot!" I ducked down and followed a row of canned vegetables to Smitty.

"Hey, Smit? Remember you said I could have a little plywood?"

"Yes, ma'am, that there's a five-day cooler. Just take it up front, and my wife'll ring it up," he said to the lady before turning to me. "Yes, yes. I gotcha covered, Harley. God, it's sticky today." He pulled out a handkerchief and wiped the back of his elephant-sized neck. "I got it around back next to the livewells."

"Just checking," I said. "You're busy. Leave it there, and I'll get it a little later. I need to pull a few traps out of the water first."

"If you need fuel, get it now. People are sucking that stuff out of the ground like the oil wells have finally run dry. News people got everybody whipped into a frenzy."

"Hurricane mania."

"Hurricaniacs. Just look at them go," he said.

I have to admit, the fever was a little contagious. I pumped twenty-four gallons into my boat.

The water in the Sound wasn't that bad, a light wind, but not much. Seemed very peaceful compared to the chaos at Smitty's. The normal lazy, white puffs had left the sky. Instead, thin gray clouds raced from east to west, the first visible warning that something unusual was headed our way.

I gunned the boat, making a beeline for the nearest trap.

After I pulled all the traps off four lines, the *White Stripe* had a full load. Forty-three chicken wire boxes, stacked three high in some places, left barely any room for Hammerhead to get around. I zoomed back to Palmetto Cove trying to keep my head above the reek of rotting bait.

I had taken pity on the trapped crabs and released them all. No way Smitty's could get to them. With no catch to sell, I went straight home, offloaded the traps, and went back for more. I kept on going like that all morning up until 11:00. That's when I buzzed over to the ferry dock.

The ferry from Cayo Costa hadn't come in yet, so I waited. I waited a long time, too. It gave me plenty of time to try and figure out who had swiped the gold.

It had to be someone who knew I had found the doubloons. Thanks to my sister, that was probably a lot of people. And, unless it had been a random crime, the thief had also known that I rode to the Pelican with Bill, that I was a friend of Bill. Maybe they had guessed I left it in the car. I tried to recall all the conversations I had in the Pelican. Did I slip up and say something to point someone in that direction? I didn't think so.

I formed a mental list of people I knew with scruples low enough to steal. My dad certainly qualified. There was this weird kid from school who looked like a caveman. He blew pepper in my eyes for no reason once. Nobody trusted him. Dustin Majors wasn't out of the question either. Although I've never considered him a thief, he was, without a doubt, a world-class dork. He was also still hot about the Eden thing – additional motivation.

I got mad at myself all over again. How could I have been so stupid? I, of all people, should have anticipated a pirate attack. My mom was going to be devastated. I had to get that gold back.

Waiting on Eden's boat was pure agony. No matter what else I tried to think about, my brain always came right back to the stolen loot. I was about to go completely insane.

The Island Queen finally showed up just after noon. A few frightened campers hurried off with their gear. Eden, Lori, and the scouts were not among them. On the dock, a group of scout parents started to flip out when they didn't see their daughters. They mobbed the boat captain after the other passengers had cleared out. I jumped onto the dock and walked down to listen.

"Hold it! Hold it! Just settle down, and I'll tell you all I know," said Ray, the captain. "We waited and waited. The scouts never showed up. I had to get these other folks back. The rangers are still there, and they're doing their best to locate the girls."

"Locate the girls? Are they lost?"

Moms and dads shoved each other to get closer.

"The rangers have boats. When they find the girls, they'll bring them back over. I guess they're still over at the campground, but I don't really know."

"Will you take us back now, so we can find them?" asked one dad as he pulled out a wad of cash. "I'll pay double."

"Takes me a long time to run that far. Cayo Costa's a small island – easy to search. The ranger's will find them. And, believe me, their boats run a lot faster than this old tub."

The parents fired a bunch more questions at the captain that he couldn't answer. I had heard enough. It was time for action.

"I'm going over there," I said loud enough to be heard.

The group quit squabbling with the captain and turned to me. I had their full attention.

"I can take four more if anyone wants to go."

"I'll go." It was Mr. Newberry.

"Me, too," said another dad.

The captain tried to talk me out of it, but five minutes later, four men, Hammerhead and I roared up the canal to open water. This was an emergency. I didn't baby the boat up that canal. I floored it.

Out in Pine Island Sound, the wind had picked up considerably. White caps rode the tops of waves as the boat hammered its way across the hard water. We were okay, though. It could have been bumpier. Most of the way, the wind worked at our backs, pushing us with the waves. We made better time that way.

Between the motor, the surf, the wind, and the water pounding my hull, I couldn't hear anything the men were yelling at each other below me on the deck. They must have been forming some sort of plan.

Trying anything to get my mind off the missing gold, I had called Eden's number several times while I waited for the ferry. Her message had picked up every time. At her home, the phone just rang and rang. I had even called the rangers out on the island. They didn't pick up either. And, the sheriff's department said they already had all the trouble they could handle. The desk sergeant laughed when I asked about the doubloons.

Up in the tower, speeding away from Pine Island, I finally worked up the nerve to make one more call.

"Mom?" I screamed into the phone.

"You almost here, Harley?"

I could barely hear her.

"No, Mom. Actually, there's been a change in plans."

"What? Harley, there's a lot of racket. Where are you?"

"Mom . . . Eden and the girl scouts didn't make it back from Cayo Costa."

"Well they have rangers out there, Harley. They can handle it."

"No, Mom, they can't. They don't know where the girls are. I'm taking a bunch of the dads back to the island to look for them."

"Harley! Are you crazy?! That storm's coming right at us."

"Mom. It's going north. It's just going to brush us," I said hoping that was still the case.

"It changed course, Harley! Oh God, turn around, turn around! It's accelerated! It's going to hit Charlotte Harbor in three hours!"

I looked at the time on the phone. It was 12:30pm. We didn't have long.

"Harley, it's getting stronger, too."

"What're the winds?"

"What? I can't hear you."

I slowed the boat a little to kill the noise some.

"The wind speed. How fast are the winds?"

"Over a hundred and twenty-five miles per hour! It's not done yet. They're saying it could turn into a Category four before it hits. Harley, for God's sake, please turn around!"

If what she said was true, it was going to get pretty rough. Smitty had showed me plenty of pictures of Homestead after Andrew hit. A McDonalds with all the windows blown out. Trees chewed into stumps. Houses missing entire walls and roofs. And the worst image, the one that really stuck in my mind, a trailer reduced to its I-beams. And Homestead sat a few miles inland from the Florida coast. Cayo Costa was on the coast. If Charley hit the island directly as a Cat four with 145 mph winds, not much would be left standing.

"I'll be fine, Mom. I gotta go." I closed the phone.

Mom was absolutely hysterical. I hated to do that to her, but I had no choice. At first, I had only been concerned about Eden. But, seeing the terror in the eyes of those parents when their little girls didn't come home just nailed me inside. I had to help.

Besides, I'd been in storms before. I'd be okay. I just had to keep my wits about me and stay smart. I knew the island pretty well, probably better than most of the rangers. I would find them. I just hoped I could do it fast. Cayo Costa sat at the mouth of Charlotte Harbor, directly in the path of the worst hurricane to threaten my town in almost 50 years.

Something's Watching

Pelican Bay didn't do much to calm the water that sloshed in from Charlotte Harbor to the east. Even on the small, inner bay, the waves were getting big and nasty. I took the *Stripe* and my passengers past the dock at the Cayo Costa ranger station and into a canal that ended in a clump of mangroves about a hundred feet later.

Two boats were tied to the dock. A small skiff that belonged to the rangers and a stone-crab boat owned by Jake Baker, Eden's dad. The unexpected sight of Mr. Baker's boat caused me to run straight into the mangroves.

"Look out, kid! Almost killed us."

"Sorry."

While the fathers jumped off to find the rangers, I secured the boat as well as I could to the nearby tree trunks then followed the men up to the ranger's quarters, that stilt home with the chain-link fence. Hammerhead trotted next to me, his nose sniffing and his eyes scanning.

"Nobody's here," said Mr. Newberry. "Place is deserted."

"Did you guys try upstairs?" I asked.

"Locked. Nobody inside."

"How about the office?" I pointed across the yard to a small trailer the park rangers used to check-in campers.

The trees and bushes around it shook like they wanted to pull up their roots and run away.

With wind shoving us along, we walked over to the trailer in a group. One guy banged on the door. No one responded. I looked through a small window. Inside was dark.

"Must be looking for them," said one of the dads.

I think his name was Mr. Simon.

"Maybe they found them," said another. "Let's fire up the tractor and head to the beach."

He ran off and cranked up the tractor, which sat in the same place that it had been sitting on Wednesday. The rest of us followed him and piled into the trailer behind. The canopy of oaks swayed and popped in the roar over our heads as the tractor carried us down the sandy road to the campground on the beach side of the island. Every now and then a gust would find its way down inside the trees to punch the saplings and palmettos like an invisible fist.

"Up there! Look!" shouted Mr. Simon.

A quarter mile away, a second tram driven by a ranger slowly came around the bend with its lights on. The scouts sat on benches in the trailer with another ranger.

"It's them!" yelled Mr. Newberry.

I squinted my eyes and scanned all the girl's faces. Eden wasn't there.

Mr. Newberry jumped off our trailer before it even stopped and ran up to the girls. He pulled his daughter down and hugged her like he hadn't seen her in five years. In fact, all four dads grabbed their daughters, just as relieved. Lori sat in the trailer with her arm around a shivering scout. She looked over at me, and I saw tears in her eyes.

"Where's Eden?"

"Oh, Harley. Am I glad to see you guys. How'd you know?"

"Lori, Eden's not with you. Where is she?"

"We don't know, son," said one of the rangers. "She took off after one of the girls a few hours ago. We've all been looking for her. Two more of my men out there right now."

"We don't know where they went, Harley," said Lori. Her voice sounded high and squeaky.

"They?" I asked her.

"That scout's still missing, too," said the ranger.

"Kimberly," said Lori. "Eden and her just disappeared."

"We gotta get these girls off the island now," said the ranger. "That storm's getting close. Williams, here, is going to take them over in the skiff before it gets any worse. How'd you get here?"

"My boat."

"What is it?"

"Twenty-two foot mullet boat."

"You're that kid with the tower?"

"That's me."

"Well, I tell you what, kid. You're gonna have to be the one to take everyone back. They way this wind's kicked up, that skiff's gonna have a time with all these people.

"I really want to help you guys look for them."

"I'm afraid I'm gonna have to insist, son. This storm ain't nothing to mess around with. We got it covered. Plus, we already got Mr. Baker and his son out here looking. And God knows where they are. Gotta find them, too."

Eden didn't have a brother. She was an only child.

"Mr. Baker's son?"

"Yeah. You gotta know him. He's from Palmetto Cove. 'Bout your age, too."

"Dustin?"

"Yeah, I think that's it. Now quit wasting time. Do me a favor, son. Get these folks home."

So, the old man had brought his gravy train to help track down his investment. Figures.

A rain squall hit us with no warning. It came in sideways, blowing so hard it stung. One minute we were dry, the next, we looked like we'd just showered in our clothes.

"This stuff's only gonna get worse and worse," the ranger shouted. "Our boat's just not big enough. Not in these conditions. Get out of here – NOW!"

I didn't move. I didn't blink. I just stared at him, eyeball to eyeball while my heart hammered away in my chest and my feet grew roots into the sand.

"Son. Look. I know you want to be a hero. But, me and the other rangers are staying put. We'll find them." He lowered his voice just a little as he put a hand on my shoulder. "Be a hero, son. Take these folks back home."

"How do you know where to look?"

"We think they went south. One of the girls said she saw the Baker girl go that way. It's only five miles to the southern tip. Plus, the island gets pretty narrow in a couple of miles. We're searching in a criss-cross pattern. We'll find them."

"Then what?"

"We can ride it out in the house. It's built like a fort, and it's up fifteen feet. We'll be fine."

I still didn't budge.

"Son, I'm ordering you off this island. The lives of these people are depending on you. Now git!"

I looked at the dads holding their daughters. I looked at the shivering girls who didn't have anybody to hug them. A couple were crying. I looked at Lori. Her eyes did the talking. They wanted to go home.

"Okay," I said. "Let's go."

We swapped tractors with the rangers and drove everyone back to the dock. I made the six little girls sit down in the back of the boat. Lori sat with them. The waves wouldn't be so bad back there. I put three of the men on the bow in front of the tower to distribute the weight. I asked Mr. Newberry to sit next to me up top. Hammerhead curled up next to Lori and the girls.

I couldn't go back the way I had come. The waves were just too big. Instead, I went south to the other end of Pelican Bay. The water got a little calmer as I fired up the *Stripe* and zoomed away from Charlotte Harbor.

For a couple of minutes, I hugged the mangroves in the deeper water on the west side of the bay. When the cut to Manatee Cove appeared on the right, I veered off the channel that would have taken us home and drove the boat into the narrow waterway instead.

"Where the hell are you going?" yelled Mr. Newberry over the noise.

"Back to the island!"

Mr. Newberry had lived in Palmetto Cove his whole life. Like me, he had driven a boat since he was twelve. Everyone would be safe in his hands.

"I need you to take them back, Mr. Newberry."

"I can't let you do this, Harley."

The cut quickly gave way to a small natural cove, a pocket of open water in the gut of Cayo Costa. A single dock stood on the far side. I slid up to it sideways and gunned the motor in reverse to stop the boat.

"You don't have a choice, Mr. Newberry."

I vaulted off the tower onto the gunnel.

"Come on, boy!" I shouted to Hammerhead.

He jumped over to the dock with me.

"Storm's coming fast, Mr. Newberry!"

"What do I do with your boat?!"

I didn't answer. I had already reached the trees at a dead run. The White Stripe roared away behind me.

Cayo Costa was a long, skinny island that ran north to south, wider to the north, skinnier to the south. On the west side, near the beach, a fire lane had been cut just to the inside of the buffer mangroves and scrub that grew in the dunes by the Gulf of Mexico. That fire lane led from the beach campground to the south for a couple of miles before it turned and cut east across the thick part of the island, all the way to Salt's canal.

Since the state owned almost the entire island, only three or four homes stood next to the fire lane. That was the obvious area to search and probably where the rangers were. They couldn't ignore the north end of the island, though, and probably sent at least one guy on an ATV to search the miles of trails in that direction.

That left the dense, east side of the island for me. There used to be an old road on the east side that ran north and south, but that must have been before I was born because it had grown over with trees and vines. Even so, I could still make out what was left of the road in the forest – barely.

Between this side of the island and the beach on the west side, lay a large, freshwater swamp with a lake in the middle. With all the rain we had gotten over the summer, it had to be full.

Hammerhead and I made it to the old road and stopped. The treetops danced and twisted as Charley's winds hammered down in big gusts. Dead branches were snapping off and hitting thc ground all over the place. I had to watch the sky and look for the girls at the same time. A rainsquall dumped more buckets of cold water onto us. I wiped my eyes every five seconds. I wished I'd worn a hat that day.

Using the overgrown road as a reference point, we began to zig-zag between the edge of the island and the swamp. The pattern slowly took us south. The rangers weren't likely to go through the swamp either. They'd circle around the opposite side towards the south and, if they didn't find the girls, they'd keep coming towards me. I would run into them eventually if I kept moving south on my side.

Hammerhead made better time through the jungle than I did, easily jumping over vines and ducking under dead trees.

"Wait up, boy!"

I didn't want to lose him. As the storm got closer and the sky got darker, that black furball was getting harder to see.

"Over here, Hammerhead. We're looking for Eden. I need your nose."

He ran over and wagged his tail, looking at me like he knew what I was talking about. We kept slogging around trees and vines and weeds and palmettos and God knows what else until the tangle got so thick I could barely see anything. The ground had gotten very wet. In fact, I looked down and saw that the water was over my sneakers. We had come to the edge of the swamp. The sky over the lake had turned to gray mush.

"Let's head back to the road."

He walked off ahead of me.

We had to parallel the swamp for a little ways because of the brush. The forest took some of the storm off us, though, and for that I was thankful.

You ever feel like someone or something is watching you? Could be a person. Could be an animal. You just feel it when it happens. Well, I got that feeling then and there, and froze in my tracks.

"Hammer!" I yelled at my dog and signaled for him to stop.

I looked around slowly. For the moment, the rain had quit. The jungle drip dried in the wind. I was hoping that the feeling came from the girls. It didn't.

I looked down and saw a ten foot alligator about six feet away.

The gator sat there cocked, like the hammer on a gun, mouth wide open, between me and the swamp, eyeing my labrador. Gators sweep animals into that mouth with their tails and – CHOMP! – dinner is served.

Hammerhead started to come back.

"Stop, Hammerhead," I said, keeping my body as motionless as possible.

Hammerhead stopped and bent his head to one side. His nose worked the air, then he spotted the gator and he barked.

"Shhhhh!"

It's well known that dogs are near the top of the list on an alligator's menu. Most of the time they don't even have to run a dog down. They just let the mutts yap away and wander closer and closer. Then they lunge with those huge jaws, and it's all over.

Hammerhead had better sense. He shut his yap.

The gator moved. He did it slowly, but it still scared the pooh out of me. That big gator head just swung around right at me. The end of his snout was now half the length of a man away.

If I moved, he'd run me down. With speed up to thirty-five miles-per-hour, those things can easily run down people. I looked up. A limb stuck out of a tree over my head about as high as a basketball goal. At school, I could barely grab the rim, but it was my only shot, and I took it. I leapt straight up with all the spring my *white boy* legs had in them.

The gator jumped, too – right at me. My foot even kicked him in the nose on the way up. Adrenaline must have been pumping, because both my hands latched onto that branch, and I hung on for dear life. The gator snapped his jaws shut and settled to the ground directly underneath.

My hands started to slip off the wet limb, so I swung my legs and wrapped them around the tree trunk.

"Back up, Hammerhead!"

I didn't have anything to throw as a diversion. Instead, I hocked up a luger and spit it on the gator. Hit him right between the eyes, but he didn't even blink. He was focused on my butt. I probably looked a lot fatter and juicier than the dog anyway.

Hammerhead backed up a few feet and stopped. He wasn't going to leave me alone with the gator. Good dog. I was just worried that he'd get tired of sitting there and attack.

The tree started rocking as another rain band beat down on us. I hoisted myself onto the branch and checked on the huge reptile. He hadn't budged an inch, just sat there waiting in the rain for his free meal to fall out of the tree.

The trees in that part of Cayo Costa were bunched up enough so that they wove themselves together. Like a spider monkey, I jumped from branch to branch until I'd put about five or six trees between the alligator and me. He still hadn't moved. Maybe he thought I'd come back and lay down in his mouth. Gators are dumb.

I jumped to the ground and ran with Hammerhead another thirty yards through the twisting jungle back to the old road. Thankfully, the way behind us was gator free. I made a note to be a little more careful.

"Good job, boy." I petted my faithful protector on his wet head while I caught my breath.

Submerged

A lot of people think that a hurricane is a bunch of constant wind and water. It is, but not necessarily all at once.

Rain and wind come and go as thunderstorms circulate around the eye in bands. The areas between those spiral bands, the gaps, can be much calmer. Sometimes, in a storm's outer bands, blue sky will even pop out for a minute or two. That's how Charley had gone so far. Around the eye, conditions would be much worse.

The periods of thunderstorm activity grew longer and more intense. Wind blew harder, driving rain drops through the air like bullets. Lightning flashed and thunder crashed everywhere. A funnel cloud briefly dipped out of the sky over the island before some unseen hand reeled it back in. I was running out of time.

Compared to a storm surge, those things were nothing. If a wall of water hit the island before I could find them, none of us stood much of a chance.

The wind had shifted a little from the east to the south-east, still blowing water up onto the island's east side. When it hit, the core of the storm would push more water in from the west. Cayo Costa would be caught in the middle.

As hurricanes move close to land, all the water they push ahead of them rises up when it reaches the shallow coast. The greatest impact is usually felt in the storm's right, front quadrant because the winds are onshore. I hadn't seen a weather report since early in the morning and didn't know precisely where the eye was going to come ashore. I said a silent prayer for it to come in to the south and lessen the punch by putting Cayo Costa on the left front, but I figured things would get pretty nasty no matter what.

I resumed the zig-zag pattern from swamp to shore until I ran out of swamp. The distance became shorter and shorter as the bay swallowed the island's east coast. Every now and then, I shouted Eden's name as loud as I could. Between the rain, thunder and wind blasting through the trees, the hurricane created an amazing amount of noise. I didn't know how far my voice would carry. I just kept yelling.

Without the swamp as a western border, I began counting my steps each time I crossed to the west of the old road. I went one hundred paces to the west and then turned back to the east. I had just made another easterly turn when I heard someone yelling.

My hopes shot sky high as I stopped to figure out which direction it came from. The call rose and fell in the storm, getting a little stronger each time. Then, as the voice got closer, I realized it was a man.

I ran toward it, and as I did, the tangled trees opened up onto a dirt fire lane. I had busted through to the lane that cut over from the beach. A ranger in a yellow rain slicker came around the bend with his hands cupped to his mouth. He saw me and stopped. It was the same guy who had ordered me off the island.

"What the heck are you still doing here?!" he yelled.

"Same as you, sir. Searching for the girls."

"I told you to take those people back to Pine Island!" He was furious.

"I'm sure they're there by now, sir," I said with an extra dose of politeness. "Mr. Newberry took them back in my boat."

Anger pinched his face together like a crab.

"I ought to tie you to a tree and leave you there until the storm's over!"

"Sir. I really can help you guys. I know this island very well. You haven't found them, have you?"

He wiped his face and pulled out his radio.

"No, son, we haven't." He raised the radio to his mouth. "Carl. You there?"

"Yeah, Dave. Go ahead," the radio said.

"That kid who was here earlier is back. Wants to risk his life and help us out."

Carl didn't answer immediately. I figured he was the boss, mulling things over. I got ready to run back into the woods in case they wanted to stick me in the ranger station or something.

"At this point, Dave, we could probably use him. That thing's getting on us. Tell him to go south, down the east side, but not too far. That'll keep him away from the waves."

"Roger that, Carl," Dave said. "You heard him, but you need to know – it's at your own risk."

"Yes sir."

"The eye is only an hour or two out. Storm's moving pretty fast now. Up to twenty miles-an-hour. Winds at 145. That's a cat four, son. They're calling for it to go straight over us. This island could be under water."

"If it hits a little south of us going that fast, we might not even get much surge."

"That's a big if, son. When Donna came through in the sixties, we got fourteen feet. You got waves on top of that. You better keep those big oak trees handy if that happens."

"I'll be okay," I said, although I had trouble believing it anymore.

"You got a phone?"

"Yes sir."

"Give me your number and I'll give you mine. Don't know how long service will hold up, but if you find them give me a shout."

We swapped numbers. He even gave me a plastic baggie for my phone.

"And remember, son, we're still looking for Mr. Baker and his kid, too."

"I'll keep my eyes open, sir."

"What's your name, son?"

"Harley Davidsen Cooper."

"Welcome aboard, Mr. Cooper. Give yourself one hour then high-tail it back to our house. Godspeed."

He shook my hand and sloshed off down the firebreak. The rain had become constant, just heavy rain mixed with heavier rain. The world looked very wet and very gray. The trees and scrub bushes thrashed around as if nature had gone nuts.

I heard something crack to my left and looked up just in time to scc thc top of a pine tree snap off and come flying down right at me. I dove behind a clump of palmetto as the wind drove it into the sand where I had just been standing. I had to stay on my toes. Things were beginning to happen pretty fast.

To continue south, I had to get off the firebreak and fight my way through the woods. It really wasn't woods anymore but just a tangle of scrubby oaks, vines and palmettos that stuck up about ten feet out of the sand. Hammerhead knew better than to wander too far off. He trailed behind, letting me take the lead.

The going was slow as brush and vines got thicker. I wondered what rattlesnakes did in a storm. In the racket that Charley was making, I wouldn't even hear one if I stepped on him. I hoped that Hammerhead's nose could warn us sooner that my ears.

I'd tromped around this part of the island before, so I wasn't traveling through that stuff with no plan. I knew it thinned out a little further south. I didn't know if the rangers had searched the area yet or not, but the land on that end of Cayo Costa opened up into low dunes and grass. If the rain wasn't too bad, I'd be able to see for a ways.

The fire lane, that ran from the beach campground to Salt's canal, forked before it turned east. That southward fork led to the dunes and grass. Maybe Kimberly and Eden had taken that fork. Equipped with ATV's, the rangers had surely searched the firebreak and beach side. I intended to keep covering the east side, like the guy on the radio said.

Five minutes later, I hit water. This part of the island was low, but never wet on a normal day. I tasted the flow with a finger – salty. The storm had pushed the stuff in from the Sound. The depth quickly went from a few inches to over a foot. Lightning flashed *white hot* against the black sky and blinded me for a moment. I blinked wide several times. When vision returned, I saw the water moving from left to right around my legs. A snake swam by and crawled up into a bush. I couldn't tell what it was.

I pushed through a tangle of bushes and all at once the brush ended, and I stood in an area that was relatively open. The sand had disappeared underwater, only the tallest bunches of grass bent in the wind over the new, salty river.

I turned to the left towards the eastern edge of the island. The tops of the mangroves that formed the island's fringe stood out in the distance a little darker than the sky. Lightning flashed again, and I saw them better for a second.

"Come on, boy!"

Hammerhead and I fought our way towards the mangroves against a current that got stronger with each step. A thicker band of rain pelted us, and I couldn't see the mangroves any longer. I just went in the direction I had seen them. Then I went down.

I must have slipped into a hole because I went completely underwater. It took me by surprise, so fast I didn't have time to take a deep breath. I couldn't feel the bottom, and I couldn't find the top. I ran out of air quick. My foot got wrapped up in a root or something, and for a second I thought I might drown. Then I yanked it loose and kicked. My face broke the surface, and I sucked in air so hard I almost drowned a second time on the rain.

Finding the edge was even harder since everything was flooded. Luckily, Hammerhead started barking. I spun around and spotted him standing a few feet to my right. The water pushed me in his direction and helped me out of the hole. I tried to stand and regain my balance just as a gust nailed me and knocked me back down. Hammerhead licked my face as I waited on my hands and knees for the burst of wind to subside.

When I finally got to my feet, I looked back over at the mangroves. I could see the tree line again, the last of the island, sandwiched between a nasty sky and a sea of choppy waves. If someone was alive out there, they'd be hanging onto one of those trees. I had to check it out. The problem was the water. I had no idea what it was hiding below those waves.

Back at the edge of the brush, pine saplings grew with the scrub. I backtracked and broke off a dead one. With the small limbs removed, it became a six-foot pole – an early warning system for hidden holes.

Now I moved more slowly, testing the sand under the water as I took a different route to the trees. The closer I got to the mangroves, the deeper and faster the water flowed. Soon, it was up to my waist. Hammerhead had to swim. The wind blew so hard that little whitecaps formed on the new lake. I held my ground against the current and looked up at the trees. An odd color, something blue, caught my eye in the strobe of the next lightning.

Then I saw a face lift up out of the water.

Another band of rain hit, as I kicked and half swam my way over the submerged island to the patch of blue. Saltwater washed over my head, and, as I neared the trees, I glimpsed a monster wave smashing through from the bay. The mangroves barely even slowed it down.

The incoming surge swamped the person entirely. A few seconds passed before I spotted blue material again, this time much closer. It floated in to me on the top of the flow – empty. In chest-deep water, I snagged it with the stick. When I pulled it out, the wind almost ripped it away before I could grab it, but I had it, a men's windbreaker, bright blue.

Sharp claws raked the back of my neck. I spun around to find Hammerhead paddling for his life against the tide. I wrapped my arms around him and pulled him close as my eyes searched the trees for the owner of the jacket. But the storm had already cleared the roots and limbs of anything that had sought safety there. I watched as it took the leaves.

Another huge wave barreled in off the bay and washed over us. I saw it coming and dove below it just before impact. The water forced Hammerhead out of my arms. When I broke the surface, he popped up next to me. I grabbed his collar and pulled him along as I swam with the current back to the middle of the island.

After a time, my feet hit the soft ground and I walked with the flow. When it became shallow enough, we both started running and we didn't stop until we were back at the brush. The island was sinking fast. Daylight had dwindled to nothing. The rain stung like wasps. The time had come to find some shelter.

Into thc Eye

The world whipped around in a frenzy on all sides. The more I watched the thrashing bushes and low trees, the more disoriented I got. The place looked less and less like any Cayo Costa I knew. I kept my head down and splashed along ahead of Hammerhead.

Something stung me under my shirt and then stung again on my fingers. My hand was covered with fire ants. I leaned over and tried to splash them clean in the storm surge. More ants floated on the surface, washed out of their nests by the hurricane. I brushed the insects off and bounded ahead through the brush to lose them as quickly as possible, but that was easier said than done – ants were everywhere.

The way back to the fire lane took longer than I expected, or maybe we had gone the wrong way. In the confusion of the storm mistakes were easy. The speed of the wind suddenly increased. This time it roared like a freight train, a long freight train. It just kept coming and coming, pressing us like little bugs into the shallow water, and into more ants. There was no way I could stand up against it. Just had to stop and ride it out. I grabbed Hammerhead's collar, pulled him around in front of me, and closed my eyes. It came so fast and hard, I could barely breathe. Stuff snapped and broke all around us. It sounded like a war. All kinds of stuff blasted into my back.

I quickly learned that when faced with a hurricane's intensity, there are two choices – bend or die. Trees that weren't supple enough to double over just broke in half and flew away. God had sent a giant weed whacker down to Earth, and its blades chewed away the island. I felt like an ant, myself, as we hunkered down trying to dodge those blades and the shrapnel it threw at us.

The wind finally began to taper a little. I heard it blasting other places near by, but, for the moment, we caught a break. I could stand. We had to move. And if what we just survived was any indication of what was to come, we had to get out of the storm fast, or that weed whacker would cut us down like dandelions.

Hammerhead seemed okay, wagging his tail at me a little. I think he even smiled. Some dog.

After what seemed like an hour of ducking and dodging and picking our way through, we finally popped out onto the fire lane that cut across the island from west to east. The roadbed had been completely submerged under flowing seawater. A wild hog, a big black sow, stumbled by in front of us following the current west towards the beach. Blind to us, she kept going through belly-deep water without pausing to notice. Behind her, a tiny shoat, probably her last, fought for air as the current swept it along after its mother.

We went to the east, into the wind, into the current, to the only place I knew that could withstand this kind of beating – Salt's cabin.

All kinds of objects whistled through the air as we stepped down into the salty river. Hammerhead stuck to the edges where the dirt rose above the water.

The palm trees over our heads rocked back and forth with every frond flapping to the northwest like a bunch of insane flags. We kept as low as we could, avoiding wind and projectiles. The sky just grew darker and darker. I prayed for Eden under my breath.

An eternity later, the firebreak turned left, to the north. I knew the oak trees around Salt's place would be coming up next. I wondered if they were still there. I couldn't see them until we were almost under their branches. And, man, those things were rocking out of control! God was pruning the snot out of the tops, spitting down twigs and leaves. But, those squatty oaks stood tough. And their dome cut the wind. How long they would last? I didn't know.

As the ground rose to form the mound under Salt's house, the water receded, and we stepped onto the first patch of dry ground I'd seen in hours. The round house sat there without a scratch. I figured old Salt would be long gone. Not the case. His boat pitched in the water next to the dock. The sight of it lifted my spirits. I was stoked. Salt was inside. Maybe Eden had found his place, too.

I ran to the porch and pounded on the door.

"Salt! Open up! It's me, Harley!"

The door cracked open a couple of inches. Salt's eye filled the gap.

"Who is it?" squawked Aruba, then he whistled.

"Are you crazy? Git your butt in here!" Salt said as he opened the door just wide enough to let me in.

Hammerhead darted through in front of me. Salt slammed the door and bolted it shut.

"You know, boy," said Salt, "it's not the best day for a slumber party."

As I fought to get a hold of my breath, I saw we were not alone. Jake Baker, Eden's dad, sat there next to a candle staring at us. He didn't look so good.

"I found him out there a little while ago staggering around," said Salt. "Said something about a boy with him."

Mr. Baker didn't say anything. He looked angry. He dropped his head down and dabbed at the side of it with a towel.

"Salt . . . Is Eden here?" I asked.

"No, son. Rangers been by, too, looking for her and the scout. I rode around on the ATV a while, but no luck." He handed me a towel.

"Your fault she's here! You miserable runt!" Mr. Baker exploded. "Came out to get away from you!"

Mr. Baker tried to get up, then fell back in the chair. He looked like a bear had mauled him, cuts and scrapes all over. His shirt was torn in three places and the side of his fat head was plastered with blood.

"Simmer down, Jake. We got bigger fish to fry," said Salt stepping in between us. "Press down hard. I'll be right back." He moved towards the kitchen around the corner.

I followed him in as he rummaged through a drawer for something.

"Spose you're out here looking for that girl, too?" he asked me.

"She's still out there, Salt.

"Came all the way out here. In a hurricane." He shook his head, then he said, "Yeah. Baker didn't see any sign of her either."

"Neither did I, and I searched the whole east side from south of the ranger station down to the dunes. Salt, the whole south end of the island's under water!"

"If it passes south of us, we should be okay. To the north?" He held the candle down to look in a drawer. "Well . . . we'll just have to see."

"I've got to find her, Salt."

He stopped rummaging and looked at me again. "Love bug's done bit you worse than I thought. A word to the wise, though. Keep your butt parked here for a while. We're getting to the meat of that thing now. Wind's shifting around to the south. Wouldn't be surprised if it passed dead over us."

He pulled out a pair of scissors and a roll of tape from the drawer and ripped off a couple of paper towels before going back to the main room.

"Fold these up and press down hard," he told Mr. Baker as he passed him the towels.

As Mr. Baker applied the bandage, Salt cut strips of duct tape. He wrapped a couple around Mr. Baker's head, frowning as he pulled them tight.

"Trying to kill me?" Mr. Baker complained.

"That'll hold you," Salt said then pointed his finger at him. "Just keep your butt planted in that chair, you hear me?"

"You got anything to drink in this dump?" asked Mr. Baker.

"You know I don't, you old fool. That's the last thing you need anyway. Better start thinking about how you're gonna find your daughter when this blow is over."

"Aw, to hell with it. I'm done," Mr. Baker grumbled. "That damn girl's caused me enough trouble for one day – her and her godforsaken mother. Shoulda had better sense to come home when she had the chance."

As a rule, I try not to argue or tell people what to do. At that moment, however, everything came to a head. The frustration, the pain, the anger that had dogged me the last few days just welled up.

"*She was trying to save a girl scout!*" I shouted at Mr. Baker.

He turned on me quick as a snake.

"Shut your mouth, boy!" he spit. "I told you to stay away from her once already. Am I going to have to make that a little clearer?" Mr. Baker made a fist and shook it at me.

Salt sailed across the room and got in his face. "Baker! You ain't gonna be doing jack! Except sitting in that chair and keeping your mouth shut! Or your butt's back out there in that storm!"

"Sorry," Mr. Baker said to me around Salt. "Didn't know your nurse maid was here." Then to Salt, he said, "Take it easy, Joe. Since when did you give a flip about anyone but yourself?" He let out a rough chuckle, but didn't say any more, just sat there like a beat up old toad.

In fact, for a while no one spoke. We sat in the gloom and listened to Charley howl at us outside. The storm screamed through the trees and whistled in through the cracks. The wind must have put tremendous pressure on the walls because, every now and then, the entire house shuddered. The clatter outside got louder as branches snapped and popped like gunfire. Limbs and logs and anything else the storm could find to throw bombed the wooden planks outside. Silvery veins of water snaked in under the front door and around the windows. Stuff crashed against the roof.

But, the architect and builders of Salt's round house had done a good job. The old place took everything the storm threw at her. Even at the height of the fury, all remained calm inside the round house.

I told Salt about losing the gold. He didn't react as much as I thought he would. He said we'd work it out after the storm. I didn't know how you could possibly *work out* a million dollars of stolen treasure, but he didn't elaborate. He just sat there. Nobody said anything for a long time, except the one they called Charley howling outside.

And then, in a matter of seconds, the storm ground to a complete halt.

"The eye's upon us," said Salt looking up at the ceiling.

He stood and listened. For a full minute, nothing moved outside. God had hit the kill switch to take a break.

In the middle of the dead calm, someone walked up on the porch and knocked on the door.

I jumped to my feet and flew to the door. In an instant, I had it open. A very wet little girl stood on the porch in tattered clothes.

"Kimberly?" I asked.

The girl burst into tears. Hammerhead walked up and licked her face.

"Kimberly?" I asked again as Salt picked her up.

The girl nodded.

"Where's Eden?" I asked her.

Kimberly sobbed uncontrollably, shaken by the wind and rain, or something worse.

"It's okay, girl," said Salt gently. "Come in. You're safe now."

Outside, past the porch, leaves slowly helicoptered to the ground through mist.

With a roof over her head, the girl slowly calmed down. "Is it . . . gone?" she asked.

"No, child," said Salt. "Just taking a break. Where's your friend?"

I'd never seen him be so tender. He smoothed her hair, coaxing her words.

"In the tree."

"Eden's up in a tree?" I asked in a rush.

"Not up – inside. The big one down the road by the beach."

"I know the one," said Salt easing Kimberly down in a chair. He looked at me. "We don't have long. Let's go."

Salt took off through the door.

"Stay here, Hammer-dude. We'll be right back."

I slammed the door shut. Salt fired up his four-wheeler, and an instant later he hauled butt around the house.

"Get on, boy! We gotta go!"

I jumped off the porch and landed behind Salt on the gear rack. Two seconds later, we were flying towards the beach.

Above us, the sun shined through a bright, blue hole in the storm. The water had receded off the firebreak, only a couple of inches remained. Branches littered the ground. Most were small enough to roll over. Some were too big and we had to detour around, but once we got out from under the oaks we started to make good time.

Cayo Costa looked like Iraq on a bad day. As far as I could see, the island was twisted and mangled. Some trees hung like broken skeletons, dripping in the air. Others had fallen to the ground hundreds of yards from their stumps. I thought about home and what was happening there.

"There's only one tree over there with a hole big enough to crawl inside," Salt yelled back over his shoulder. "Big black mangrove just off the beach. Used it myself a time or two."

"Think she's alright?"

"We'll find out soon enough."

"Why would she stay there and let Kimberly go?"

Salt didn't answer. And, since he drove that ATV faster than I had ever seen one go, I didn't bug him by repeating myself. The wreckage blurred by and we reached the beach about three minutes later.

The sky churned in nasty shades of purple and black way out over the sea. Overhead, the hole of blue had slipped away to the east. The beach looked much wider than it should have. At the spot where it finally met the water, enormous white capped breakers chewed on the exposed bottom. The wind began to come in again, this time from the northwest, driving the waves closer.

Salt bounced to a stop beneath a giant black mangrove. It's top was gone, but the sturdy trunk remained intact. I followed him around to the far side, the side facing the beach.

Something stopped him. His expression chilled my blood, sending shivers through my back. I followed his eyes into the hollow of the tree. Eden lay there, her sweet head against the inside of the tree, her eyes closed.

I dropped to my knees and took her hand out of her lap. It felt cold and lifeless. The flesh had become discolored and swollen.

My heart stopped, and I couldn't breathe anymore.

I looked over at Salt. He slowly shook his head, and hot water flooded the sight of him away.

"I'm sorry, son."

I wiped my eyes clear and coughed. My lungs took in air I no longer wanted.

"Help me with her."

He began to drag her out over the sand. As I set her limp hand back down on her body, her sleeve slipped up, and I saw the marks, two red punctures side by side. Fangs.

Then, she moaned.

"Eden!" I cried.

"Something got her good," said Salt.

I put my ear to her nose. "Oh my God. She's breathing."

Salt pulled the sleeve further up her swollen arm. The wounds were about a half-inch apart.

"Snake," he said. He put a hand to her throat. "Weak. But it's there. Let's get her back."

Something pounded the ground and screamed behind me. Before I could turn, it was on my back, its claws pulling me over by my neck.

"GET AWAY FROM HER!!!!"

I rolled over to see Dustin swinging a club at my head. His eyes looked crazy. The limb crashed down an inch from my skull, and I kicked out. My foot caught his gut causing him to stumble backwards off balance.

As if a hand pulled him backward towards the sea, he staggered towards the incoming waves unable to regain his footing. Finally, he fell, and, after he had hit the wet sand, I saw why. He wore my backpack.

"I'm going to kill you, Cooper!" He got to his feet and charged.

"Boys, we don't have time for this," said Salt like we were two brothers in a slap fight.

"He took the gold, Salt," I said as stood and braced myself.

"What?"

"He took my gold!"

"Aaaaayyyyyy!"

Dustin had clearly snapped. He bull-rushed me and nailed me again before I could move. The blow took me down a second time, and we locked up, fists flying, rolling back down the beach.

Because of the gold's weight on his back, I had a little advantage. I used it to claw my way on top. I saw the water just before it knocked out my lights and put stars in my head.

The wave crashed down and flipped us in a knot of knees and elbows up the beach. When it returned to the gulf, the surf rolled us with it like ragdolls. I grabbed a lung of air as the next one hit. It drove my face back into the shells. My body moved with the water, but I couldn't tell you which way.

I lost track of Dustin, then his hand clamped around my ankle like a steel trap, dragging me up. I tried to kick it away. My head left the water and I heard Salt yelling.

"Take it easy, boy! I'm pulling you out!"

Salt dragged me out of the surf up to the ATV. I spit and gagged and tasted the sea. When I finally cleared my eyes, I saw Salt dive into the waves. The Gulf of Mexico looked angry again. Wind blew against giant waves as they slammed onto the beach. I used the ATV to haul myself to my feet. Eden was lying across the rack on the back, unconscious, with her hair whipping around her head.

Cold water swirled around my ankles and down into my shoes. Salt emerged from the breakers dragging Dustin up the beach by the leg. My backpack was no longer over his shoulders.

"Salt! The gold! It's gone!" I screamed above the storm.

"Forget it, kid. It's on us again. We've got to get her back!"

Dustin fought against Salt's grip even as the next wave washed over him. Salt waited a moment for the water to recede, then threw Dustin next to the ATV. He scrambled to his feet like something wild, a raccoon or a stray dog. His eyes shot back and forth between Salt and me, not sure what to do, or what we might do.

"Take it easy, son," Salt said. He had his hands stretched out towards Dustin. "We're all gonna be okay. Let's just take a ride back to my place and get out of this weather."

Dustin took a half step backward. I thought he was going to bolt.

"Now, let's not do anything stupid. Come on, now. Hop up on the ATV."

Hurricane Charley spoke next with crashing surf that brought the sea in around our knees. I held onto the ATV as the water sucked back out. I could feel it tugging on our ride as it went.

Down the beach, I spotted something.

"The gold!" I yelled.

Salt turned and saw my pack sitting on the sand all by itself about forty yards away. That old sparkle lit his eyes.

"Wait here," he said.

Salt took off down the beach in a dead run.

That's when I saw it. A spindly black funnel descended from the clouds and touched down on the raging Gulf of

Mexico – a waterspout. The twister licked the waves like a nasty tongue. The storm yanked it up, and I thought it was gone, but a second later, it dropped back down, even closer to Salt.

I yelled at the top of my lungs. The tornado roared back, louder. Salt didn't see it. The spinning vortex came in behind him.

I ran. I had to beat that thing to Salt, had to warn him.

A wave pushed my pack higher onto the beach, easier for Salt to reach, but directly into the tornado's path. That same mountain of water tossed me into the weeds at the top of the beach like an empty shell.

When I looked up, it was too late.

It happened so fast. The pack was there. Salt grabbed it. He turned with this huge grin on his face and held it up. And then, the evil funnel roared through and wiped him off the face of the earth like an eraser.

He was gone, just like that.

"Saaaaalt!"

I screamed his name more than once, but it didn't do any good. He wasn't on the beach anymore. He wasn't bobbing around in the surf. I didn't see him spinning around in the sky. He was just gone.

Darkness

Storms don't care. They don't bargain. They take what they want.

Charley had swallowed my best friend. It had stolen my gold. And, now, the storm gobbled up the entire beach.

I remembered Eden on the back of the ATV. I had to get her inside. I ran along the brush line at the edge of the beach, but the ATV was gone. Wind driven currents pushed the sea into the fire lane where the vehicle had been parked.

Heavy gusts knocked me forward as I splashed down the lane after Dustin. Did the coward have enough sense to take Eden to Salt's cabin? I hoped so.

The water seemed to come at me from everywhere, out running me. I had to squint my eyes nearly shut to block out shredded leaves, sticks, and airborne sand. Nothing stopped the hurricane from invading my ears, though. With the storm blowing in over nothing but water, its sound was even more deafening than before.

I wanted my room. I wanted my bed – to hide under my covers. I wanted to be anywhere but inside that storm. They say dreams come true. Well, so do nightmares. That day was living proof.

Rain choked off the air, and I could barely see the edges of the fire lane. I almost stumbled directly into red tail lights. The ATV had stopped in the middle of the storm river.

I found Eden's soaked body on the back. So much rain washed over her face that I thought she might have a problem breathing. I turned her on her side, using three big bungee cords to hold her in place.

I spotted Dustin in the bushes to the left. A branch had knocked him out of the driver's seat, and part of it had punctured his pants up around the thigh. A stain had already darkened the material around the wound. He screamed out when I pulled the projectile out of his leg.

As he laid in the bushes, his eyes still looked wild, like a cornered rat. I was spent, done, in no mood to fight anymore. We could settle things later.

"Come on, man! We got to get her back! I'm going now! You can come or stay here!" I held my hand out to him.

Dustin just stared for a second, then tried to stand on his own. It didn't work. He fell back with a groan.

"A stick stabbed your leg! Take my arm!"

He looked like a scared little kid. He could have been crying. I couldn't tell with all the water. Finally, he grabbed my hand. I helped him through the current back onto the ATV. Water was up to the top of the tires.

"Hold on!" I shouted.

Like a barge, we pushed through the surge until the mound rose up under the trees at Salt's house.

I lifted Eden off the back of the ATV under oaks that bucked like wild horses again. On the porch, I kicked the door with my foot.

"Open up!" I tried to shout over the storm.

When no one responded, Dustin limped up and opened the door enough for me to carry her in.

Salt didn't really have a bedroom, just an area in one corner with a small bed next to a nightstand. I lowered Eden down on it.

Mr. Baker was already starting in on me.

"What'd you do to her, boy? She looks dead," he demanded from his chair.

The man didn't even bother to get up. I ignored him and turned to Kimberly, who had joined Dustin and me by the bed.

"Kimberly, do you know what happened to Eden?"

"Yes, sir, a snake bit her."

"When did this happen?"

"Right after she found me."

"Was that before the storm or after it started?"

"The wind was blowing, but it wasn't raining. I got lost trying to find the beach, and she found me."

Hammerhead nudged Eden's face with his nose. She didn't move.

"Do you know what kind of snake it was?"

"There were two of them. They made this buzzing sound. I was scared because they were right next to me when she came. I thought they were going to get me. Eden made one go away, but while she was doing that, the other one bit her arm."

Even in the dim candle light, Eden's hand looked swollen and bruised like an over-ripe pear. The areas around the fang marks appeared darker than the rest. The time for a tourniquet had passed. There wasn't any ice I could use for the swelling. She needed a shot of antivenin. The best I could do was to make her comfortable until the storm passed, then get help.

A tree limb or something smashed down on the roof. Dustin jumped like a cat, and Kimberly threw her arms around my neck as I knelt next to Eden's bed.

"This thing is bad, man," Dustin whimpered. "How much longer is it going to storm?"

"Dustin. Go sit down and rest your leg. If that thing starts gushing blood again, we don't have any way to close it up," I said.

He limped over to a chair, whimpering like a baby.

The storm hit every corner of the house, banging and wailing like a flock of demons. Vibrations traveled down the walls to the beams under the floor. I could feel it in my knees.

"Kimberly, can you stay here with Eden in case she needs anything?"

"Yes, sir," she said bravely, even though her eyes didn't hide how scared she really was.

"Hammerhead will stay here with you and help."

"Yes, sir." She petted my lab on the head.

I went to a window where I could see through a crack. Outside, water continued to spill in over the island as the winds blew from the northwest. Under a blanket of raindrops, the sea crept through the tree trunks and up the short hill to the house. It didn't look good out there.

"Where's that no good excuse for a fisherman?" asked Eden's dad from his chair.

"He's gone, Mr. Baker."

"Gone? What'd ya mean? Run off or something?"

"Storm took him on the beach." I fought to block the vision. It came anyway.

"Serves him right," Mr. Baker muttered under his breath.

My nerves were shot. All I had left was emotion. I wheeled on him. "What did you say?!"

"I said he had it coming," he barked back at me. The side of his head was slick with bleeding that had soaked through the bandage.

"Let me tell you something, Mr. Baker," I said through my teeth. "That man just saved your daughter's life. And Dustin's life. And my life! And he died doing it! And you don't even care!"

"Let me tell you something, you pin-headed punk, he ain't nothing but a murderer who oughta be in jail! He killed a man in cold blood over a little money!"

His words stunned me like a boat oar to the face. I stood there trying to sort through what he just said. Was it true?

"That's right. He's scum. If my head wasn't already bashed, I would have kicked his sorry butt as soon as I laid eyes on him today." The veins in his neck bulged to the point that I thought they might start popping. "In fact, I think it's high time I started knocking some sense into you for good measure."

He tried to stand up, but a grimace washed over his face, and his hand immediately found the side of his head. The pain closed his eyes, and he forgot all about me as he winced and blotted his gash with a towel.

I backed away from him, remembering what Salt had said when I asked about jail. He had avoided the question. Had he been hiding something? Was Salt a murderer?

My mind darted to the storm surge approaching outside.

In my hurricane discussions with Smitty, I heard stories about what happens when storm surge hits a community. Basically, nothing stops the water. Surge can lift entire houses off their foundations and smash them, and everyone inside, into oblivion. I doubted that the waves from the beach could reach us across a half mile of island, but who knew. If enough water came in, it could easily float us off the pilings below and send us right out into Pine Island Sound like a supply barge. Then we'd have no protection at all.

I looked over at Eden and Kimberly. The little girl must have seen something in my face because she frowned.

"Is everything okay?" she asked, timid as a mouse.

"Everything's fine," I lied.

"Is the storm over soon?"

"Soon."

"I hope my mommy's okay."

"You're from St. James City, right?"

"Yes, sir."

"Well, I'm sure she misses you, but don't worry; the police got everyone off the island before the storm."

A blast of wind broke through the oaks and pounded the roof. Kimberly started crying. I went over and settled down on the floor next to her.

"It's okay," I said. "Sit on my lap."

She sat on me and buried her face against my chest. I tried to think of what kids liked, what would take her mind off things. Bill had a little sister. She always wanted to hear a story. The only stories I knew were the pirate tales I heard from Salt.

"You know who lived near this very spot a long, long time ago?" I asked her.

"No . . . who?" She sniffled.

"A big, bad pirate."

"Really?"

"Really. His men called him Gasparilla, and they had a fort up on Boca Grande, the island just north of here.

Well, one day Gasparilla looked around and realized he was getting old. Now, that's a rare thing for a pirate. Most of them are killed off young in battles or fights. But, not Gasparilla. He was tougher and smarter than all the rest.

So, this day, he decided he'd been a pirate long enough."

Little Kimberly settled even closer to me. I still felt her warm body shiver, but I couldn't hear her sniffles anymore.

"Gasparilla told his men he was done, no more pirating at all. They didn't know what to do. Most of them had never been anything but pirates before.

He told them not to worry. That they would be rich beyond their wildest dreams and could live out their lives anywhere they wished and do anything they wanted. Then he led them down to a room in his mansion that only he knew about, a room they had never been allowed to see – his secret treasure room.

Now, pirates didn't have banks. They had to hide their treasure. That's why they were always burying stuff and making maps. But, old Gasparilla liked to keep an eye on things, so most of his treasure was right under their noses in a secret room under a hidden door. On that day, he showed it to his men."

Kimberly's breathing had become slow and regular. I peeked around and saw her eyes were closed. I kept going with the diddie anyway.

"Gasparilla shoved aside the big table in the dining room and threw back the rug. There lay the trap door in the floor. The pirate captain called for a lit torch; then he pulled open the hatch, and his men followed him down.

They had never seen so much gold and jewels in their lives. Heavy wooden boxes overflowed with gold and silver coins.

Other chests contained long ropes of gold chains. He opened velvet bags and showed them handfuls of emeralds, rubies, and diamonds. Everything sparkled in the torchlight. The treasure seemed endless. Stacks of crates and chests stretched to the far corners of the room, and it was a big room.

Gasparilla stood before his men and shared the news they longed to hear. All the treasure belonged to them. They would divide the loot evenly between each man."

I stole a look over at Dustin. He caught me and quickly turned his head. He was listening. He was just as scared as the rest of us.

"Gasparilla's men were delighted to hear the news. In fact, they were so happy they threw a big party for their captain. They put out the word, and all the hearties from nearby islands sailed their boats and joined them for a huge feast. The celebration lasted for days.

The men were too worn out to divvy up the treasure on the appointed day, so they slept off the party and did it the next day. Pirates really don't stick to their schedules very well.

On that bright morning there wasn't a cloud in the sky. Gasparilla and his men hauled all the treasure out of the secret room and stuffed it into twenty barrels, one for each of the men. It was quite a sight, glimmering and shining in the sun.

The men were about to carry their portions off to their boats and sail their separate ways, when someone spotted a merchant ship on the horizon. Being a greedy pirate, Gasparilla suggested that they go on one last raid for old time's sake. He didn't have to twist any arms to get the rest to agree. Once a pirate smells gold it's worse than a shark sniffin' blood. Nothing shakes him off the trail.

Gasparilla shouted, 'Hoist the sails!' And they all climbed aboard their captain's boat, the Florida Blanca, except a few who stayed on shore to keep an eye on the loot.

Soon, the beautiful ship had set the jolly roger to fly and charged out to sea. The lookout in the crow's nest called down that it was indeed a merchant vessel sailing up the coast towards Tampa.

'Soft, be their bellies,' the pirate assured his men, 'and weak be their will.'

They readied their swords for a short battle with frightened merchants who were sure to surrender without much of a fight.

As they drew close to the other ship, Gasparilla brought up his spyglass to watch the victims cower. But, instead of running, the other ship turned towards them. Gasparilla looked again. The crew wore uniforms, military uniforms. All at once, the opposing ship dropped the cloth facades that disguised its hull, and Gasparilla stared down a U.S. Navy Man-of-War.

'Ready the cannons!' he yelled to his men.

But it was too late. The warship was faster than it had first appeared. It turned broadside to the Florida Blanca and began blasting Gasparilla's ship with cannons of its own. The fight was indeed quick, as Gasparilla had said, but the tables were turned.

With his ship broken and in flames, the old pirate captain saw the navy men rowing over to capture him. Instead of allowing that to happen, he decided upon his final act.

With his men helping him one last time, he gathered up a length of anchor chain and wrapped it around his body as he stood on the bow of his beloved ship.

With his sword held high, he yelled to the Navy men, "Gasparilla dies by his own hand, not the enemy's!"

And with that, he plunged to the bottom of the sea never to be seen again."

Kimberly was asleep. I laid my head back on the bed and listened to Charley beat the snot out of the island. I wondered what the storm would do with Salt's body. Would someone find him washed up on a beach or stuck in a tree? Would a boat pull him from the gulf? Would he be lost forever, like Gasparilla?

I remembered his eyes, how they had sparkled on the beach. Why did he have to go after the gold? I told myself that if he hadn't, I would have. But, I doubted I could have been as brave.

Another voice, a quieter one filled with shame, told me that he did it for me.

The treasure had been snatched away again, but this time, I didn't miss it. I missed Salt. To think he had left my life forever, well, it just left a huge hole.

I wondered how Mom and Tori were making out in LaBelle. I tried to envision what the storm might be doing to Palmetto Cove. I worried about the hurricane washing us off the island. And then, I must have fallen asleep.

When I woke up, the wind had died down some. The room seemed darker. The candles were still lit, but they had burned down low. I felt something poke me in the back of the head. I felt around and found Eden's knee. She moaned a little at my touch.

I gently rolled Kimberly onto Hammerhead. He sniffed her a little and stayed put. I tested the floor with a hand. Dry. The surge hadn't invaded the house. I decided to check on Eden.

I moved what was left of the candle to the edge of the nightstand, close to her face. Her eyes fluttered open and she scowled at the light, trying to get her bearings.

"Harley?" She spoke my name weakly.

I nodded and smiled at her.

"Kimberly?" she asked, a bit stronger.

"She's right here. She's okay."

Mr. Baker snored in his chair. I didn't raise my voice loud enough to wake him.

"We found you on the beach," I told her. "You and Kimberly. You've been bitten by a rattlesnake."

She tried to raise her arm, but groaned and let it settle back down.

"The poison's got it all swollen," I said.

"Thirsty."

I went to the kitchen and brought back a bottle of water. She took little sips as I held it to her lips.

"I feel awful."

"You don't look much better," I tried, hoping the small joke might help.

"Where?" she asked from somewhere far away.

"Salt's cabin on Cayo Costa. Your dad's here, too. He was looking for you."

"No…the storm…where are Lori and the girls."

"Safe." I hoped it was true. "Mr. Newberry took them back in my boat."

With that bit of information, she drifted off again. I took it as a good sign that she had regained consciousness and was alert enough to ask the right questions. Maybe she'd be okay.

I looked around the room. The candle nearest Dustin had gone out, but I could see his outline on the floor. I pulled out my cell. Even with the baggie, it was trashed by the storm and wouldn't turn on. Salt didn't have any clocks on the wall so I could only guess at the time. It was after sunset, probably about 8:00pm.

Hurricane Charley hit hard, but it moved fast. The worst was over. Thanks to Salt and his cabin, we had survived – well . . . most of us.

Empty

Just before dawn, I woke up on the floor. Eden's breathing came slow and steady as she lay on Salt's bed beside me. The candles had burned themselves out. The cabin was pitch black and quiet. But Mr. Baker's buzz-saw ripped that silence every few seconds and, over in the other corner, Dustin snored as well. I still felt Kimberly's warm hand across my leg. I guess I had been her security blanket through the night. Hammerhead sensed that I was up, stretched and yawned.

The air had calmed down outside like the world had stopped or blown away. Inside my body, I felt the same, nothing moved, no emotion, no sensation, nothing.

I made it to my feet. A moment later, I felt my hands work the latch and open the door. The storm had taken the oak bench from the porch so I sat on the boards and let my feet hang down. I had never felt so grim in my life, as if Charley had washed away all the jokes and fun, all the color, and left only gray behind.

Hammerhead wandered up and nudged my shoulder with his nose. I reached around and grabbed him in both arms and squeezed him to me and held on. He stood still and let me hold on as long as I needed to.

I buried my face in his fur and let it come. My shoulders shook around him, and he stood there like a rock. The sounds I made were weak and small, nothing close to the size of loss that ate my insides. I let it go. In ugly, ragged gasps, my misery found a way out. Next to my nose, his fur got wet with it. Anger, guilt, grief, you name it, every bad emotion, he soaked it all up in his black coat. I cried on that dog until my guts hurt.

Salt was gone. And I just stood there and let that hurricane take him. I should have grabbed him, ran sooner, anything. But instead, I sat there in the weeds like an idiot and watched it swallow him whole.

As for what happened to the gold, I was glad. It was cursed. I had known it and done nothing. From here on out, hardship was the only thing I deserved. Pain and punishment would be my lunch and dinner.

I had come out to save Eden, but I couldn't even do that. A nine-year-old had to walk through a hurricane to find me! As I thought about Eden lying in that tree with snake venom running through her veins, I became even more disgusted with myself. Why hadn't I looked there? It was an obvious spot.

I let go of Hammerhead and stared into the blackness. Nothing moved. For a moment, I experienced total emptiness, no thoughts, no emotion. Then it hit me again – my best friend was dead. I hadn't really ever thought of Salt that way before, but that's what he had been, my best friend. Over the years, I hadn't wanted to hang out with anybody more than him. Outside of my mom, I hadn't trusted anyone more than him. And when I recalled all the advice, all the lessons, all the understanding, I knew no one had given to me more than him. And I repaid him, how?

A warm, little hand settled on my neck.

"Is it over?" a girl's voice asked.

I turned to the question. The eastern sky glowed pink behind the maze of branches. "Yes, Kimberly. It's over. He's gone."

"Can I sit with you?"

I nodded my head. Hammerhead trotted down the stairs, and Kimberly sat on the porch floor beside me.

"What's your name?"

"Harley."

"What are we going to do, Harley?"

I hadn't really thought about that.

"I guess we go home."

Home. What did that look like today? How many people lost their lives? Or was Salt the only one? Did anyone else get killed because some idiot stood by and did nothing?

"Harley?"

"Yes."

"I'm glad you found me."

"I didn't find you."

"Yes, you did. You opened the door and let me in."

"You knocked."

"What if you didn't hear me? Or, what if you weren't there? And you found Eden, too."

"Salt did that."

The sky had brightened enough to show details around the cabin. I stepped to the ground and moved away from the porch. Most of the water had receded leaving behind only a few dark puddles. Dead leaves had been swept into a long row just short of the cabin, a tide line showing the water's highest point. The surge had risen to the edge of the cabin, but no more.

Above, some limbs were snapped and shattered, some left to hang, others blown away completely. Although Charley had stripped away the leaves and removed random chunks, most of the squatty oak canopy had survived, twisted but intact.

Debris littered the ground below. A few of Salt's stone crab traps had ripped away from their tie downs and mixed with the fallen branches. A styrofoam cooler bottom sat wedged under one of the amputated hunks of tree where the water had left it.

I walked down the rise towards the dock. Salt's old crab boat, the Costa Blanca, floated on the canal next to the dock where she had been moored. Tree limbs hung on her ropes and her railings, and one had even smashed a window in the wheelhouse, but she looked reasonably seaworthy. The automatic bilge clicked on sending a rope of water into the canal.

As the light improved, it brought shapes of mangled vegetation in every direction. Hammerhead hurried around sniffing the ground. He stopped at a lump and wagged his tail. A fish, a large snook, had been washed up and left to die in the storm's wake. Its dry eye stared up at the dawn. Its gills didn't move anymore.

I suddenly felt like I needed to puke. I tried to swallow the sensation. It didn't work. I hurled next to an oak. Afterwards, I had to lean on the tree for quite a while.

The ATV was parked next to the cabin where I left it. Amazing. I thought it would have been long gone, blown across the sound by now, but there it was, waiting. I thought it over for a moment. Everyone inside was still asleep except for Kimberly. I told her to go back in.

Then, I broke into a run, hopped on the ATV. It started like the storm had never come. I roared off down the rise to the fire lane that would take me back to the beach, and hopefully, back to Salt.

As I dodged the trees and pieces of trees that obstructed the trail, hope returned. If he was anything, Salt was a survivor. He had told me about terrible storms he'd lived through at sea as a merchant marine. Car crashes. And even a plane crash he escaped from while he was in the service stationed in Guantanamo. He could land on his feet. And, he definitely had nine lives. No way he'd used them all up. I'd get to the beach, and there he'd be, walking up the shore to me with another amazing tale.

I got lost in those thoughts as I drove, and before I knew it I was by the tree where Eden had hidden, but Salt wasn't asleep inside. I searched the beach in both directions. No one walked along the shore. Only waves moved among the logs and chunks of siding, roofing, and insulation that had washed up.

I stared south at the spot where the tornado had carried him off. The hurricane had left its mark. Morning sunshine beamed over a shoreline that had been gouged out in some places and piled up in others. The usual morning birds, the ones the waves chased to higher ground as they pecked the sand, were gone. A lone, limping heron with one wing stretched to the sand was the only sign of life.

Still, I turned the four wheeler south and worked my way around the storm junk, not ready to give up or give in. He had to be down there somewhere. He just had to.

Not a single boat cut the water out on the gulf. On a normal Saturday, I would have passed twenty already. Not a single bird flapped through the sky. I felt marooned. Charley had stolen the Gulf of Mexico's aquamarine rollers and polluted the sea with brownish humps that broke into dirty foam when they hit the sand.

I drove on for about a mile more. He wasn't there. And then, I began to hope that I wouldn't find him, because he'd probably look a lot like that snook Hammerhead found, and if he did, I couldn't take it.

I didn't search the twisted grass to my right quite as thoroughly. I didn't scan the calm sea behind the surf anymore.

Far off, down the coast, a helicopter beat its way along the water's edge. I stopped to watch. The people inside were probably surveying the damage on Upper Captiva, the next island in the chain. I waited. Instead of continuing to Cayo Costa, it turned east over Captiva Pass to circle around the backside of the resort island. A lot of rich people had vacation homes down there. Money talks.

I watched a wave break past the wheels of the ATV, and something caught my eye, something small sticking out of the sand. I hopped off and plucked it up before the next wave cruised in. After a moment, I almost threw it back to the sea. But I couldn't. I stared at the thing in the palm of my hand until a fresh tear splattered across it. A gold doubloon shimmered wet like it had been minted that morning.

I had been so happy, so excited to find that coin in the swamp muck. But, as I held it then, on that black morning, its curse brought pain. Its *too happy* shine mocked me, reminding me of my greed. That's where greed can take your life. That's where it took mine.

I didn't deserve that coin. I deserved only to suffer. But, I didn't throw it back. I shoved it in my pocket. That small hunk of metal was now a lesson. If I kept it, it would keep me from destroying any more lives, maybe even my own.

Salt always said, if you make a mistake, do your best to make it right – and then some. I had a long ways to go. My future looked like a barefooted expedition up Mount Everest.

"I will never forget you, Salt."

I felt stupid. I felt dramatic. And I felt corny. But, I also realized something for the first time in my life that morning – love. I had loved Salt without even knowing it. Not the *mom love* you grow up with. And, not like having the hots for a girl. Something deeper. Something that's so close to you, it is you. It's like the air you breathe. You're so inside of it, you don't even notice it until it's sucked away. Then, you get it – big time.

How come I couldn't see the best thing in my life when it was staring me in the face the whole time?

Something bumped into my leg, and I nearly jumped out of my skin. I whirled around and saw Hammerhead wagging his tail at me. I dropped to my knees and hugged his soggy neck. He licked my face.

"Come on, boy. Let's go get those guys to a doctor."

Back at Salt's house, I drove up to find Aruba, the parrot, standing out on the bare porch. He side-stepped away from Hammerhead towards the open door.

"Come here, guy."

I held my hand out and lowered it down to the floor. He hopped on, digging his claws into the skin of my index finger as I lifted him up.

The parrot squawked. "Hello! Hello!"

"Good morning, Aruba," I said as I took him inside.

The place was empty. I set him down on his perch and ran back outside and around the house. The boat was gone!

I jumped to the porch and tore back into the house to look for a note. There wasn't one. They had just left without me. I was such an idiot. I should have taken the keys to the boat. Now what?

I un-shuddered the windows and poured Aruba a big bowl of food and a big bowl of water.

"I'll be back to check on you in a few days, buddy."

He told me good-bye as I shut the door then Hammerhead and I struck off for the ranger station on foot. Considering all the junk I'd have to avoid on the ATV going the long way on the firebreak, a bee line north through the woods would get us there the quickest. We could follow the old roadbed. I'd just have to steer clear of the *not so friendly* swamp creatures.

The day got hot and sticky fast as I picked my way along Cayo Costa's bay side. When my mouth began to dry out, I wished I'd brought some water. I wondered how my mom was doing. I had seen her just the morning before, but that seemed like a year ago. Deep down, I knew how she was doing. She was worried sick. I needed to let her know I was okay.

Less than an hour later, we arrived at the ranger's house. My heart sank when I saw the roof missing. But then, I spotted three rangers down by the docks. We ran over to them.

"Would you look at that!" said one. It was Dave. "Where did you come from?"

I gave them my story, told them what happened to Salt, but left out the part about the gold. They wouldn't believe me anyway.

"Hard to believe that old guy would be so careless on the beach," Dave said. "At least you found the girls."

Anger flashed up inside me. He didn't understand. Salt wasn't stupid. He was helping me. I rolled the doubloon around in my pocket.

"That man did more than all you guys put together!" I screamed at them. "He found them all! Cut him some slack!"

"Easy, guy," said one of them. "We know he was your buddy."

"Well, can't you send out a search party or something? Maybe he's out there treading water."

"Look. We're doing all we can. Our resources are a little limited right now," said Dave.

I looked around. The place was a disaster. Both tractors had been flipped on their sides. One was missing its trailer. The surge had floated trees under their big tires. The dock looked like someone had shaken a piano keyboard like a blanket and left all the keys at crazy angles.

"Where's your boat?" I asked.

"You tell me," said Dave. "Mr. Baker's is gone, too. We radioed headquarters over on Boca, but they got problems of their own. Said they'd send somebody out when they got a chance. You hungry?"

I hadn't noticed that I was starving. They led me back to what was left of their house. The stairs had been washed away, so we got up by way of a makeshift ladder one of them had strung together. All they had was a bunch of granola bars and oatmeal cookies wrapped in foil, a few canned goods. The water had gotten to everything else. I ate some and washed it down with warm Pepsi.

Cell phone service was down. Dave radioed the sheriff department and gave them my grandfather's number in LaBelle. Hopefully they'd get a message through. He told the cops about Salt, too. It was awkward, though, because none of us knew his real name. I told them his first name might be Joe, since I had heard Eden's dad call him that.

The rangers did have some records that gave a legal description of Salt's property, however, and the officer said he could look it up from that. They were sending out a rescue boat that morning, and they'd do what they could. I heard the dispatcher mention recovery. I couldn't eat anymore after hearing that.

The ranger's boat showed up at noon. An hour later, they were ready to leave the island. Dave asked me where I wanted to go. I could only think of one place – Palmetto Cove, home. I had to see it.

Hammerhead and I sat in the back of their boat. I wondered if he saw what I saw. Did he know Charley had wrecked our beautiful sound? Her waters were littered with aluminum siding, insulation, chunks of wood. Whole trees had been uprooted and tossed into the bay like twigs. We had to go slow to avoid the wreckage.

As the junk slid by, I realized that each piece floating in the water had once been part of someone's home, part of a life. A picture in a frame bobbed on the surface. I leaned over and scooped it up. In it, a little girl held onto a yellow cat. Her arms wrapped the cat around its midsection, and she lifted it up straight-legged, with her back bowed as if she barely had the strength. Water had worked its way under making the girl's grin stick to the glass. I let it slide back into the dirty water, watching as her face disappeared below the murk.

The men barely spoke on the way over to Pine Island. Everyone seemed shell-shocked. Occasionally someone might have said "Oh my God," or "Will you look at that," but mostly, the destruction was so massive it forced us to stay quiet.

Useppa was smashed. Roofs torn off. Big trees split in half. Boats flipped over in the marina. A couple of men milled around inspecting the damage, and the rangers called out to them. They were fine. A boat was coming.

Most of the small uninhabited mangrove islands had been chewed and twisted beyond recognition. I still hadn't seen a bird. I spotted a trail cut right through the center of one clump of trees. Must have been another tornado. My guts hurt.

Even the water below us had been bruised. The normal clear green that lapped over the sea grass was gone. The boat pushed through a brown, muddy soup instead, and I couldn't even see the bottom.

The channel markers leading into Palmetto Cove stood in the water at crazy angles. A couple were gone altogether. The first house I saw belonged to Mrs. Rovich. A sailboat sat on its side in her yard, and her roof had been skinned down to the plywood. The screen cage over the back patio was missing, too.

We had to slow down even more when the boat entered the canal. Someone's trailer had blown into it. The single-wide hung off the edge of the seawall, half in, half out. We barely had enough room to squeeze around.

The town seemed way too quiet. I didn't see a soul as we inched along the canal dodging patio furniture and sheet metal. At the ferry dock, I spotted something that looked both familiar and alien at the same time. The tower of a boat leaned out of the nasty water. I knew the name on the sunken hull read *White Stripe*. My eyes welled up. I shut my mouth and blinked to look somewhere else.

The roof over Smitty's place was gone. Two large trees now leaned against the walls with their roots sticking up through the busted ground. Other trees had lost all their leaves and most of their branches.

After a hurricane passes through, you always hear people on the news say that it looks like a bomb went off. Those people are right. That's about the best way to describe it. Palmetto Cove had been blown to smithereens.

I told the rangers where I lived, but it didn't matter. We couldn't go any further. Two more sunken boats prevented that. They offered to take me with them over to their station on Boca. I refused. I had them let me and Hammerhead off at what was left of Smitty's, and we walked. This was my life now. I needed to see it.

Palmetto Cove looked like a Halloween trick. Anything left standing had been turned like it was about to slide off the earth. Hammerhead growled, and I spotted somebody's dog rummaging through a pile of twisted metal and fiberglass insulation that had once been a trailer.

Telephone poles and wires crisscrossed the street. Car windows were smashed clear or had lumber or tree limbs sticking out of them. The playground that Mr. Connelly built for his kids had taken out the midsection of the Parker's trailer. Mr. Henley's mobile home, on the other hand, had disappeared completely.

I barely recognized my own neighborhood. I kept hoping that I'd find something the way I'd left it, but that didn't happen. I stopped in the middle of the street when I came to our place.

Home was gone. Only two things remained in our entire yard – our trailer's twisted metal I-beams and the concrete pad they were set on. Everything else had been stolen by Charley. Even the light pole down by the dock was snapped off.

We didn't stay long. I couldn't. I felt like a ghost. This was a graveyard, and I was vapor. The thinnest breeze would scatter me, too. I just started walking, not even knowing where.

The Last Pirate

We weren't allowed to live in Palmetto Cove anymore, at least until the town could be rebuilt. It had been declared "unfit for human habitation." The whole island was ruled a federal disaster area. The cops and National Guard let residents back on during the day to salvage what we could, but they'd run us off before night.

We didn't have anything to salvage, so Mom brought lunch, cold drinks, and ice to people, and I helped folks straighten out their messes. Even Tori was able to forget about her needs for a while and pitch in.

That went on for a week or two. Each night we'd drive back to LaBelle because we didn't have anywhere else to go. The county delayed the start of school since Charley had also damaged a few school buildings. I watched the news with my grandpa at night until I thought my eyes were going to pop out. I had no choice. His house was tiny, and the living room couch was my bed.

Mostly, the news was bad. Charley had turned out to be a category four storm at landfall. It had spun up more powerfully than any of the weathermen predicted and sliced a path of destruction all the way across the state to the Atlantic. Then it re-strengthened and slammed into South Carolina.

The only thing that prevented the hurricane from doing even more damage was its smaller size. But, it wrecked plenty.

Punta Gorda, a town on the southeast side of Charlotte Harbor, had been devastated. Whole office buildings had been destroyed. Homes were wiped out. No power. No food. No ice. Life was horrible. Everything had to be trucked in. I felt lucky to be in LaBelle.

Fort Myers did a little better, though the city received its share of destruction. A news camera had recorded the storm as it peeled off the roof of the downtown post office. Across, the river in Cape Coral, the footage looked worse – roofs gone, boats flipped or sunk, trees ripped away.

Every night while I watched with my grandpa, I braced myself for the one story that never came. Although the news people said the storm had killed ten people, they never reported finding the body of a man who had once lived on Cayo Costa. I figured that was fitting. Salt had been a mysterious man and also a man of the sea. I'm sure he was fine with a no frills burial in the Gulf of Mexico alongside Gasparilla. Didn't make me feel any better about it, though.

About the only bright spot in the news seemed to be the small number of deaths and injuries. They said that was due to the evacuations before the storm and the new rescue equipment that had been purchased just that summer. A ten million dollar donation in June by someone identified only as Joseph G., had allowed emergency services to purchase rescue boats, gear and a helicopter the month before the storm hit. The newscasters had dug up records of the same man donating millions more over previous years and said they were trying to track him down for an interview.

That's the kind of news people needed to hear. News like that jump-starts generosity.

A funny thing happens when disaster strikes. Some people become bitter. But, more become generous, not just with their money, but also with their time, with themselves. Our community came together every day as we helped each other. People forgot their issues for a little while, got along, and helped out.

And, I think a lot of folks understood for the first time just how much they had, not before the hurricane, but after. And they were truly grateful. I could not have predicted that. It was a good thing to see, and it did me good to be a part of it.

Now, why does it take a huge storm to make that happen?

Mr. Baker even let go of his grudges. I figured it was just temporary, but after the storm he actually acted human towards me. I ran into him out on the island a couple of days after.

"Cooper," he said, "I've still got old Salt's boat. Not sure what to do with it. Thinking maybe you'd want to hang onto it until the law figures out where she goes."

I told him I'd be glad to and asked him about Eden.

"She's in Lee Memorial. I'm sure she could use a little company," he told me.

He gave me her room number at the hospital, and the next day Bill took me down there while his folks were at work. She seemed fine, or at least getting better. The swelling in her arm had gone down some. She didn't have much memory after the snakebite, didn't remember us finding her at all.

She looked great to me, though, even with those sleepy eyes. I wanted to hold her. I wanted to send Bill out and tell her everything. But, I kept it in. I told myself that she had enough to deal with. I'd give her some space. At the same time, a little voice deep down inside called me a chicken.

I promised to stay in touch, but left feeling like she had slipped even further away.

A day after that, I took Salt's boat and made a run out to Cayo Costa to rescue Aruba. What a wreck. I was shocked all over again – so much for paradise. I just loaded up the old bird in his cage and left.

Days ran into weeks, and we were still stuck out at Grandpa's place in LaBelle. I'd heard a rumor that the Federal Government was going to send some trailers for hurricane victims to live in while they got their places back. Mom checked into it and found out it was true. She filled out the paperwork and sent it in. The government said it would take a few weeks for the trailers to get set up somewhere near Punta Gorda.

She had taken the loss of the gold better than I expected. I think she was just glad I wasn't killed. She was pretty mad at first, but that kind of melted away when she heard what happened.

When school finally started, I had to catch a ride into Cape Coral with Mom on her way to work. Somehow, she talked me into working at MegaMart with her in the afternoons. What's the difference? I couldn't fish if I wanted to. Not a single trap survived the storm. There was mullet season. That only required a boat and a cast net. The season was a few months away, though, and I had no boat. Sure, there was plenty of clean up work, but I didn't have any wheels.

So day after day, I put on a vest with one of those smiley faces and worked at MegaMart in the sporting goods department. I answered stupid questions from stupid customers about which tennis ball bounced better or if the sleeping bags came in extra large. I tolerated idiotic supervisors with bad breath and worse hair dos. And I did it all for $5.15 an hour.

Mom said the insurance wasn't going to bring much towards a new trailer. I just pinched my nose and swallowed each day like a bad pill knowing that every dollar I made went towards getting us back at home on the water. But, honestly? I felt like a snail trying to cross the whole United States. My life had become a climb up Mount Everest in more ways than one.

Then one day, this red neck came rolling in. He's got his back to me checking out the fishing rods, so he doesn't see me. But, I'd been there a couple of weeks. I knew the type. His gray hair's all matted under a nasty *I Cheer For Beer* ball cap turned around backwards, and he's got on a flannel shirt so full of holes, the moths have run out of cloth to eat. These people were always trouble.

Then, right in front of me, the redneck takes down a rod and starts whacking it against the rack, lightly, at first, like he was just testing it, then a lot harder. I couldn't believe it.

"No good piece of Chinese junk!" he said. Whack! Whack! Whack!

I wasn't a real company guy or anything, but I had developed a low tolerance for morons in that store. I started around the end of the counter.

"Couldn't even pull up a pin fish with this piece of garbage!" Whack! Whack!

"Sir! Sir!" I followed corporate policy of customer respect, at least for the moment. "Sir, put the rod down."

He wheeled around on me like some kind of lunatic, and, using the rod as a sword, he poked me in the center of the chest.

"Aha!" he yelled. "Got you, you swarthy swab!"

The tip hit me so hard that the whole rod doubled up as he continued to come towards me. I grabbed the thing and snatched it out of his hands. Just as I reared back to wrap it around his neck, I looked up into the eyes of a grinning ghost.

"Salt?" His name came so weakly out of my throat; it barely had enough power to make it past my lips. My jaw dropped, and I heard the rod hit the floor.

"Salt! You're aliiiiive!" I screamed. I wrapped my arms around that nasty plaid shirt and squeezed him like there's no tomorrow.

"What're you doing in here, kid? There's a whole world waiting for us outside the door. Let's go!"

He ripped the smiley face button off my vest and flipped it like a frisbee over the customer's heads.

"How . . ." I started, but he stopped me.

"There'll be time for that. We got to git. Got to dodge a couple of folks, then I got something to show you."

I dropped my MegaMart vest onto the floor and followed Salt straight through the women's lingerie department to the front doors. I waved at my mom as we passed her cash register.

"I guess I got a ride today, Mom!"

She froze there with a bottle of ketchup in her hand over the scanner and her mouth hanging wide open.

Outside, I squinted my eyes against the daylight. Through the glare I thought I saw a limo with a mob of people around it.

I veered to the left, but Salt steered me directly towards the black stretch. He didn't look pleased.

"No matter what they do, just keep going to the car," he said.

They looked like reporters. One of the cameramen spotted Salt.

"It's him! Here he comes!"

And it was on. The whole mob detached from the limo and rushed us like a pack of hyenas.

"Is it true?" shouted one. "Are you the benefactor?"

"Sir, are you behind all the medical and rescue donations in Lee County over the past decade?" screamed another sticking a microphone in Salt's face.

"Where did you get the money?"

"Sir, why did you keep it anonymous?"

Salt didn't even seem to notice them. He kept his mouth shut and pushed me towards the car.

"Did you build the new hospital?"

"Sir, are you really the . . ."

Salt slammed the door shut on the crowd. Faces appeared along the windows. Hands beat on the glass, but Salt kept his eyes on me.

"Well. Ask away, kid. Questions are still free."

I didn't know where to begin.

The car started rolling.

"Salt, you're alive!"

"You seem surprised," he laughed.

"What's up with all those reporters and TV people? Where did they come from?"

"You," he said.

"Me?"

"You told the rangers I was dead. You made 'em dig up the records. Right?"

"I guess so. Salt, I had to! You were dead, man!"

"Well, the secret's out. They found out who I was."

"Who are you?"

"There'll be time for that. Besides, you know me better than anyone else on this planet. You know who I am. Wouldn't you rather know how I got out of that twister?"

The visual that I had struggled so hard to shake out of my head came again – Salt standing there with the pack, the tornado, then nothing.

"Take more than a little thunderstorm to get rid of me, lad," he said with his gray eyes twinkling. " She tried, though, she tried. Plucked me up right off the sand, she did. For a few moments there, I couldn't tell up from down – not a feeling I'd recommend. When she finally spit me out, I found myself flailing around in the sea."

He pulled out a pack of saltines and ripped it open.

"Cracker?"

"No, thanks."

"Sorry, kid. I think it was somewhere in the water when I let go of your gold. It was kind of weighing me down." He bit a cracker. "And then, there I was, clawing and gagging and spitting out minnows. Somehow, I had to figure out the way to the shore. Well, that old Gulf? She did it for me. Sent a big swell that rose up and washed me to the sand.

I thought I was back on the Cayo. Started looking for you. But then, I noticed all the fancy tourist homes flapping in the breeze, and I knew I'd landed down south on Upper Captiva instead."

It was like the clouds had evaporated, and the sun actually shined again. It was the new happiest day of my life.

"Don't tell me that's where you've been all this time, living it up with the blue-bloods!" I joked. "I suppose they paid for this ride."

"Well, I dragged my aching bones up the beach, what was left of it, and found one of those houses to crawl into. Rode out the rest of the gale in there. When it was over, I took a little walk around the island. Do you know that all those chickens had flew the coop? Not another single living soul out there. Had the whole place to my self. No boats, either, though. Not even a raft.

Thought about swimming the pass, but then I figured these people had better food and softer beds, so I just made myself comfortable. Took 'em a few days, but a few of them made it back. They sniffed me out, and when it was finally convenient enough for them, one of them carried me back over to the house.

And guess what, my little swab? My ship had already sailed without me. Any clue how it got tied up to your dock, sonny?" He shut his mouth and gave me the hairy eye.

Now it was my turn to start yakking. I filled him in on the events that took place after the storm had killed him. He already knew most of it, but seemed taken by all my grief and misfortunes as he nibbled another cracker.

"And my bird? Storm blow my girl away, too?"

"No, Salt. She's with me in LaBelle. I went out and got her a couple of days later."

Salt nodded, then looked out one of the limo's dark windows. Our talking had gotten us all the way to Matlacha.

"Those media buzzards are right behind us, I'm sure," he said. "Now they're in for a surprise."

He knocked on the window up by the driver, and the stretch pulled off the road at Matlacha Seafood Company.

"Step lively, kid."

Salt threw open the door and shot out like a bolt of lightning straight for the big building with blue tarps on the roof. I followed him. We ran up the steps and through the front doors. A man looked up from his desk. I expected him to yell at us to slow down, but he didn't seem the least bit surprised.

"She's already running, Joe," he said as we hurried by.

"Much obliged, Benji," said Salt.

We shot through to the back where they clean and sort the fish, and we didn't stop. Salt kept going out the door and down the docks between the shrimp boats. At the end, he jumped aboard a huge sport fisherman.

"Untie her and shove off, boy. Time's a wasting," he shouted over his shoulder.

"Salt! We can't just take somebody's boat because a few reporters are after you."

"We're not, sonny. She's mine."

If I had been a cartoon character like Sponge Bob or Bart Simpson, my lower jaw would have literally hit the dock with a cute sound effect. This was not the Salt I knew before hurricane Charley.

"Now!!" he shouted.

At the far end of the dock, reporters and cameras spilled out of the building and onto the planks. I sprinted to the bowline and spun it off the cleat. Salt was already pulling away when I reached the stern. I barely had time to undo the rope and jump over before he gunned the boat off the dock.

A woman reporter led the charge to the end of the dock. I recognized her from the local news. She put on the brakes at the last plank with a microphone in her hand and an exasperated look on her face. Unfortunately for her, being first on the scene was a bad thing that day. The rest of the paparazzi kept coming and off she went, high heels over hairspray, into the bay.

The diesel motors hummed away under my feet as Salt took the massive boat out to the channel. I climbed the ladder to the flybridge. The windows were so dark, I couldn't even see inside. When I opened the door, Salt sat in the captain's chair with one hand on the wheel and the other on the throttle.

"Welcome aboard, kid."

"Salt. This thing's bigger than my trailer was."

"Hatteras 77C. Brand spanking new." He was beaming.

"Seventy-seven feet long! Oh my God!"

"Well, she's really just seventy-six and ten inches. They like to round up. Twenty-two feet wide, though. And, she draws less than six."

"She's gorgeous."

"Four bedrooms, plus crew quarters. Flat screens everywhere. And a tower on top. Comfortable, yes, but built to fish."

"Yeah. I saw the fighting chair. Salt, what are the payments on this thing?"

"No idea. Paid cash. Got a better deal that way."

Maybe the storm had killed us both. Maybe I'd been stuck in purgatory, and Salt had just snatched me up to Heaven. It just didn't make any sense.

"Go ahead," he said. "Take a look around."

The flybridge alone looked bigger than any boat I had ever been on. In the front, two small couches flanked the captain's chair. And behind that, another couch long enough for ten people curved around a black granite table. A TV big as a dining room table hung from the ceiling.

"Check out the other decks," said Salt.

"Other *decks*? As in plural?"

"Sure. There's two more below us."

Outside the dark windows, Matlacha slipped away behind us. I spotted the curving staircase that went down to the next level. Nothing looked like any boat I'd ever seen. The carpet on the stairs felt so cushioned; it belonged in some fancy hotel.

At the bottom, another huge room, larger than the flybridge, spread out before me. On the left, a galley waited behind another hunk of granite that hung over a few barstools. And on the right, an elegant table set for three. Wooden blinds covering the windows were opened enough to let in a nice view of Matlacha Pass. Another wrap-around sofa began under the windows and curved around the back of the room.

Eden Baker sat in the corner with her legs crossed and her arms stretched out along the cushions.

"Well, it's about time, sailor," she said.

Yep. I was right. I had died and, somehow, a limo had taken me from MegaMart to Heaven.

She stood up and walked straight to me.

"Why, Harley. You look like you've seen a ghost."

But, her lips didn't belong to any ghost. They felt way too hot on mine.

Either the boat hit a wave or my knees gave out. I don't know which. Something brought us down to the couch, and she hung on to my neck. Her body felt amazing inside my arms.

"Oh, Harley. Salt told me everything," she said to my ear. "What Mrs. Rovich did. How you rescued us."

I let her keep going. She pulled away to face me.

"How much you care," she said softly.

Her nose brushed mine, and she kissed me again.

"I . . ."

"I know. I know. You tried to tell me, Harley. You did. And I was such a bull-headed idiot. But, that's over. I know the truth now. Oh, Harley. Can you forgive me?" She grabbed me again and put her head to my chest.

Could I forgive her? I could certainly try. I didn't think it was going to be much of a problem.

The motors were thumping away, though not as fast as my heart, as I took Eden's hand and led her back up the stairs to the flybridge. The first thing I needed was answers.

"Okay, Salt. Time's up," I said. "You got a lot of explaining to do."

"You like the ship?"

"I'd like a few answers even more."

"Oh, I didn't know the boat came with mermaids. " He grinned at Eden as she came up beside me. "A thousand pardons, my lady. I apologize for this clod's impertinence. Allow me to introduce myself . . ."

"Salt."

"That's it. My friends call me Salt."

"She knows who you are. And you apparently know her. Now spill the beans, man. What's with the limo, the boat, all the sneaking around? Give it up, dude!"

"Harley, I ever tell you how Captiva Island got its name?"

"About a thousand times. What's that got to do with anything?"

"Well, perhaps, I'll tell you again. Maybe Miss Eden would like to hear. Why don't you two have a seat?"

We took the small sofa to the left of Salt's chair. He pushed the throttle forward and brought the Hatteras up on plane. He made us wait until the channel straightened out into Charlotte Harbor before he finally began to speak.

"See that island way over there? That's Boca Grande, old Gasparilla's home and castle. Truth be known, he treated all these islands as his own. Cayo Costa, Upper Cap, Captiva, Sanibel. He had outposts on them all.

Some held treasure. Some, stockpiles of freshwater, dry goods and food. Captiva held people."

"People?" asked Eden.

"That's right," Salt continued. "Prisoners, captives. Hence the name." He leaned over and shot us a wink. "Women mostly. Gasparilla was a big believer in the ransom system. When he plundered merchant ships, he took more than gold and silver. If there were any good looking women, he took them, too.

Now, he didn't treat them harshly. Quite the contrary, he set them up on Captiva in high style, with armed guards, of course. For their own protection, you see."

"So they wouldn't escape," I added.

"Well, whatever. The guards were there and the women were taken care of until their husbands or fathers or uncles delivered the asking price to Boca; then Gasparilla, true to his word, set them free.

This little business went along just fine for years until one day a fellow by the name of Henri Caesar stirred things up. Caesar had been captured by slave traders in Africa and, upon arriving in the Caribbean, escaped to become a notorious pirate who called himself Black Caesar.

By the way, he had a clever way of attacking a ship. Him and his buddy would row out to sea in a little boat and make like they were shipwrecked. After a kindly captain invited them aboard, they set the ship on fire when the moment was right and grabbed all the loot they could stuff in their pockets before jumping back into their rowboat while the crew fought the fire.

Well, eventually, Black Caesar kept one of those ships and worked his way up the islands until he reached Florida. When he got here, he ran into Gasparilla. Instead of fighting, the two pirates decided they could help each other in a profitable alliance. They teamed up and plundered many merchant vessels together. Business was good.

But one day, Black Caesar and his men got bored. They had heard about Gasparilla's beautiful prisoners down on Captiva and figured they'd go have a look. Off they went, and when they arrived on shore, they were met by Gasparilla's guards. A scuffle broke out that soon turned bloody. Black Caesar and his men overpowered the guards and set off for the women.

Now the women had heard the commotion and they were ready for Caesar and the other scallywags. One especially beautiful woman named Joseffa had come up with a plan.

When the men burst into Gasparilla's little jail, they found all the women on the floor dead, or so they thought. Blood splattered everywhere.

"Some bad thing happen here," said Black Caesar. "Some bad voodoo thing!"

Just then, Joseffa came out of the closet wailing like a banshee, her arms held straight out and her skin pale as a ghost. She went for Black Caesar.

Caesar screamed, "Zombie, it is! Run for your life!" He and his men couldn't leave fast enough. They splashed through the water, jumped into their boat, and sailed south, never to return again.

By the way, old Black Caesar finally got captured by the U.S. Navy, and they hung him up in Virginia. But that's a different story." Salt picked up a bottle of water and chugged it.

"And this explains your current situation how?" I asked him.

"MegaMart didn't do much for your patience, did it? I'm getting to that. " He smiled over at Eden as he set the water down. "He's a bit over anxious. Perhaps you can help him with that."

Eden crinkled her nose at him. Salt cleared his throat.

"Anyway, Gasparilla was furious when he heard what had happened. But, he was mightily impressed by the cunning

Joseffa. So impressed, that he invited her up to the big house to explain what she had done.

Joseffa said it was simple. She figured old Caesar was superstitious. Almost everybody back then was afraid of the supernatural. She just sprinkled a little chicken blood on her fellow prisoners and a little flour on herself before she hid in the closet. Caesar's imagination did the rest.

Before he knew it, Gasparilla took a shine to Joseffa and, since no one had shown up to pay her ransom, let her stay on there at the house. After a while, they fell in love.

Now, I'll tell you, it isn't fitting for any self-respecting pirate king like Gasparilla to keep a lady around his place permanently. It's a bachelor pad, after all. So once he had defeated the Calusa, he built her a fancy house down on what's now Useppa."

"Joseffa Key," said Eden.

"Exactly," said Salt. "La Isla de Joseffa. Even the history books know that. What they don't know is that Gasparilla and Joseffa had a child, a boy named Jose after his dad, and his mom. Gasparilla's real name was Jose Gaspar. Their son was Jose, Jr.

Now, that's the real reason Gasparilla had decided to retire. He wanted to settle down, become a family man and all. He had seen the world and lived the life. But that greedy side did him in before he could live the last.

Joseffa was left to raise the boy alone. The Navy pretty much put an end to pirates in this area when they cornered old Gasparilla. What Spanish were left drifted off or became fishermen. Joseffa did a good job and raised a strong lad. Little Jose became a very successful fisherman in these parts. Started one heckuva seafood company, too.

Well, he had a son. And his son had a son, and so on. Gradually, all the Spanish blood worked its way out and the family just became plain old American."

Suddenly, I got goose bumps all over my back, and the hairs on my neck stood up.

"Joe G.," I whispered.

"Where'd you hear that?" asked Salt.

"The news," I said. "They said all the donations came from a guy named Joseph G. Salt. Is that you?"

"Joseph Gaspar at your service."

"Holy moly! You're Gasparilla's grandson?!"

"Great-great-great-grandson to be exact. How'd you think I knew all those pirate tales. Think I made 'em up?"

"You're the last pirate," said Eden.

"Well, truth be known, I'm not much of a pirate. But, I am the last of the line. Only one still holding the name. The real name. Gasparilla was his pirate name. He took it when he became one.

Anyway, I got no brothers and no sisters. No aunts, uncles or anybody else. Just me, myself, and I."

"Dude."

"Never married, either. No kids . . . that I know of."

Awestruck. That's what I was. It's like discovering your best friend is secretly the lead singer and guitarist of the *White Stripes*. But it all made perfect sense – a life of adventure on the high seas when he was younger; living out on Cayo Costa in that old house, being one of the last hold-outs when the rest of the island had been taken over by the state; Aruba, the parrot. Of course! Pirates always have parrots. Even the name of his crab boat, Costa Blanca. How could I have missed that? Come on! He must have mentioned Gasparilla's boat, the Florida Blanca, at least a thousand times. Wake up Cooper!

I must have asked him a million questions about his family history. Salt patiently answered each of them as he drove that big boat to Cayo Costa. By the time we finally pulled into Pelican Bay, it dawned on me to ask why he decided to spill the beans now.

"Mind if I tell you another story?" he asked with his gray eyes twinkling at me and Eden. "But this one's no pirate diddie. It's about me."

"Sure."

"Well, give me a hand with this barge, and I'll get to it."

Family Secrets

Eden and I helped Salt anchor the Hatteras in Pelican Bay. We had to leave her there and break out the dinghy since there was no way a seventy-seven foot boat could make it up his canal. The dinghy alone was almost as big as my boat had been. I had my doubts about it bottoming out on the way to his house.

As we eased off the Hatteras, the big boat had turned on her anchor line into the northerly breeze, putting her stern to the dinghy. For the first time, I saw her name in big blue letters across the transom – Florida Blanca.

"I'll tell you kids something," Salt began. "Maybe you've thought of it before. Maybe you haven't. As you make your way through this thing we call life, you write your own history. Some things sneak up on you, but for the most part, you have the major say so as to what that book says when it's all over. Every decision you make, every action, they're all in there.

When I was younger, some of the decisions I made weren't so bright. Eden, I've known your dad forever – since we were splashing around out here like finger mullet. Used to be pretty good friends in those days, too."

I watched porpoise work the calm edges of the bay next to the mangroves. Salt's words flowed as smoothly as those animals slid through the water, laying a spell over the late afternoon as we idled past the sailboats.

"Then having fun turned into trying to make a buck. One thing led to another, and money came between us. Now, I'm not one to point fingers or even get into it. I'll just say that, at this point, I'm not proud of what I did.

And, yes, Harley, I went to prison for it. Served my time. Luckily for me, I had an understanding father. Took me back when I got out. Taught me the family business.

I felt real bad for the things I'd done. He didn't raise me that'a way, and I knew it. I decided to set things right. And not with just the people I had had disagreements with, but with mankind and God above.

Before my pappy shared the family secrets, he waited until they wouldn't go to my head. He didn't have to worry, I was past that then. Life had humbled me."

Salt didn't look at either one of us as he spoke. He kept his eyes ahead of the boat on the water.

"When he showed me the family heirlooms, I wanted to use them in the name of what's good, not greedy."

"Treasure?" I ventured. "You have treasure, Salt?"

"Kid, you have no idea."

The boat leaned a little as we turned into Salt's canal. The great blue heron squawked at us, but didn't fly.

"Old Gasparilla's men, what was left of them, were very loyal. Besides, they had over twenty brimming barrels and a lot more buried away. They made sure their captain's wife, and only son, were set.

Well, Joseffa and her boy lived their lives like they didn't have a nickel of it. Passed it down, and they passed it down.

I didn't have to look far to see need for it, right here in this neck of the woods. Over the years, I've given back. Thanks to the sea turtles, I figured we might be getting a little blow this summer, so I beefed up the EMS squads around here some more."

We turned the corner in the canal. Salt's stone crab boat floated by the dock. The stacks of crab traps were still tied down behind the house. Charley hadn't moved many of them. As I stared at those traps, something clicked.

"You put that map in my trap!" I blurted. "Didn't you?"

"Family heirloom. Didn't know where the gold lay, though," he said with a smile. "You found that fair and square, kid. Can't say I hadn't tried, though."

How many other things had he done for me over the years?

Instead of tying it next to his crab boat, Salt eased the dinghy up on the soft mud at the end of the canal. He killed the motor and hopped off the bow to give Eden a hand down. I followed them up the rise under the oaks, where Salt stopped between the house and a stack of traps.

"I did me some thinking while I was marooned down there on Upper Cap after the hurricane. I'm not such a young snapper anymore. I figure that someplace somewhere, there's a bait well that's been holding all my days. That twister lifted me high enough off the ground to sneak a peek in there, and kid, that well is running low."

He stepped over to the traps.

"My account with the Man upstairs has been paid and then some. I figure it's time to have me a little fun.

Help me with this line, would you?"

With the toe of his boot, he tapped on a rope securing the traps to a big stake that had been driven into the ground at an angle. I worked the knot until it came loose. Salt heaved the rope over the top of the traps.

"Slide that stack over there."

I grabbed the bottom trap and slid a stack out of the line. Salt knelt down and brushed away the leaves. He tapped his knuckles on something like he was knocking on a door. His hand reached under a board and pulled it out of the loose dirt.

Six dark-green garbage bags sat in the hole, square shapes, not round.

"Pull one out," he said. "If you can."

I dropped to my knees and felt around the nearest one for something I could grab onto. My hands found what felt like slots in the sides of a wooden box. I gripped them and pulled backwards. It took every ounce of strength I had to wrestle the thing out of the hole.

"Go ahead. Open her up."

I untied the bags. There were three of them, one inside the other, covering an old chest. The top opened easily.

A beam of late afternoon sunlight came in through the branches over my shoulder and sparkled off a shimmering pile of gold doubloons.

"Oh . . . My . . . God," said Eden.

"I'm retiring, Harley. This is all yours."

"No way, Salt! I can't deal with this, man. Not your money! It's not right!"

"Relax, relax. This isn't all my loot," he said with a grin. "I've got plenty more."

"Still, it doesn't feel right," I said as I stood up.

"Of course it doesn't. That's why I'm giving it to you, Harley." He put his hand on my shoulder and looked me in the eye. "Look, kid. I know you pretty well. Of all people, you can handle it. I don't have a single doubt.

Besides, I don't have any kids. Who else would I give it to? Guess that makes you the last pirate!" He let out a laugh and slapped me hard on the back.

"But what'll happen to you, Salt?"

"Me? I'm sailing to Aruba, naturally. Didn't I always tell you I was going? Already got me a place staked out. That's why I'm giving you the house and the boat as well!"

I looked over at Eden. "Did you know about this?" I asked her.

"No clue," she said.

"Look, boy. All those glittery palaces down there on Upper Cap? That's not the real deal. The real deal's in here." He patted his heart. "And out there." He waved his hand at the island. "This loot can do good things. And I'll help you do them, but I need you to help me.

The way I see it, this treasure's been a secret too long. Originally, way back, it was taken from hard working Indians, right? Let's give it back to people. Let's put it back to work.

Why, there's a million things we can do with this money that'll make a difference to people all over the world."

He put his hands on his hips and looked at me. His eyes twinkled.

"Me and you. What do you say?"

I thought about that mountain I swore I would climb. Even though Salt had come back, my history was still waiting to be written. Why wait for another storm or a death to get me started up my own Everest?

"Okay, Salt."

"That a boy. Now. You've got to keep your head on straight. Finish school." He started jabbering away, a million miles an hour. "Good grades. College degree. We're gonna need all that. In the meantime, fish. It keeps you honest."

I was actually looking forward to stone crabs the most.

"Of course, you'll have to provide for your mom, too. Get her back on her feet. I hear the Rovich place is for sale. The fair widow bugged out back to Russia after Charley."

As I listened, it hit me. Salt was moving away.

"Dude, I thought I'd lost you. Now, I'm losing you again?"

"Don't get all mushy on me. You'll see plenty of me. We're partners now! I've got a great lawyer who'll set it all up." He pointed at the gold. "This stuff's going to the bank. Lot's of banks. It needs real security now that everything's out in the clear."

I had never seen Salt so jazzed. I never thought that giving money away would make him so happy. But maybe that wasn't it. Maybe finally coming clean with someone did the trick. Whatever it was, it was good. I slung my arm over Eden's shoulders, and we let him go.

He kept gibbering and jabbering about all these things until he finally got it out of his system. We promised him we'd keep quiet until he said everything was good to go. He finally quit talking long enough to let us take a spin in my new crab boat as the daylight started to fade. We promised to meet him back at the Florida Blanca for dinner.

"Wanna catch a sunset?" I asked Eden as we waved good-bye.

"Love to."

We roared out to Boca Grande Pass and cut the motor just as the big, orange ball touched the water. We were the only boat.

"Two and a half minutes," she said.

"Two forty-five," I said.

She slugged me in the arm. "You don't even have a watch," she laughed.

"Well, neither do you."

"Know what else you don't have?"

"What's that?"

"A first mate," she said.

"You looking for a job?"

"More like a partnership."

"Seal it with a kiss?"

The tide carried us out to sea.

Life is a roller coaster, right? Hang on and enjoy the ride. And write some history you'd let anybody read. That's my advice.

At that moment, I was hanging on with both arms and all my heart. And out on the sea next to his island, I finally understood what turned that old pirate around.

Some diddie, huh?

About the Author

Wilson Hawthorne lives in south Florida with his wife, Gail, and a house full of children.

In addition to writing, Wilson has enjoyed a lengthy career in television production filled with many interesting characters and far away places.

Around the Hawthorne household, story-time is a daily occurrence. Sometimes the tales flow from a large collection of books, but more often than not, they spring directly from the storyteller's imagination. And - as the kids insist – those are always the best.

Please direct any correspondence for the author to:

Wilson@TheLastPirate.net

The Cajun Pirate

Like *The Last Pirate*? Join Harley, Salt and Eden for another non-stop adventure in the sequel, *The Cajun Pirate*. Check it out at

www.TheCajunPirate.com

Made in the USA
Middletown, DE
21 July 2021